# DIRTY BOSS

CRYSTAL KASWELL

# Copyright

This is a work of fiction. Similarities to real people, places, or events are entirely coincidental.

# Also by Crystal Kaswell

### *Sinful Serenade*

*Sing Your Heart Out* - Miles

*Strum Your Heart Out* - Drew

*Rock Your Heart Out* - Tom

*Play Your Heart Out* - Pete

*Sinful Ever After* – series sequel

### *Dangerous Noise*

*Dangerous Kiss* - Ethan

*Dangerous Crush* – Kit

*Dangerous Rock* – Joel

*Dangerous Fling* – Mal

*Dangerous Encore* - series sequel

### *Inked Hearts*

*Tempting* - Brendon

*Hooking Up* - Walker

*Pretend You're Mine* - Ryan

*Hating You, Loving You* - Dean

*Breaking the Rules* - Hunter

*Losing It* - Wes - coming 2019

more coming in 2019

Sign up for the Crystal Kaswell mailing list

# Chapter One

TODAY

The elevator doors slide open. I take a deep breath, cultivating every ounce of badass I can muster. Either I nail this interview and get this internship, or I slink back to Stanford for dull classes and three thousand miles between me and everything I love.

Here goes nothing.

The woman sitting behind the reception desk is pure New York City cool. Slick straight black bob. Sleek red dress. Perfect makeup.

"You must be Elizabeth Wilder. I'm Jasmine Lee, the office manager." She shakes my hand with a strong grip.

"Lizzy."

Jasmine smiles. "We mostly go by last names here. It's a lot more formal than the Bay."

She leads me through the modern office. It's sleeker than a typical San Francisco startup. Modern art hangs next to huge windows. The room glows with the soft January light.

We stop in a corner office.

Jasmine motions for me to sit in the leather executive

chair. "I'm going to leave you with this programming test. Then Mr. Marlowe is going to come in and ask you a few questions."

My stomach twists. Phoenix Marlowe is the company's CEO, a billionaire programming genius. How am I supposed to impress him?

"He's excited to meet you. He couldn't stop talking about your AI projects." She points to the monitor, now displaying a programming test. "Good luck."

She nods a goodbye on her way out the door.

The second it clicks shut, my attention shifts to the computer screen.

I get lost in the hard but doable questions.

Until I hear his voice.

That same voice I heard that night in San Francisco.

"I hope I haven't surprised you," he says.

That's him. It can't be possible, but that's him. I spin in my chair so we're eye to eye.

What the hell is Nick doing here?

"No," I say. "It's fine."

He closes and locks the door. His gaze drifts to the résumé in his hands. It's like he doesn't recognize me. Maybe he has one-night stands all the time. Maybe it meant nothing to him.

My head fills with the feeling of his body sinking into mine, the taste of whiskey on his lips, the smell of his cologne.

He's wearing the same cologne today.

His eyes flash with something. Anger, I think. He's hard to read.

It's something. Something bad.

He does recognize me. He must.

His voice is rough. "Who is Marie?"

I take a deep breath. "My middle name. And Nick?"

"Phoenix. My friends call me Nick."

"I didn't realize." I press my hand against the slick surface of the desk. "I'm sure this kind of thing has happened before."

His eyes narrow. "No."

"But you're very—"

"I don't go around fucking college students." He places my résumé on the desk and takes a seat behind it.

"I don't go around fucking billionaire programmers." My nostrils flare. My heart pounds. Anger fills my veins. As much as it hurts, meaning nothing to him, I need this opportunity. It's the only way I can stay near Kat. And Kat's the only person I trust. I clear my throat. "Can we start over?"

Frustration spreads across his face. "This project means everything to me."

"Your assistant, Ms. Lee—"

"She's not my assistant."

"Whatever she is, she told me how impressed you were by my board game bots. Is that true?"

"Yes." He stares at me like he's expecting me to back down.

I don't.

"Your programming skills are not up to the standards of Odyssey Industries. Your code is sloppy and inefficient."

"You didn't even look at my programming test."

He taps the monitor.

"You can see the test on your computer, can't you?"

Nick nods. His eyes meet mine, and his expression shifts. It's softer. "You're stubborn and overconfident."

"I am not." Objecting doesn't help my case. But he's wrong.

"I'd like to hire you, Ms. Wilder. You're the only candidate with any grasp of artificial intelligence." Nick stares back at me. "But there are other issues to consider."

"I fucked the boss, so I'm shit out of luck?"

His expression is impossible to read.

"Are you even going to deny it?" I will myself to stay logical. This is a good opportunity. Not worth wasting over a romantic connection, not when there are three million men in Manhattan.

It doesn't help.

I can't look at Nick for another second. How can this be the same man I met last September? That man was calm and collected, but there was warmth in his eyes. His voice was stern and strong, but it was caring too.

This guy is a narcissistic asshole.

I push myself out of my seat. "I'll spare you the awkwardness of explaining it to HR." I sling my purse over my shoulder and march to the door.

"Lizzy, wait."

That's not happening. Not when there's a tear welling up in my eye. This opportunity is everything to me and it's nothing to him.

There's no way I'm staying in New York.

Dammit, I'm not crying in front of him.

Head down, I rush to the elevator. Jasmine says a frantic goodbye, but I pretend I don't hear her.

There are footsteps behind me. I can't bring myself to turn and find out if they belong to Nick. I duck into the staircase and race all the way to the first floor.

I disappear into the Wall Street subway station.

---

MY SISTER, KAT, LIVES WITH HER FIANCÉ BLAKE Sterling on the Upper East Side. He's wealthy. If I tell him about this internship, he'll offer me the money to stay in New York.

But I'm not accepting help from either of them. Kat spent the last four years taking care of me. For once, she's going to live her life. I'm going to stand on my own two feet. Even if it kills me.

I collapse on the modern black couch and scan my streaming options. All the sci-fi movies make me think about Nick's project. The Haley Bot (named for Hal, the evil computer in *2001: A Space Odyssey*) is a virtual assistant far beyond any of its competitors. It's an amazing AI project. It's the best opportunity I'll ever have to learn about AI.

This internship is the only way I can stay in New York without dropping out of school.

I can swallow my pride, apologize, and convince Nick to keep our relationship professional.

But I'm not so sure I can be around him without melting into a pile of desire.

## Chapter Two

THREE MONTHS AGO

Happy freaking birthday.

September in San Francisco sucked.

Everything in the Bay area sucked. My Stanford dorm room was tiny. My roommate hated me. Some of my classmates were receptive to my *let's hang out and study* suggestions, but none of them got me.

My friend from high school—the one who had moved to San Francisco to pursue a music career—was supposed to join me for a birthday dinner.

But her cancellation text sat there on my phone. *Sorry, Lizzy. I can't make it. Happy Birthday XOXO.*

Raindrops dotted my screen. I slid my phone back into my purse. To protect it. Or maybe myself. I wasn't good with feelings. Or disappointment. Code? Yeah. I could ace any test. But figuring out if the guy sitting next to me wanted to study or wanted to *study*? I had no idea how to do that.

I scanned the dark city. The downtown skyline looked less impressive up close. Like some cheap imitation of Manhattan. I never loved Manhattan the way Kat did, but

I appreciated its prominence. New Yorkers made sense to be. The weird combination of preppy, laid back, smug, chill, and money-worshiping—the Bay made no sense to me.

I stepped under the red awning of a massive hotel. One with gold doors and clean windows.

There he was, all tall, dark, and handsome, standing on the sidewalk with a wide stance, his shoulders pulled back, his gaze on his cell phone.

Without a word, he slid his suit jacket off his shoulders and offered it to me.

A stranger offering me his coat.

That was an invitation, wasn't it?

Like those guys who raised their eyebrows after they said *study*.

My eyes fixed on his. They were dark. Like coffee. And just as rich and bold.

He was the perfect way to spend my birthday.

I could even flirt a little. In theory.

I stared back into his beautiful eyes. "I can't take your jacket."

"Why not?"

I rubbed my fingers over the fabric. It was a finely woven wool. Expensive. "I don't know you."

"I'm Nick."

We shook hands.

He was clearly rich and important. There was no way I'd ever see him again. Better to give him my middle name.

"Marie." I slung the jacket over my shoulders. It was thick. Warm. And comforting in another way. It was a way to try on a role for the night. Marie, the confident, bold girl who accepts strangers' jackets and invitations for one-night stands.

"I'm going inside for a drink." He pulled the door open as if to invite me.

I nodded a thank you and followed him to a booth in the corner of the lounge.

The walls were cream, the lights were soft, the furniture was purple. It wasn't the kind of place I'd expect to see a guy like Nick.

His deep brown eyes fixed on mine. "What brought you into the city today?"

"How do you know I'm not a local?"

He gave me a long once-over. "People in San Francisco rarely wear—"

"Tight dresses and heels?"

"Not on this side of town."

"I got that impression." My gaze drifted to the dark carpet. "It's my birthday."

He looked back at me. "Is it?"

"What? You think that's a line I use to get guys to buy me drinks?"

"No. I don't think you have any trouble getting guys to buy you drinks."

My lips curled into a smile. He liked me. In a *let's chat until we're ready to fuck* kind of way. "I was supposed to meet a friend. She canceled."

"Not everyone is reliable."

"True."

The way he looked at me was understanding. Sweet, even.

"Are you from the Bay?"

"No."

"So you can't explain the appeal?"

His eyes lit up as he chuckled. It was a strong, deep laugh. He was a strong, deep guy. He had a certain stoic vibe to him. I wanted to peel back his layers. I wanted to understand him. At least for a while. "It can't be the weather."

"You don't enjoy the frigid summers?"

"No." I pressed my lips together. Was this sharing too much? Was I about to insult his beloved city? No. I didn't think so. "I don't get it here. Everyone you meet is a snob or, worse, some programmer who thinks he's better than you because he knows C++. Is there anything good about this city?"

"The rents are making landlords rich."

I laughed. "You would know."

He nodded.

"You don't like it either?"

"You get used to the self-importance."

The cocktail waitress stopped by our table to take our drink order. She accepted my fake ID without batting an eye.

"Let me guess." I slid his jacket off my shoulders and set it in my lap. "You're a venture capitalist and you have to fly here twice a week to hear desperate pitches from egotistical start-up founders."

Nick's eyes were fixed on me. His gaze was already so intense and captivating. I was losing interest in our conversation. What did I need to know about him besides how much I wanted him to take me to his room?

I never reacted to men like that. I'd only been with two —a boyfriend before the accident made everything complicated and a classmate I dated for a few months the previous summer. Neither was worth remembering.

My heartbeat picked up. I shifted back in my seat. "Was I close?"

"Yes. And you're a student as UCSF. A science major. Chemistry."

"Something like that."

The waitress returned with our drinks. Whiskey for him. Rum and diet for me. Nick slid two twenty-dollar bills into her hand. She smiled the way I always smiled after a huge commission.

I took a long sip. It was a perfect mix of sweet and bitter. "What brought you into the city?"

He copied my words. "How do you know I'm not a local?"

"You're staying in a hotel."

"I could be going through a divorce."

I shook my head. I took his left hand and pointed to the base of his ring finger. "You don't have a tan line."

His brows rose. He smiled, impressed. "That's a neat trick."

"It doesn't absolve you of being thrown out by your girlfriend." I met his gaze. "But I can't imagine that."

"Why not?"

"I can't see you letting a woman have that much control of your life. Living with you even."

"That's quite the accusation."

"I guess so. You learn to read people pretty well when you work retail." I pressed my lips together. "Am I wrong? Have you ever lived with a woman?"

"Not one besides my mother."

"Do you have girlfriends or just—" I motioned to our seat in the lounge "—do things like this?"

"Do you have boyfriends?"

"Not since high school."

"Me either."

"You had a boyfriend in high school?"

He looked back at me curiously, like he wasn't sure if I was joking or not.

"Just kidding." I smiled. "Where are you from?"

"Los Angeles. Just as self-important." His gaze went to the jacket in my lap. "But the weather is more tolerable."

That sealed it. He was from Los Angeles. There was no way I'd see him again. There was no reason to hold back anything.

I was so lonely that first semester of college. It wasn't abnormal for my temper and strong will to get me into trouble, but it was so much harder with my sister, my best friend in the world, three thousand miles away.

Nick was listening to me. He was honest. It was my chance to let my guard down for a night, to have a conversation that wasn't bullshit.

I promised myself I'd take advantage of the opportunity. "I'm from New York. I can deal with weather."

"You go out like that during New York winters?"

"You sound like my sister."

"Not your mom?"

"My parents died when I was fifteen."

His voice softened. His expression filled with sympathy. "I'm sorry."

"Thank you." I nodded. For once, it felt like someone meant it. Like someone actually cared about me. It filled me in places that usually panged with emptiness. I wanted to talk to him forever. "Why are you in the city today?"

"I had to deal with a problem."

I leaned in closer, studying his dark eyes. They were hard to read but they were honest.

"Is it dealt with?" I asked.

His eyes flared with concern. He nodded and finished his drink. "Hopefully."

"Was it business or personal?"

He looked back to me. "Both, unfortunately."

"You don't seem like the kind of guy who mixes the two."

"I don't. Not usually."

"What happened this time? Seduce your secretary, then kick her to the curb?"

He raised a brow, studying my expression as if he was deciding if I was joking. He must have decided yes, because he smiled.

His voice lightened. "No one is called a secretary anymore. It's administrative assistant."

"Would you?"

"That's an open-and-shut sexual harassment case. I don't need the headache."

"Afraid of litigation?"

"Have you ever dealt with lawyers?"

I shook my head.

"I hope, for your sake, that you never have to."

"What if you were sure she wouldn't sue?"

"It's not a risk worth taking."

We were almost flirting. I had to elevate it. To tease him. "You're chicken?"

He pulled back, his expression hardening. "No. When you're older, you'll realize that there's a difference between bravery and foolishness."

I bit my tongue. I didn't need to be polite with him. I could call him on his bullshit. "So you think you're smarter than everyone younger than you? There's a difference between cowardice and caution. I could say that and make you sound like the one who is wrong."

He smiled. It did things to me, made me dizzy and flushed.

"You called me a chicken," he said.

"So I started it? Very mature, Nick. I thought you were old and wise." I reached out and ran my hand through his soft hair. "Is this all dyed? Are you naturally grey?"

His smile widened. "No."

"Can you prove it?"

He raised an eyebrow. "Yes." He set his hand in his lap.

Oh. That would prove it.

I blushed, unable to do anything but imagine him naked. That sounded like an invitation. I needed to take it. There was something about him... he made me feel safe. Understood.

Like, for once, I wasn't completely alone in the world.

"Then you should," I said.

"Are you a chemistry student?"

"No. But I am in STEM."

"You're naturally skeptical."

I nodded. "I have a hypothesis, and I need to test it. To find proof." Finishing my drink pushed my boldness. "It's very trendy to tell women to study STEM. No one approaches it like this though."

"You'd rather colleges tell women they can use STEM to get laid?" He laughed. "I hope you aren't going into politics."

"No." I bit my tongue just in time to keep from admitting I was a programmer. That would make it easy for him to find me. "I'm a science girl, through and through."

"You're a beautiful, smart young woman. I doubt you need STEM to get laid."

My cheeks flushed. "Thank you." My tongue was tied. I had to regain control of the conversation. "It does improve my odds. My classes are eighty percent male. The guys love talking to me because they think I'm a ditz."

"You don't carry yourself like a ditz."

"I wear heels."

"And glasses."

"You can't be an idiot in glasses?"

"An idiot, yes. I have the misfortune of working with

many idiots in glasses. But a ditz? No. You'd lose your glasses."

I laughed. "That's your argument?"

He nods.

"It's flimsy."

"I'm not a lawyer."

I nodded and took a deep breath. I was done with teasing. I stared back into his eyes. "Will you prove it?"

"If you want me to fuck you, you should ask."

Well, shit. He was blunt.

"You want to fuck me," he said.

I nodded a yes.

He smiled, charmed. "You don't play coy."

"Should I?"

"No." He looked into my eyes. "Do you want to have another drink in the lobby or in my room?"

"Your room."

———

HIS HOTEL ROOM WAS A CORNER SUITE. IT HAD A PLUSH king bed, a wall-mounted TV, and a side room with a couch and a desk. That paled in comparison to the view outside the long windows.

The Bay Bridge was lit up in white, a gorgeous contrast against the dark blue water and sky around it.

San Francisco was beautiful.

I was being unfair, writing off the entire state of California. It had a lot to offer.

But none of it appealed as much as being able to meet Kat for brunch every Sunday.

His fingers grazed my neck as he clicked the door shut. His touch was soft. Commanding.

He went to hang his jacket on the wall.

My eyes stayed fixed on the view.

Nothing could have stopped me, definitely not the fact that I had no business poking around Nick's room without his permission.

I went straight to the balcony door, pulled it open, and stepped outside.

Cold air rushed over my skin. The rain had stopped, but the floor was still slick. I pressed my hands against the railing and peered to the mostly empty street thirty floors below me.

I was up high.

Too high for anyone to see me.

Inside the room, Nick poured two glasses of whiskey on the rocks. He was methodical about it. No rush, like he had all the time in the world.

It gave the nerves racing around my body time to catch up to my brain. The only thing I knew about him was his first name, and I was in his hotel room, ready to throw myself on his bed.

Was I reckless or brave?

His eyes met mine as he stepped onto the balcony. He was tall. Even in my heels, I was three or four inches shorter.

He handed me my glass. I drank quickly. I didn't need the taste. I needed the release from my inhibitions.

I set my empty glass on the side table sandwiched between two patio chairs.

His eyes passed over me. He moved closer, so he was three inches behind me, his body heat chasing away any goosebumps on my arms.

"I want to fuck you, Marie, but you need to understand that I do things a certain way."

I made a mental note that I'd told him to call me Marie. "What is that?"

"I'm always in control."

I squeezed the railing to steady myself.

"Am I mistaken, or do you want that too?"

"Yes." I bit my lip. It overwhelmed me, how much I wanted him in control. It had only been a passing fantasy. Something to go to when I couldn't sleep. Not something to seek out. "But what if I stop wanting it?"

"Say stop, and I'll stop."

"That simple?"

"Why make it complicated?" He leaned down, his mouth inches from my ear. "Take off your dress."

I turned so we were eye to eye. Or eye to chin, given our height difference.

His expression was intense, hungry.

I pulled the straps of my dress off my shoulders, first the left, then the right.

My bra was nothing fancy, but his eyes opened wide like it was the best thing he'd ever seen. Those eyes followed my hands as I pushed the dress to my knees and kicked it off my feet.

They made their way up my body, back to my eyes.

"Take off your bra." He stared back at me.

I unhooked my bra and tossed it aside.

He looked me over slowly, like he was taking a mental picture. "You're beautiful."

Heat surged through my body. I'd never stripped like this for someone, and I was doing it for a stranger. I was standing on the balcony in nothing but a thong and heels.

He traced a line over the cherry blossom tattoo on my side. "What does this mean?"

"They're just flowers."

"Not true." His fingers rested on the Latin quote next to the petals. "*Memento mori*. Remember your mortality." He looked at me as if to ask for an explanation. "You're a little young to worry about dying."

"I almost died when I was fifteen."

"When your parents did?" He traced the lines of my tattoo again and again.

My chest panged. Usually, I avoided talking about the accident. Usually, I avoided sharing anything that made me vulnerable.

But there was no reason to hold back. We only had that night. I was going to make the most of it.

I stared back into his eyes. "Yes. It was a car accident. It left me in the ICU for a week. When I got out, I couldn't walk, and my back was messed up. It took six months of rehab and physical therapy to get back to normal. I have to be careful, do all sorts of exercises and yoga, but I mostly manage okay."

"Is there anything you can't do?"

I took a deep breath. He was asking about sex, if there was anything he needed to be careful about. It was a concern and the main reason why I'd never considered anything casual. I didn't want to have a back spasm on a stranger's bed.

But, mostly, I'd been fine. I shook my head. "I'll let you know if it starts acting up."

"Did you have anyone to help you?"

I nodded. "My sister. She's done a lot for me. Worked full-time instead of going to college. I owe her everything, and I'd do anything for her." Like take a merit-based scholarship at a school across the country so she wouldn't feel like she had to help.

"Where is she?" he asked.

"In New York."

"Far away."

I nodded. "Too far."

The wind picked up. It was cold and I was nearly naked.

Nick must have recognized it in my expression. He rubbed my arms to warm me up.

It was incredibly effective.

I ran my fingers over the metal railing. "She's not like me. She's an optimistic, romantic person who sees the good in everything."

"What are you like?"

"I don't know. A cynic, I guess." I shifted so I could feel his chest against my back. "After that accident, I was struck with this knowledge that I could lose everything at any moment. I didn't want to forget that feeling." Or to ever hurt like that again. If I didn't let people in, they couldn't hurt me. It was lonely, but it was safe too.

He looked closer. "You never forget something like that."

"Do you assume you know everything?"

"Only most things." His smile faded quickly. He pressed his fingertips into my skin. "My mother had ovarian cancer. Stage four. She had a chance of survival, but it meant invasive surgery and a year of chemo and radiation."

"She decided to die instead of fighting it?"

"That is a pessimistic way of looking at it."

"And how did you look at it?"

"I was only nineteen. I was terrified."

I looked back to him. "You get scared?"

"Not anymore. Losing her, it made everything else feel trivial."

I nodded. I understood exactly what he meant.

"It was over fast. Two months."

I swallowed hard. "So you know too, how little the

world gives a fuck about you or anything you want? That you need to grab it and hold onto it before it's gone."

"I care what you want." He brought his body against mine. "You want to come?"

Heat surged through my body. Somehow, I didn't feel self-conscious. "Yes."

He moved closer. My bare skin pressed against his suit. Even with the thick fabric between us, I could feel the warmth of his body. I slung my hands around his neck and rose to my tiptoes.

He pulled my glasses off and set them on the side table. Almost. He leaned down and brushed his lips against mine. The kiss threw gasoline on the fire raging through me. Any doubts I had were burned away. I opened my mouth to make way for his tongue. He was an amazing kisser, aggressive and in control.

His hands slid around my waist and held me close. My sex clenched. When his hands drifted to my ass, I almost screamed.

The kiss broke, and he stared into my eyes. His expression was so intense.

He pressed his lips to mine, and I knew we were done with the conversation part of the evening. Thank God, because I was quickly losing my ability to form a coherent thought.

Nick pushed my panties to my feet. I was naked on that balcony. The air was cold against my bare skin, but I didn't mind. My body was on fire. He was so close to touching me.

Then he was touching me. His hand skimmed my sex, stopping on my clit. The pressure was already intense. I slung my arm around his neck to keep my balance.

He moved a little faster, a little harder. His other hand went to my chest. He traced circles around my nipples.

His kiss broke, and he stared into my eyes with equal parts care and demand.

I stared back the best I could. It was too much. I had to close my eyes to contain the orgasm building inside me.

There.

My body clenched. I tugged at his oxford shirt, moaning as I came.

All my muscles relaxed at once. My knees buckled, but he caught me.

He lifted me into his arms, carried me into the main room, and laid me on the bed.

Slowly, Nick stripped to his boxers.

His body was a work of art. Hard and defined.

And not a grey hair in sight.

He pressed his lips against my neck then kissed a trail down my chest and stomach. "Spread your legs."

I did.

His fingertips brushed against the sides of my knees. They trailed up my thighs, getting closer and closer. He pressed his lips against my inner thigh. Then closer. Closer.

Then he was sucking on my outer lips. My legs rose of their own accord. Nick dug his hands into my thighs to hold them against the bed.

He was in control.

It was hot as hell.

Pleasure built as he licked me up and down. I groaned, my free hand digging into the cool cotton sheets. His tongue was soft and his movements were confident.

Finally, I understood all the fuss about oral sex.

It was amazing.

My sex clenched, tighter and tighter, then so tight I wanted to scream. His next lick sent me tumbling into an orgasm.

"Nick." I groaned his name as I came. It encouraged him, made his tongue faster, more desperate.

He kissed his way back up my body, not shy about pressing his lips to mine.

It was strange tasting myself. Intimate.

I ran my hands down his stomach. When I got to his belly button he recoiled. His fingers curled around my wrist.

"Wait." He pressed my hand flat against the bed.

The look in his eyes was clear. He didn't want me touching him.

It was a shame, but I could manage it.

He grabbed a condom from the bedside table and rolled it on. I leaned back, spreading my legs to give him access.

I took a deep breath, bracing myself. He was big.

Nick slid one hand under my ass, holding me in place. His cock strained against my sex. The latex tugged for a moment, then he slipped inside me.

Fuck yes. My body cried out with relief. I dug my nails into his strong back as he thrust into me. He started slow, then went faster, harder, deeper. I rocked my hips to match his movements.

There were no words, but his body communicated so much.

Maybe I'd drunk too much of that whiskey, but I felt more than his cock inside me. There were no pretenses. This was Nick, the real Nick.

And it was the real me. I'd given him a fake name, but I wasn't holding anything back.

I was giving myself to him. For the night.

Every thrust sent me closer to another orgasm. This tall, dark, handsome stranger's body was pressed against mine.

The anonymity of it had me breathless. He was never going to see me again. There was no reason to be shy.

I clawed at his back, panting and groaning. He had to know how good I felt, how much I wanted him.

Every time I scraped my nails against his back or screamed his name, Nick moved faster or harder. His body was shaking. His eyes were heavy. He groaned and dug his teeth into the skin on my shoulder.

I bucked my hips to meet him. My heart was racing, my breath was completely out of my control. He felt good inside me. His skin felt good against mine. His lips felt good against mine.

And the night was ours.

When I came, I held back nothing. I screamed and panted and rocked my hips as quickly as I could.

Nick dug his nails into my ass, holding my body against his so he could go deeper.

He wasn't far behind. He nipped at my shoulder as he came.

Our bodies untangled. I relaxed into the bed as he took care of the condom. He shifted back, next to me. His expression was soft, like we were old lovers instead of strangers.

"Have you eaten?" he asked.

"No."

"Then allow me." He pressed his lips to mine, pushed off the bed, and stepped into his slacks.

———

THE REST OF THE NIGHT WAS A BLUR, THANKS VERY much to the powers of rum and Diet Coke.

We ate at some fantastic hole-in-the-wall Chinese place. The food was spicy, authentic.

I let everything off my chest, told Nick things I'd never told anyone. About the accident. About how lonely I was at school. About the things I wanted for my future, the way it only included me and my sister—no husband, no children, no pets. No concerns but my career. No one I could lose forever.

Back in the hotel room, we had sex. I fell asleep in his arms.

When I woke, he was gone. There was a change of clothes, all in my size, on the table. Next to it was a present —a white box with a sheer red bow. The card was simple.

*Dear Marie,*

*Happy birthday. Think of me when you wear this.*

*Sincerely,*

*Nick*

I pulled at the bow until it unfurled then opened the box. Inside was a set of lacy black lingerie. It was exactly like him—classy, elegant, refined.

I changed into my new threads. Knowing the lingerie was under my simple jeans and t-shirt made me feel racy, like I had a secret from the world.

I did. We did. We'd had this night together, and even though we'd never see each other again, it was ours.

# Chapter Three

My cell phone's ring rouses me from my daydreams. Sarah.

"Hey," I answer.

"Meet me at 8:30 for dancing? Pretty please."

My friend's brand of dance-until-you-find-someone-to-take-home fun is exactly what I need. "That sounds perfect."

"Robin is still fucking that guy from The Gap. She went over there twenty minutes ago."

"Maybe they're having a nice conversation."

"You're not that naive, sweet thang." She laughs. "Club is all ages tonight. Leave your fake ID at home."

"Done." My mood lifts. I latch onto my desire to lose myself in music. Not as good as losing myself in Nick's groans, but it's all I've got. "See you then."

"Ciao, bella."

I hang up and toss my phone on the bed in the guest room. The silence of the apartment amplifies my thoughts.

I dig through my bottom drawer to find the lingerie set he gave me. The sight of it is enough to make my heart race. My sex clenches, my body remembering the finesse of his touch.

I do away with my clothes and pull on the lacy black bra and panty set.

It's almost like he's here. Like he's on the other side of the mirror, staring back at me with his eyes wide and his lips parted. Like he's about to press me onto the bed, peel my thong to my knees, and bury himself deep inside me.

But he's not here.

He's not fucking me.

He's not going to fuck me.

There are half a million eligible men in New York City.

Tonight, I'm going to find one, and I'm going to forget all about Phoenix Marlowe.

———

I MEET SARAH AT A CLUB ON THE LOWER EAST SIDE. Her hot pink dress makes her easy to spot.

She bounces over and throws her arms around me.

I hug her back. It's been a while. It's nice to see her.

"You look hot as fuck. You're out for cock tonight, huh?" She throws her brown hair over her shoulder. "Oh shit. Your job thing was today, huh?"

"It was a nightmare." I need to think about something else. Now. "How's Pixie Dust?"

"Same old shit." She takes my arm and pulls me to the entrance. "What happened?"

"The guy who owns the company doesn't think I'm good enough for it."

"Fuck him then."

God, how I want to.

At nine on a Wednesday, there's no line. We show our

IDs at the door—the backs of my hands are marked with swanky black Xs to signify that I am absolutely not to be served any alcohol—and walk inside.

The warehouse-turned-club has tall ceilings and soft red lighting. The dance floor is packed. The room is warm with body heat.

Sarah whispers in my ear, "I'll get you a rum and diet. Meet you on the floor."

She crosses to the bar. I follow a few paces behind, stopping in the middle of the vinyl. It only takes a moment for someone to approach me—a guy in his mid-twenties with strawberry blond hair and a navy shirt. It's a good combination.

"I'm Jason." He offers his hand.

I slide it around my waist. "Let's dance."

Okay, Jason. Let's do this. He's no Phoenix Marlowe but he's cute. He seems nice. I sling my arm around his neck and get close.

My body refuses to respond to his. Instead, it whines *tell Nick you're over the internship. That you'd rather get under him.*

Dammit, I thought my body and I were finally on good terms. I try, hard, to find a connection with Jason, but it's not happening. I try to lean back, to let him lead, but he can't handle it. He looks at me with uncertainty.

"You want to come to my place?" he asks.

Okay. Maybe I can work with that. I go to nod, to say yes, but my head fills with the image of Nick naked on that bed, his perfect, hard body pressed against mine.

Jason will not do.

Nothing but Nick will do.

"Thanks but I... I have a boyfriend." Can't get over someone. Same difference. I take a step backwards. "My friend, Sarah. You're her type." She has a thing for blonds but he's close enough. I scan the room for her but her pink dress is nowhere to be found. "I'll point her to you later."

Jason nods enthusiastically. Great. He's not even pretending like I'm more than a lay. Not that I can talk. I'm more than willing to use him to forget about Nick.

Only nothing will make me forget about Nick. It's been four months and he still drifts into my head every night.

I excuse myself and dance alone. It's not quite as fun, but there's nothing limiting my movement. One thing about almost losing your ability to walk—you learn to appreciate everything your hips can do.

I make figure eights, rolling my shoulders, shifting my weight between my legs.

My attention focuses on the pounding music and the motions of my body.

It's like a record skips.

There's this tall man thirty feet away. Dark hair, sleek black suit, perfect posture.

Nick.

His eyes find mine. They're just as demanding as they were in his office, as they were that night in San Francisco. He walks to me with a patient gait. His hand brushes against my shoulder. He leans in close, so his mouth is inches from my ear. "Let's talk."

I rise to my tiptoes so I can speak into his ear. It's the only way to communicate besides screaming. "What are you doing here?"

"This isn't a private club."

"Not your scene either." I step back. "Unless you're here to find a woman to take back to your place."

His eyes bore into me. He points to the red couch in the corner.

I step to the side. "We don't have anything to talk

about. You have your company, and I have nothing. You don't have to rub it in."

"This is important."

His grip tightens around my shoulder, more protective than forceful. Heat rushes through my body. It's like I'm on fire. That demanding look in his eyes is enough to undo me, but his hands on my skin?

My breath catches in my throat. I take another step sideways. Nick wants to talk. I want that job. This opportunity is more important than my pride.

That doesn't make it easier to look at him without melting.

"Fine." I follow him to the couch in the corner. It's still loud, but not loud enough to overpower a conversation.

Nick sits next to me. His knee connects with mine. He turns his body towards mine, planting his hand just outside my thigh.

His thumb brushes against the hem of my dress. He moves his hand an inch, like it really was an accident. "I can't have this information get out."

"Which part—that you fucked me or that you chose not to hire me because of it?" So much for swallowing my pride. I really need a better handle on my temper.

"My personal life needs to stay private."

"Next time try using the telephone instead of stalking a girl to a club. How did you even know I was here?"

"Your friend tagged you on Instagram."

"You looked for me on social media?"

I go to push myself off the couch but Nick grabs my wrist.

"I called the number from your résumé three times."

I dig into my purse and find my phone to see if he's telling the truth. He is. One call while I was getting ready, another around the time I got off the subway. Which means call three happened sometime while I was underground.

One point in the Nick-isn't-an-asshole tally.

"I did a background check," he says.

"Why?"

"Standard procedure for all potential Odyssey employees." He stares into my eyes. "You're only nineteen. You have a fake ID."

"I plead the fifth." I hold up the back of my hand to show off my nifty X. "This is an all-ages club."

"You're eight years younger than I am."

"Yeah, well it's not like we're going to get married." I throw my brown hair back. I have a goal here, and it's not to insult Nick as much as possible within a fifteen-minute span. It's to get a job at his company. I clear my throat and offer a polite smile. "If you don't trust me, I understand, but I'm not going to tell anyone about the night we spent together."

"Your sister?"

"Do you have a problem with Blake Sterling or just with me knowing him?"

"Both."

"Blake is the one who told me about your company. He's not interested in stealing your trade secrets."

"How can you be sure?" His eyes bore into me.

"You think I would do that to you?"

"I don't think with my cock."

My chest pangs. That's all I am to him—some girl he fucked. I clear my throat, holding strong. "He wouldn't send me as a spy." I press my palms into my thighs. "He knows I don't trust him."

"You're staying in his apartment."

"How the fuck do you know that?"

"You listed it as your address in your application."

30

"Oh." My back softens. "I'm staying for winter break. Our old place is sublet, and I don't exactly have the spare cash for a hotel. If I don't get this internship, it's back to California, to the Stanford dorms."

Nick's shoulders relax. "You'll need to sign a non-disclosure agreement."

"Of course." It's standard procedure at every tech company.

"It will include our personal relationship."

That's not as standard. I take a sharp breath. "What personal relationship is that?"

"I'm not going to fuck an intern."

Great, I'm an intern. In his head, I don't even have a name.

Wait.

I'm an intern.

I have to sign an NDA.

He's offering me the job.

Well, I guess it's technically an internship. Since it's for school credit.

I tug at the hem of my dress, accidentally revealing my purple tights all the way to mid-thigh. Okay, maybe it's more my subconscious taking over. "Are we... friends?"

"We're colleagues. I'm expecting you to keep this professional. As far as I'm concerned, we met today. Do you understand me?"

I nod. I want to tell him to go fuck himself, but I know enough about working to hold my tongue.

His expression softens. "I want you, Lizzy. You're the best candidate. And the only one who isn't as dull as a doorknob."

The way he says it, *I want you, Lizzy*—it does things to me. Makes it difficult to breathe.

As if on cue, Sarah approaches us. She hands me a half drunk rum and diet and shakes Nick's hand.

"I'm Sarah."

"Lizzy's new boss." He turns to me. "I'll send an offer in the morning. You start immediately."

"I haven't agreed to take the position."

"You will."

His hand brushes against my thigh as he shifts off the couch. It sends a wave of heat through my body.

The way he's looking at me, the stern tone of his voice —I want to close my eyes and drink it in.

I want to throw myself on this couch and spread my legs as wide as they'll go.

Fortunately, my libido isn't quite as unchecked as my temper. I smooth my dress and take a small sip of my beverage.

Nick's eyes go to my drink. "You're nineteen."

"And it's a Diet Coke."

"Diet Coke is almost black. There's rum in that drink."

Sarah looks at me, her eyes wide with wonder. She mouths *holy shit*.

Okay, so Nick has the observational powers of a god. That will make it more difficult to keep my list under wraps.

He slides his hand into his pocket. "I am not understanding about employee indiscretions."

I slurp the last drop of my rum and diet. "Still didn't take the job yet."

My snappy comeback does nothing to soothe me. He's still so cool and collected. That night must not have meant anything to him.

I make a point of bending over to set my drink on the floor. My dress shifts down, revealing the top of my lacy black bra. The one he gave me.

He licks his lips. His pupils dilate. He doesn't hide that he's staring.

Doesn't hide that he wants me.

My cheeks flush. I should feel victorious—Nick wants me—but I feel deprived. Empty.

I can't have him.

I want him. He wants me. But we have to stay professional.

Sometimes, I loathe adulthood.

Nick nods goodbye to Sarah. "Nice to meet you." His gaze catches mine. "Take the morning to finish arranging everything. Ms. Lee will expect you in the office by 1:00."

"Okay."

"Goodnight, Lizzy."

He leans in, close enough that I can smell his cologne, and kisses me on the cheek.

My lungs empty. He was close enough to kiss me. He did kiss me. On the cheek, yeah, but his lips were on my skin.

And now he's walking away.

"Goodnight." I press my hands against my tights.

Sarah fans herself. "Holy fuck, Lizzy. That's your boss? He sure puts Robin to shame."

I turn back to the dance floor, but it's like all the energy is being sucked out a black hole. I don't want to dance with any of these guys. Not when I can still smell Nick's cologne.

My eyes flutter closed. I can almost taste his lips. I can almost feel his hands on my skin, his body pressed against mine, his cock—

"Snap out of it. Go after him or forget about him. You're not moping on my watch." She leans in to whisper. "He was looking at you with fuck-me eyes." *You should go after him.*

"He's my boss and this opportunity is important to me."

Sarah pouts. "Then let's find someone who will get your mind off him."

I nod, determined to prove I can want someone more than I want Nick. Anything is possible. "And if you see Kat—"

"My lips are sealed, sweet thang."

————

I TRY HALF A DOZEN DANCE PARTNERS. ALL OF THEM PALE in comparison to Nick.

My body remains flushed and wanting. All the dancing in the world will do nothing to release the tension between my legs.

I sit on the couch with a drink while I wait to approve Sarah's fuck of the night as safe enough to leave with.

He's a tanned surfer boy. Harmless and likely high on weed. I text her my approval and a reminder to use protection and I head home.

The air outside is cold, a few degrees below freezing, but my skin keeps sizzling.

Back at Blake's place, I go straight to the spare bedroom. My room for the time being.

I unzip my boots and peel off my tights. I do it slowly, the way Nick would.

He's not going to fuck me. That much is clear. It's a good thing for our professional relationship. I can learn a lot from him, about programming and about AI specifically.

Deep, slow breath. Not fucking Nick is a good thing. It's absolutely a good thing. Totally, absolutely a good thing.

I press my eyes closed and drag my hand up my thighs.

He's never going to fuck me.

I need to get over how badly I want him.

I slide my panties to my knees. I need the release. A healthy way to deal with all the desire coursing through my body.

My fingers slide over my clit. I'm already so sensitive, like my body remembers how much it enjoyed Nick.

Memories fill my head as I stroke myself to an orgasm. The release is there, but I don't feel any more satisfied.

I'm only more desperate to have him.

# Chapter Four

The intercom buzzes at 7 AM sharp. There's a mountain of paperwork waiting for me at the front desk. I spend the morning finishing it and dealing with Stanford administration.

I arrive at Odyssey at exactly 1 PM, just as Nick requested. Jasmine helps me set up my desk and get familiar with the company software.

The office empties around five-thirty, but I stay, lost in my work.

At six, an instant message pops up on my computer screen.

*Phoenix Marlowe: Miss Wilder, please come to my office at your earliest convenience. I need to speak with you.*

I bite my lip. Does he have to be so formal?

We're colleagues. That's it. I can do that.

I power down my computer, collect my things, and knock on the door.

"Come in," he answers.

I do. He's sitting behind his desk, all his attention on his computer screen. His office is huge. There's a couch, a wet bar, and an amazing view of the buildings on the other side of Broadway.

His focus shifts to me. "How was it?"

"Amazing." I clear my throat and try something a little more professional. "I expect it will take me a few days to get familiar with everything."

"Interns are allowed to be excited."

"I'm aware that I'm an intern, Nick."

"Please address me by my last name while we're at work." He shifts out of his seat, all business. "We need to discuss your living arrangements."

"I'm pretty sure that where I live is none of your business, Mr. Marlowe."

"You can't stay with Blake Sterling. I won't punish you for your sister's engagement, but it doesn't look right, an employee staying with the CEO of a competing company."

"I don't have anywhere else to stay. Do you have any idea how much it costs to rent a place in the city?" I fold my arms over my chest. "No, I suppose you're too rich to care about little trifles like rent."

"I'm aware of the market."

"Own enough buildings that it matters to you?"

"Don't insult my wealth. The money doesn't matter to me."

"Money never matters to people who have it." *Go to hell for telling me what to do.*

I take a deep breath. This is an important opportunity. I'm not throwing it away, even if it kills me that he's this calm and collected.

I press my palms against my skirt. "I can't accept a salary without losing my school credit. The two-thousand-dollar-a-month stipend is more than generous."

He scribbles something on a memo pad and hands it to me.

It's an address.

"A leasing company," he says. "We offer employees discounted apartments."

Nick rises to his feet. He looks even taller and grander standing in his sleek, modern office.

"For you, I'll pay the extra." He stares at me.

"You're paying for my apartment?"

"The company is. It will be yours through June." His voice is stern but his expression is protective.

Does Nick really care about my well-being? This can't be cheap.

But then he's a billionaire. It's all relative.

I stare back at him. It doesn't help. He's unreadable.

"Is that legal?" I ask.

"Yes. I can refer you to the company lawyer—"

"No, I trust you. About work." And about sex. But that isn't happening. I need to stop thinking about it.

"I'll take you to sign the papers tomorrow."

*Did that night mean anything to you? Even a little bit?*

I swallow hard. As much as I love my sister, I hate feeling like a third wheel crashing at her fiancé's place.

I've always wanted my own apartment.

I make eye contact with Nick. "Fine. But I can't go tomorrow. My sister gets back from St. Barts tomorrow."

"Lucky her."

"Yes, she's very lucky and very happy and very in love. But, really, Blake is the one who is lucky to have her, because she's—"

"Caring, sweet, and idealistic?"

His face is smug, like he's satisfied with his memory.

"Yes." I fold my arms. How can he remember such a specific detail and still act like we're strangers?

Nick moves out from behind his desk. He grabs his coat

from the rack and slides it around his shoulders. "We'll go now."

———

We go straight to the apartment building.

The elevator ride is unbearable. His hand skims my lower back. It's enough to send heat racing through my body.

Nick is ten inches away. Close enough to touch. Close enough to rip off every one of my four layers, press me up against the elevator, and bury himself deep inside me.

He's wearing that same fucking cologne.

My thoughts do nothing to straighten once we're inside the apartment. I try to focus on taking in the small yet elegant place.

The high-tech, stainless steel kitchen serves as a hall-way. Hardwood floors. Just enough room for a desk, a TV, a bed, and a yoga corner.

He could press me against the wall. He could peel off my coat and unbutton my blouse and tease me until I'm panting.

We're alone.

No one has to know.

I swallow hard. I'm the one with everything to lose. I can't fuck this up.

There are low clouds in the sky. A storm on the way. But nothing is stopping me from going out on that balcony.

I unlock the glass door. Frigid air nips at my nose and chin.

I button my coat and shove my hands into my pockets as I step outside.

It's slick. There's a small puddle a few feet from the

built-in drain. Leftover from the New Year's Day snow. Or as simple as a drunk upstairs neighbor spilling his cocktail.

I hold onto the railing to peer over the edge. Ten stories is still plenty high. In one direction, the river is dark and choppy. In the other, the steel and glass reflect the grey sky.

Nick steps onto the balcony. His hands go to my waist and he holds tightly. "Careful."

"Is it bad for your liability insurance if an intern falls to her death?"

"Lizzy, you—" He stops himself. "I would be very unhappy if something happened to you."

I release the railing, shifting my waist so I'm pressed against him. "Why?"

"You know the answer to that."

"Actually, I don't." I turn to face him. "And I don't appreciate you pretending like that night meant something to you."

"It did."

I play with the button of my coat. "Should I strip right here to remind you how it went?"

"You'll freeze to death."

"Probably worse for your liability insurance if an intern freezes to death naked on the balcony while the CEO watches."

He frowns, not at all amused. "Will it make you feel better proving that I want you?"

"Yes."

"Then do it." He stares at me, daring me.

Okay. I can do that. I unbutton my coat and slide if off my shoulders. The cold air nips at my forearms. My blouse does nothing to keep me warm. There's no way I'm undressing here.

Nick's eyes are fixed on me. "Come here." He slides his arms around my waist, pulling my body against his.

Instantly, I'm warm. I'm safe. I'm whole.

It was one night. I shouldn't want him this much. Shouldn't feel like we're old lovers.

Nick pulls me inside. He grabs my coat from the balcony and slings it around my shoulders.

His touch is gentle, caring.

He leans in to whisper, "It won't help things, baiting me. You aren't going to get me to break."

"To break what?"

"I have rules about this. I don't sleep with people who work under me." His voice fills with regret. "You're a bright girl with a great future ahead of you. I'm not letting you give that up because you have a crush on me."

"It's not a crush." My temper surges. Half of me hates him for assuming he knows what's best for me. The other half is desperate for the intimacy we shared once upon a time.

Behind us, the wind howls. The balcony door pounds against the frame. Nick's expression is intense and he's staring right at me.

"You're not going to forgive yourself if you sacrifice this opportunity." He releases his grip on my waist and goes to shut and lock the balcony door. "And I'm not going to forgive myself if you give up your career for me. I don't do relationships. You really want to throw away your future to fuck me again?"

I turn to face him. There's nothing but grey sky and steel buildings behind him. It's so fucking fitting.

"What if I did?" I ask.

"That's not the girl I met last September. Or the girl I met yesterday."

"Maybe you don't know anything about me."

"Do you really believe that?" His eyes bore into me.

He is trying to protect me. But from what? He owns the company. He can make whatever rules he wants.

He can fuck me and work with me.

"It's your company," I say. "Can't you change the rules?"

"Yes, but I won't."

"Why?"

"I stay in control of my life."

He's still looking at me like he's fixed on protecting me. It's sweet... but annoying. I take care of myself. I don't need his help.

Even if I want him tearing off my clothes.

Dammit, working with him is going to be impossible.

He steps closer. "There were two dozen excellent bots in your portfolio. They were smart, adaptable. You must have spent months trying to figure out that Go AI."

"It's terrible."

"Go is considered un-crackable. I've seen worse attempts from programmers with fifteen years of experience." He holds my gaze. "You love artificial intelligence, don't you?"

"Yes."

"Me too. The last five years of my life have been about this project. You won't find a better place to learn. And you won't be satisfied interning somewhere else. You'll be a code monkey."

"Monkeys are cute. You should see the monkey keychain on my purple Kipling bag. It's adorable." I fold my arms. He's right. Most internships are grunt work. Most advanced AI projects are only accessible to PhDs. This is the best chance I'll ever get to learn about programming artificial intelligence.

"Pretend that night never happened. Archive it away in your memory."

Anger rises in my gut, pushing away my logic. I stare back at him. "Where? In my spank bank?"

"If you'd like."

I examine his expression for any sign of emotion. Nothing. "Is that what you did?" I see red. "Do you think about that night, about me, when you fuck yourself?"

His expression cracks. Finally. His lips turn down. His eyes fill with frustration. He's upset.

I should feel victorious, but I don't.

"I don't care about many people, Lizzy. That night meant a lot to me."

I swallow hard. "Then why are you treating me like this?"

"What matters more to you—proving that I want you or learning about AI?" he asks.

"Why do I have to choose?"

"You win. I want you. I want you in my bed, under my control, screaming my name as you come." He stares at me. "Do you feel better?"

"No."

His voice gets stern. "I want you working at Odyssey, but I will fire you if you push me."

I swallow hard. "Do you think about that night?"

"Yes."

"When you fuck yourself?"

"Often."

His voice is dripping with confidence. He thinks of me often? Suddenly, this coat is far too heavy. I'm burning up.

He thinks about me when he fucks himself.

How am I supposed to resist him, knowing that?

His voice softens. "Mostly, I think about our conversation." He crosses towards the door, motioning for me to follow. "As far as I'm concerned, I met a woman named Marie and never saw her again. Do you understand me?"

"I'm not a child. Don't patronize me." I understand. I've got to pretend that we never shared anything. It may as well have been a different guy that night.

Only, the Nick in front of me—the hurt in his eyes, the strength in his posture, the determination in his voice—is exactly the guy I met last year.

It's not like I work with him directly. I can avoid Nick at the office enough to pretend.

I take one more look at the apartment. That white winter light is beautiful, especially bouncing off the shiny hardwood floor. It will be my space. All mine.

"Thank you for the apartment," I say. "It's beautiful."

"It's not from me. It's a company apartment."

"Only technically."

He doesn't correct me. Once again, winning doesn't make me feel better.

I only feel empty.

Nick wants me.

He thinks about me when he fucks himself.

He's paying for my apartment.

He's fixed on protecting me.

But I can't have him.

The facts don't add up. There's something missing, something he's not telling me.

Judging from the stern expression in his eyes, he's not going to explain. I have to accept things.

Nick pulls the door open for me. "I'll have someone from my team pack up your stuff at Stanford. It may take a few weeks to clear it with the school."

"I have enough for a few weeks."

We make our way to the elevator. Then to the street. To the subway station.

Nick nods goodbye. "Your apartment should be ready by the end of next week. If there's anything specific you need—" He pulls a business card from his pocket. "My personal number."

I stare at the business card, confused.

This doesn't make sense. If we're keeping things professional, what do I need with his personal number?

He thinks about me when he fucks himself.

I'm never going to concentrate on anything else again.

## Chapter Five

Friday passes without a single Nick sighting. He's locked in his office, all by himself.

I leave a few minutes after five. A familiar voice greets me in the lobby. It starts as a girlish shriek.

"Your dress is so pretty!" Kat throws her arms around me. "I can't believe how grown up you look. I'm going to cry."

"You'll embarrass me."

"Someone has to do it." She pulls her cell phone from her pocket and snaps a picture. "You want coffee? You look tired."

"How rude are you?" I take in all the slight changes in her appearance. "You're super tan."

She shrugs, her sun-lightened hair falling off her shoulders. I get a warm, gooey feeling in my chest. My sister is so much happier than she was last year. And she's close again.

No more pretending to laugh at Adam Sandler movies with my ex-roommate. No more pangs of loneliness from being three thousand miles away. My sister, my best friend, is back.

I squeeze her again for good measure. "As long as it's on me."

"Are you really getting a two-thousand-dollar-a -month honorarium?"

"And an apartment."

"What?" She hugs her purse. "The company is providing an apartment? But don't you want to stay with me and Blake?"

No way I'm going to continue being a burden to her. "You really want me around every night when it's time to ride your fiancé?"

"You're depraved."

"Thanks." I take Kat's hand and lead us to the street. "He drop you off on his way into the office?"

"He was really good about avoiding work all vacation." Her gaze shifts to the sky. "I know you don't like him—"

"It's not exactly that I don't like him." I don't. But it's more that I don't trust him with her heart. He nearly destroyed her last year.

"Whatever it is, I love him, and I trust him with every-thing. If you have any qualms about that, let's deal with them now. The wedding is barely three months away."

We cross the street. The local coffee shop glows like a beacon of energy.

I wait until we're inside the blissfully warm shop to turn to Kat. "Are you happy?"

She beams, her eyes all goo-goo, ga-ga in love. She nods.

"Then I am happy." I whisper in her ear. "But if he does anything to hurt you, I will throw him off that gorgeous balcony."

"How are you going to overpower Blake?"

"First, I'll drug him—"

"Where do you come up with this?"

"*Law & Order*." After the accident, we watched a lot of reruns. *Law & Order* was one of our favorites.

She tilts her head like she's weighing my idea as a potential procedural plot. "What's the snappy one-liner when Briscoe investigates the scene?"

I do my best Jerry Orbach/Lennie Briscoe imitation. "Talk about a fall from grace."

Kat cracks up. She buckles, one hand going to her mouth, the other to her stomach. "Oh my God. That's perfect. I'm so glad you're back in New York."

"Me too."

We order our drinks and wait at the counter. She leans against it, dreamily staring out the window in one of her *I'm looking at the world with my magical artist powers* moments.

"Drawing a comic in your head?" I ask.

"Sorta."

Which means she's actually thinking about Blake. Her right index finger goes to her engagement ring. Yep. Definitely thinking about Blake.

Honeymoon period, love is sweet, etc., etc., etc. It's all a little much for me.

Our drinks—two vanilla lattes—arrive at the bar. I fasten the lids and hand Kat hers.

"When are you moving into the apartment?" She sips her drink. "Holy shit, Lizzy. You're moving into your own apartment. You're so grown up."

"I went to college last year."

"But it's your apartment."

"No. It's Odyssey Industry's apartment."

"When did you get so cynical?"

"This day four years ago. You might remember it.

49

Early fall, leaves were changing, weather was cold. You were at a cross-country meet."

"Glibness is cowardice."

"Did you read that off a poster?"

"No." She frowns. "I still get upset when I think about that day. Sometimes I panic to the point where I can't even breathe. How can you pretend like it didn't destroy you?"

"You're the one asking why I'm cynical."

"I don't want to have this argument again." She takes a long sip. "Where's the apartment?"

"A few blocks away."

Kat sets her drink on the counter to clap her hands together. "Let's see."

In theory, there's nothing stopping us. The paperwork is done. Nick, or his moving company, has the key. It's only a matter of asking to use it.

"Okay." I take a long sip of my sweet, creamy beverage. "But I think Nick, I mean Mr. Marlowe, has the key."

"Nick?"

"He's not into formality." Such an obvious lie. She'll know I'm full of shit the second she meets him. "He's super—you'll like him."

"He sounds great. Super, actually." She grabs my hand and leads me back to the Odyssey building.

She spends the elevator ride giving me a maternal once-over. I shrug like I have no idea what she's suggesting.

The office is mostly empty. I lead Kat down the hallway to Nick's office. I knock once. "It's Lizzy. I have a question for you."

"Come in."

I push the door open and step inside before Kat. Not the best manners, but I don't want to terrify Nick with the sudden appearance of an outsider.

"My sister, Kat—" I hold out my hand like I'm presenting a queen at her coronation.

Kat steps inside. She goes up to Nick, who is standing behind his now-at-standing-level desk, and shakes his hand. "I've heard great things about you."

Nick looks at me as if to say *really?*

I mouth *no*.

His eyes lock with mine. He raises a brow. I'm not sure what he's saying, only that I'm supposed to be in on a private joke.

My stomach flip-flops. He trusts me. Some part of him does.

Some part of him wants to be more than colleagues.

I clear my throat. "Do you have the key to my new apartment? Kat wants to see it while she's all the way downtown."

She nudges me in that maternal *don't be so rude* kind of way.

"What? You live on the Upper East Side and go to Columbia. You're very old money."

"I'm sorry my sister is such a brat." Kat shakes her head. "I'm sure she meant to say that she's excited to live on her own for the first time, and that she wants to share her happiness with the people who love her."

"I have a younger brother." He looks at Kat with understanding. "They only get more petulant as they get older."

"I'm right here." I dig my heels into the ground, but there's this lightness in my chest. Nick is making a joke about me. He's teasing me.

I study his expression. His eyes are wide, bright. He's having fun. At my expense, but still...

He likes me.

Not that it matters. I can't do anything about it.

He opens one of his desk drawers, pulls out the key, and offers it to me. "I'll have the doorman let the moving company in."

Kat's jaw drops. "You already have a moving company lined up?"

"We'll discuss it later." I take the key, my gaze fixing on Nick. "Thank you. I'll see you Monday. Have a nice weekend. I hope you think of me."

Fuck. My lips clamp together but there's no way to get the words back into my mouth. I do want him thinking of me, desperately cursing himself for writing me off, but I can't tell him to think of me. We both know what that means.

His eyes go wide. His voice gets rough, commanding. "I will."

"Great." He's going to think of me when he fucks himself. It's hot in here. "I'll think of you." As soon as I'm alone.

Do I sound as desperate as I feel?

Kat is staring at me with a concerned look. I nod another goodbye and pull her out of the room.

As sweet and polite as always, she says nothing until we're alone in the elevator.

"What was that?" she asks.

"What was what?"

"Think of me? I'm not that naïve."

The elevator opens up to the lobby. I step onto the tile floor. "It was nothing. Inside joke."

"An inside joke about asking your boss to touch himself to you?"

"No..." I try and fail to think of another interpretation.

"I wish you wouldn't lie to me."

"It was nothing. Nick and I—"

"You called him Nick again."

52

"Did I?"

"Want to tell me what else is going on?"

"A joke. Can't explain it." Because she'll freak out about my bad decisions. "It's no big deal."

She looks me over in that maternal way. "So there's no reason why you were eye-fucking him?"

"I was not eye-fucking him. Since when do you say 'eye-fucking'?"

"Since now."

We're quiet as I lead her to the apartment building. It's about ten blocks away.

Kat is just as in awe as I was. Living with a billionaire hasn't spoiled her. She looks around the room, practically pressing her nose against the glass.

"The light here is amazing." She goes to the kitchen and examines all its fixtures. "But it's so small. Where am I supposed to sleep when I visit you?"

"You mean if you can't bear to take Blake's limo back to the Upper East Side?"

"I'm aware that he's rich. You don't have to remind me every time you talk about him."

"Sorry." My gaze goes to the balcony, my body hot and cold all at once. I need to get Nick out of my head. Even if he deserves to suffer with the kind of desire that is killing me. I turn to Kat. "Meeting loverboy for dinner?"

"Not till 8:30. Want to come? There's a great Thai place across the street from his office. I'm not sure if you realized it, but Blake is rich, so he'll probably buy your green curry."

"Blake is rich? I had no idea. I thought he was squatting in the massive apartment."

"It's a shock. Do you need time to absorb it?"

I shake my head. "We've got an hour and a half. Come

shopping with me. I already wore the only two work-appropriate outfits I own."

"You know I'll only slow you down."

"Yeah, but for some reason I like your company."

———

WE GO TO CENTURY 21, A MASSIVE DEPARTMENT STORE with terrible atmosphere and great discounts. Kat approves my outfits with a bemused smile. For an artist, she knows absolutely nothing about clothes.

My first three dresses are completely work appropriate. The fourth is a clingy wrap. All I have to do is pull the bow undone and the dress slides open.

Kat raises her eyebrows. Her voice shifts to maternal mode. "You are not going to work dressed like that. Unless you work on a porn set and you're playing the secretary who wants to seduce her boss."

I laugh like I find her idea absurd. "I'd never try to seduce someone like Nick."

"No? He's tall, dark, handsome, receptive to your eye-fucking."

"He's an asshole." I swallow hard. "You think he was receptive?"

"Why do you care?"

"I don't."

"He's rich. He's smart. And he's a programmer too."

"That combination is toxic. Rich, smart, male programmers think they're God's gift to the world."

"You just described my fiancé."

I clear my throat. "Well, he's... not as bad as he seemed at first."

"Is that your idea of a compliment?"

"No. But he's... I'm glad you're happy."

My next outfit is too sexy for work. The sheer blouse shows every inch of my bra. The skirt is tight around my ass and cut high in the back.

There's no reason to buy this. Not unless I'm going to march into Nick's office, strip to my lingerie, and demand he pay attention to me as more than an intern.

My sex clenches as the scene plays out in my head.

This opportunity is everything. But I'm considering risking it to be with him again.

What the hell is wrong with me?

"You wouldn't sleep with him?" she asks.

"You want to talk about my sex life?"

She lets out a heavy breath. "I thought about it, and you were right. I had this idea in my head of you as my innocent little sister. But you're an adult woman, and that comes with certain desires—"

God, Kat is the only person in the world who can make sex sound so After School Special.

"What kinds of desires?" I change into my next outfit. This one is too racy for work, but it's perfect for dancing. It's a low-cut black dress with a shiny zipper running from the chest to the waist. It screams *undo me*.

"Oh please, we both know you're a pervert. And it's fine if you don't want to talk about that with me. But if you do want to talk about it, I won't freak out. Even if it's to tell me that you're having casual sex every night. As long as you're being safe. If you're not being safe, then I'm going to freak out."

I unlock the dressing room door and step into the main room. The sweet expression falls off Kat's face. She looks me up and down.

"Now I know you're up to something." She shakes her head.

"It's for clubbing."

"What is the point of the zipper? So strangers can grope you more easily?"

"And if you wore it for Blake?"

Her cheeks turn bright red. "I'm going to use the bathroom. I'll meet you at the entrance."

"Sure thing."

I change and make my way to the register.

This job is too important to risk with sex. But there's no reason why I can't tease Nick. There's no reason why I can't change into this slinky black dress on my way out the door. No reason why I can't make sure he wants me as much as I want him.

# Chapter Six

Monday morning, I go straight to Nick's office.

The room is awash in soft white light. He's standing behind his desk, all tall and statuesque.

His expression is stern. He really could be made out of stone.

I knock even though the door is wide open. "Mr. Marlowe?" I bite my tongue. I worked retail for almost three years. I know how to play nice with people who frustrate me.

"How was your weekend?"

"Great. I got a lot of thinking done." My cheeks flush.

His lip corners turn down. "Do you really want to continue this?"

"Continue what?" I play dumb.

"You don't know what you're getting yourself into, Ms. Wilder."

"I'm not following."

"Yes you are."

My cheeks flush.

He knows I'm following. He knows exactly what I'm

thinking. It's written all over his face. I clear my throat and smooth my blazer.

I have to ask him for something and he's not going to agree if I push him. "I apologize, sir. I'm not sure what got into me."

He nods, accepting my apology. But there's no sign he's buying my coy reaction.

He takes a step towards me. "Your apartment is ready. Fully furnished. Your belongings won't be in until the end of next week, so I had my assistant pick up a few necessities. Call if you need anything else."

"Thank you."

He steps out from behind his desk, so he's about five feet away. "Would you like a drink?" He nods to the mini-fridge.

"Alcoholic?"

"Caffeinated."

"Whatever you're having."

He kneels to open the fridge. Somehow, he looks badass and in control on one knee.

Nick pulls two cans of black iced coffee from the fridge and hands one to me.

I nod a thank you and pop it open. Not Diet Coke, but not bad.

I take a long sip. I cultivate every ounce of my courage.

I need to do this now. Before I'm too tongue-tied to speak.

Deep breath.

Here goes nothing.

I try to copy his confident posture, but my back isn't having it. "Gabriel has no interest in training me. I don't blame him, but I do expect to work with someone who is willing to teach."

His expression gets protective. "Do you have a suggestion?"

I dig my fingers into the frigid aluminum. "There are only three senior programmers at Odyssey. Somehow, I doubt that David will be any more interested in training."

Nick nods. "You'd like to work under me?"

Fuck yes. I press the can to my neck to counteract the heat spreading across my chest. "You're the most qualified person. I'll learn the most under you."

His eyes bore into me like he's examining my intentions. "I can spare two hours a day. You'll have to get to the office by 8 AM and you'll have to stay until I'm finished, so I can check your code."

I nod. "Of course."

"You'll have some twelve-hour days. Fourteen, even."

"As long as I have an hour or two for exercises. My back—"

"I remember."

"I thought that night never happened."

He frowns. "Is it going to be a problem for you, working so close to me?"

*Of course. It's a problem being in the same city as you and not begging you to take control again.* "If it was going to be a problem, I wouldn't ask. I want to learn everything I can from you."

"About AI?"

"What else would I mean?"

He stares back at me like he doesn't buy it. "You're not good at playing coy." He finishes his can of coffee in one swig and sets it in a recycling bin. "Lizzy—"

"Nick."

"I want to work with you. You're an excellent programmer for your experience and you have a knack for AI."

"Thank you."

"I've cut you slack because of your skill."

I swallow hard.

"But that ends now. I'm not making any more exceptions."

"Of course. This is professional. We're colleagues. That's all."

"Be here at 8 AM tomorrow. We'll work in my office, alone, until ten."

"Sure."

"If there is a problem—"

"There won't be. Thank you for the opportunity."

I hold his gaze for a moment. There's something in his eyes, something more than professionalism, but I can't place it.

———

My nerves are shot. I give up on coding around four and kill time playing FreeCell. When the office clears, I leave.

I go straight to my new apartment building.

The elevator is slow. I slide my key into the lock and pull the door open.

It's past sunset. Warm blue light streams in through the windows, the dark sky mixed with the yellow fluorescent lights of nearby office buildings.

I flick on the light and step into the main room. It's a small space, but it's perfect. There's a full bed against the wall. It's covered with a royal purple comforter and a lilac blanket. Paper string lights line the wall—white flowers with a pale yellow glow. The whole room is shades of cream and purple. Just like the hotel lounge where we met.

It can't be a coincidence. Nick isn't a coincidence kind

of guy.

The decorations are beautiful. Feminine, soft, under-stated. Like that lounge. Like his idea of a woman's bedroom. I turn the main light off to see the string lights in all their glory, but something else catches my attention—

The view is even better in the dark. I soak it in for as long as I can.

I have my own apartment. Even if Nick decorated it. Even if Nick arranged it. Even if Nick is practically in my fucking bed.

It's still mine.

———

THE FLOOR IS DEAD AT 8 AM. THE ONLY SOUNDS COME from the end of the hall. I slide my coat off my shoulders as I make my way to Nick's office.

He's standing at his computer, his attention on the screen. There are two takeout coffee cups on his desk.

He nods to the one on the right then to a small white paper bag on top of the mini-fridge. "Cream and sugar. There's milk in the office kitchen if you prefer that."

"This is fine." I fix my coffee with two packets of half and half and two of brown sugar. "No bagels?"

He looks at me like he's trying to figure out if I'm teasing.

"I'm kidding." I look up at Nick, motioning to my coat. "Is there some place where I should put this?"

"Anywhere is fine."

Doubtful. His office is incredibly neat. I didn't notice before, but it's well decorated. The minimalist artwork is abstract shapes in bold colors. They match the clean white walls and the sleek black desk.

I set my coat on the couch. Such a nice couch. It would

be so easy for him to throw me onto it, to pull up my skirt, roll down my tights, and press his palm against me.

My sex clenches. I can't keep thinking about him like this. I need to get a hold of myself.

I take a sip and set my coffee at the end of the desk. It's currently in standing mode. "The apartment looks beautiful. Thank you."

"I'm glad you like it. You deserve the best."

What the hell is that supposed to mean? I look for something to focus on. His office is well decorated too. Mostly black and white with hints of color. "Did you decorate your office?"

He nods. "Yes. I dabble in design."

"And my apartment?"

"That too."

"Oh."

He was in my apartment, picking out the lights and the bedspread.

He picked out my fucking bedspread.

His voice calls my attention. Back to business, thank goodness.

"Are you okay with standing?" he asks.

"Sure. Can I take off my shoes?" I motion to my black pumps. Not the most comfortable for standing.

"Of course."

I slide out of my shoes and press my toes into the squishy anti-fatigue mat.

It must be so handy having a desk that can be any height you want. There are so many possibilities. He could plant me on my back and spread my legs or press my stomach flat against the desk and take me from behind.

How the hell am I going to work with him for two hours every day? I can't think about anything but him touching me again.

I clear my throat. "Would you teach me about design if I asked?"

"Yes, but I can find someone who knows more. I mostly learned from my mother. She was an artist. Her work was modern."

"Like the guy with the paintings that are all one color?"

"Ellsworth Kelly."

"Yeah! That's it." One of the paintings catches my eye. "That's him, isn't it?"

He nods.

"He has the one at the Met—the huge, single-color paintings that make up a rainbow. My sister thinks it's genius."

"And you?"

"I don't really get art." I recall a dozen rainy afternoons Kat and I spent walking around the Met. The way her eyes lit up at her favorite paintings. It was quite the revenge for forcing her to watch so much sci-fi.

I didn't mind tagging along with her, not when it made her so happy.

His hand brushes against my side.

I try to find the meaning in Nick's expression, but I can't place his expression.

"Design is all about creating a feeling in the user." He points to the painting in the corner—it's an abstract shape in a royal blue. "What does that color make you feel?"

"It's bold."

"What about the shape?"

"It's calming but dangerous. Like the ocean. A wave even." I look back to him. "Did I get it right?"

"This isn't programming. There is no right answer. Most things don't have a correct answer." He directions my attention to the code onscreen.

"What's your office supposed to feel like?"

"Power and sophistication."

"To intimidate people?"

"Not exactly."

"My apartment?"

"Softness. Purple is your favorite color, isn't it?"

"How did you know?"

"You wear it almost every day."

I look down at my outfit. My dress and shoes are black but my tights are purple. A mental check of my wardrobe suggests he's correct. Half my clothing is purple.

He pays attention to my clothing.

My heartbeat picks up. His eyes are wide. His lips are curled into the tiniest smile.

He's interested in me.

I know he is.

His attention goes to the screen. "Why don't you explain what you see here?"

I turn to the code and explain the best I can.

Nick listens intently, nodding and explaining every technical detail.

The further we get into work mode, the closer he gets to me. Until he's right behind me, his hand hovering over mine, his chest inches behind my back.

He's warm. He smells good. That hint of cologne and Nick. I hold my breath so I won't react in a way that convinces him I can't handle this. I can already tell I'll learn a lot from him.

When we break, Nick takes a huge step back. He shakes his head like he lost track of himself. Is it possible he didn't realize how close he was? That his body was taking over?

There might be some wiggle room between forgetting about that night and him firing me for pushing matters.

I try to focus on our lesson, but I keep getting

distracted. His jaw is so strong. His lips are so soft. His eyes are such a lovely shade of brown.

By 10 AM, I'm exhausted. Half from the intensity of the work, half from the proximity of his body. I slip into a coding trance for most of the day. When I surface, Nick is checking my work, still close, still strong, still hard and soft at once.

———

THERE ARE BAGELS ON HIS DESK. TWO BAGELS, EACH ON a paper plate, each dotted with cream cheese. One is onion. One is sesame.

Nick is standing behind his computer, cool and confident and utterly untouchable. He looks so handsome.

I try to remind myself that I hate him for writing me off. It's coffee and a bagel. It's not a love letter. It's not an apology. It's breakfast.

Still.

He bought me breakfast.

It's sweet.

He nods to the bagels. "Your call."

I pick sesame. "You really shouldn't eat bagels. They're nothing but empty carbs."

"I swim two miles a day."

"No wonder you have such broad shoulders." Crap. That was out loud. My inhibitions aren't at full strength yet. It's too early in the morning for them to catch up to my mouth. "Where do you swim?"

"There's a lap pool in my building."

I pull my bagel into quarters then eighths. "I practice yoga for an hour every day. Sometimes two."

"For your back?"

"That's how it started. But then I liked how it forced me to focus on my body. And how flexible it made me."

I study his expression to see if I've caused a reaction.

His pupils dilate. His eyes go to my legs. It's quick. A few seconds, max. But it's clear as day.

I take a bite of my bagel, chew, and swallow. "I hope you don't have a lunch date. Onions will ruin your breath."

He stares at me with a look that says *try a little harder with the subtlety*. Okay, I'm reading into that. But there is understanding in his eyes.

"I don't date." He opens a file on his computer. "I don't have time."

"Do you have time for anything fun? Besides exercise?"

He takes a bite of his bagel. Somehow, he does it gracefully. He motions to his computer. "I'll tell you if you find a way to improve this code."

He steps aside. My ass brushes against his crotch as we switch positions. His fingertips skim my lower back.

I check his expression. It doesn't help me figure out his intentions.

It takes twenty minutes of concentration, but I find something. I point to it. "Here. This function is redundant."

He smiles, proud. "I play poker."

"For real money?"

"It's not about the money. It's about the game."

"Right. What's the entry fee?"

"Anything from twenty dollars to twenty thousand."

"But mostly the twenty thousand?"

"Usually, around a hundred dollars."

I examine his expression for any signs he's lying. There are none. It's awfully democratic of Nick, playing any poker game that will have him. "Isn't gambling illegal?"

"Call the vice squad."

"You're all about rules."

"No. I'm about being in control. When I play poker, I'm in control of the table."

"And when you have sex?"

"Lizzy. Don't. You're only making this harder."

I clear my throat. "You brought it up."

"Yes, when I have sex, I'm in control. But you already know that."

"How do you find women who are interested?"

"It's never been an issue."

"Every woman you've been with has agreed to you being in control?"

"Yes."

"Oh."

"But I've enjoyed it more with some women than with others."

There's something about his voice, this edge to it. He's baiting me. Getting me back for pushing him.

Maybe I'm a fool for taking the bait, but I have to know.

"Anyone in particular?" I ask.

"You want me to say it was you?"

"If it's true."

"It is."

"Nick—"

He steps aside and points to the computer. Instantly, his posture changes. All business.

Okay. Fine. This time, I earned my blue balls. Blue ovaries. Whatever they're called.

Once again, I look to his expression for some clue to his intention. Maybe it's more than bait.

Maybe he's considering us together again.

I study him for a full minute. But I've got no idea what he's thinking.

## Chapter Seven

A long yoga session exhausts my energy. I'm ready to work, to stay 100 percent professional.

The second I see Nick standing behind his desk, his tie undone, his jacket tossed aside, his sleeves rolled up to his elbows—I melt.

Is he teasing me or getting comfortable? Hard to tell.

There's breakfast again. The same breakfast—bagels, coffee, half and half, brown sugar.

We spend the morning working and making small talk. We take turns adding comments about robots over-throwing the government to the code.

———

IT's THE SAME ALL WEEK. HE HAS BREAKFAST. HE STANDS so, so close to me. He flirts just enough to drive me crazy.

I spend another weekend trying to burn off energy. This time, I volunteer to follow Kat to every museum in the city. I fill every spare minute, but I still fall asleep thinking about Nick.

By week three, I can't take it anymore. I go out dancing with Sarah and get home too drunk to care about anything but making my point.

I text Nick's personal number.

*Lizzy: I need some DVDs. Movies about artificial intelligence. To inspire me.*

*Nick: Like what?*

*Lizzy: The Matrix trilogy. Battlestar Galactica, the new one. Ex Machina. You'd like it. It's all about a robot who manipulates men using her sexuality.*

*Nick: Do robots have sexuality?*

*Lizzy: I should ask you. You're about as close to a robot as I've ever seen. Have you seen it?*

*Nick: No.*

*Lizzy: Really?*

*Nick: Really. Would you rather get a rise out of me or keep your job?*

*Lizzy: Permission to speak freely, sir.*

*Nick: Permission granted.*

*Lizzy: Right now, I'd rather get a rise out of you. I'm drunk and frustrated. Are you at the office?*

*Nick: Yes.*

*Lizzy: I can come over there. We can have this conversation in person.*

*Nick: That's unwise.*

*Lizzy: Why?*

*Nick: You know why.*

My cheeks flush. It's practically a confession. For Nick, at least. He might as well say *because I want to fuck you.*

*Lizzy: No, I don't.*

*Nick: Even if things were different, I don't fuck drunk women.*

*Lizzy: Why not?*

*Nick: It's my policy.*

*Lizzy: And if I was sober?*

*Nick: Don't play coy. I respect you too much to bullshit you. I hope you feel the same towards me.*

*Lizzy: I want to read the words.*

*Nick: Did you feel better knowing I think of you when I fuck myself?*

*Lizzy: No.*

*Nick: Knowing that I want you, that I think about ripping off your skirt and binding your wrists with my tie, will only make you want it more.*

*Lizzy: So? Sometimes it's good to want things. Reminds you that you're alive. Why can't I come back to the office? Why can't we have this conversation in person?*

*Nick: Because you want to fuck me.*

*Lizzy: And?*

*Nick: And I want to tie you to my bed, rip of your panties, and suck on your clit until you're screaming my name.*

Fuck. Heat passes through me. I rub my eyes to make sure I'm not seeing things. I'm not.

*Nick: Do you feel better?*

*Lizzy: No.*

*Nick: How do you feel?*

*Lizzy: Deprived. Was that to prove a point?*

*Nick: Yes, but it was true.*

*Lizzy: I'll come over right now. No one has to know. We can do whatever you want, as long as I get to be with you.*

*Nick: We can't.*

*Lizzy: Why? You want me. I want you. What's stopping you?*

*Nick: I told you, before. I stay in control of my life.*

*Lizzy: And sleeping with me means you'll lose control?*

*Nick: You want to work under me or you want to fuck me?*

*Lizzy: Both.*

*Nick: You only get one.*

*Lizzy: Fine. I'll be good. I'll come to the office and only talk about movies. Have you seen the first Terminator movie?*

*Nick: Never.*

*Lizzy: Battlestar Galactica?*

*Nick: I only watch police procedurals.*

*Lizzy: Why?*

*Nick: Because I like them.*

*Lizzy: Ooh, sassy today. I like it.*

*Nick: Drink some water before you go to bed.*

*Lizzy: You'll have to come over and watch with me.*

*Nick: I have to get back to work. I'll have your DVDs shipped to your apartment.*

*Lizzy: Will you watch one with me? If we do it at the office?*

*Nick: I'll consider it.*

*Lizzy: I'm sorry I said you're a robot. I don't really think that. I'm just frustrated.*

*Nick: I know. I'm frustrated too.*

*Lizzy: Really?*

*Nick: Yes. Go to bed. It's late.*

*Lizzy: I'm going to think of you.*

*Nick: I know.*

———

FRIDAY MORNING IS AWKWARD. I DISCUSS NOTHING BUT the project.

At ten, I gather my things to go back to my desk. No more Nick for two whole days. It feels like a long time.

"I'll check your work early tonight," he says. "I have a meeting."

"A date?"

He stares at me like he's saying *don't push it*.

I don't.

"A meeting with a colleague. I need to leave by six if I want to arrive at the hotel on time."

"That doesn't sound like a very professional meeting. I

didn't realize you were willing to get on your back for your company like that."

He raises a brow. "I know you like thinking of me naked, but you should know I'd never submit to someone else."

I hate to bite my lip. He's as good as flirting with me.

"Of course." I push it. "You're always in control. I... And you would never take advantage. You'd only consider something if the woman—"

"Lizzy, stop. You're already in over your head."

"I thought we went by last names."

"I'll check your work at five."

"Sure." I have to do this. "Let me look at one thing first."

He nods and steps aside.

I wait for him to turn away and check his calendar.

*Meeting with Zachary, 6:30 P.M.*

There's an address. I commit it to memory and close the window.

"Would you like something?" He rifles through the fridge.

"No thank you. I'll see you later."

I lock myself in the bathroom and call Sarah. She doesn't pick up until the third time I call.

"I have to start opening the store in five minutes. Make it quick. I'm hungover," she says.

"I need your help tonight."

"With?"

"A guy."

"Text me a time and place and I'm there, sweet thang."

———

THIS ISN'T A CUTE COINCIDENCE.

This is crazy stalker shit.

I take a long sip of my rum and diet. I smooth my dress. I try to look as if I'm sitting here for any reason other than following Nick to his meeting.

Okay, technically, I didn't follow him.

He's not even here yet.

But still...

Sarah taps my toe with hers.

"This would go much easier if you just asked him to fuck you." She sips her cherry red fruit-flavored martini. "Less games."

"I did. He said no. He's all about keeping things professional." I polish off my rum and diet and signal the bartender for another. "He was so clear, Sarah. He told me that he'd fire me if I pushed this. What am I doing?"

"I saw the way he looked at you. You'll be fine."

"You don't know Nick. He's stern. He's obsessed with being in control."

"Sounds hot."

"It is. But..."

"He wants you. Trust me."

Maybe.

The cocktail waitress drops off our next round. I nod a thank you and get to work on polishing off this glass.

My hands are shaking. It's not like me. I only get nervous when I have to get in a car. Not about boys.

But Nick isn't a boy.

He's a man. One with enough power to destroy me.

"Slow down, honey. You want to be sexy, not sloppy." Sarah pulls my drink away. She adjusts my dress a smidge. Motions for me to take off my coat.

I do. I hang it off my chair. We're at a table that seats four. So we can invite Nick and his friend to join us. Since it's so funny that we accidentally ran into them.

No way this fools Nick.

Her gaze goes to the entrance doors. He's here. And he looks even sexier than usual with a five-o'clock shadow.

I stay put in my seat, so I can play this whole thing casual.

His footsteps move closer. Then he's five feet away, staring at me. For a moment, his gaze is curious. Then it's filled with understanding.

"Lizzy's boss, right?" Sarah stands and offers her hand. "I'm not sure if you recall—"

"Sarah. I'm Phoenix." He shakes her hand, his eyes on me. "What are you doing here?"

Sarah jumps in. "My friend Carly was supposed to get into New York today. She has a rich boyfriend." She lowers her voice. "But she's not here. Out fucking her millionaire somewhere else."

Where the hell does she come up with this shit?

Nick's eyes go to the elevators. "It was nice to see you again. Excuse me."

He looks at me for a split second, his expression stone. Then he moves away.

Well fuck.

"Don't worry. He'll be back." She switches to the seat next to mine. "He was staring at that zipper the way a dog stares at a ball."

"He looked pissed."

"Pissed he wants you so bad." She pulls my zipper down another half-inch. "Trust me."

I take a deep breath, trying out my most Phoenix Marlowe badass aloofness.

A few moments later, he's back. He has a friend in tow. A tall man in a grey suit with blue eyes and sandy brown hair. Sarah's type.

Sure enough, she's staring at him with lust in her eyes.

Nick makes eye contact. "Would you two like to join us for dinner?"

I'm too tongue-tied to speak. It's too easy. Something must be wrong.

Sarah jumps in. "We'd love to."

Nick nods. For a moment, his gaze goes to my cleavage. His pupils dilate. His lips part. Then he's turning to the door, once again a wall of stone.

# Chapter Eight

After dinner, Sarah invites Zachary dancing. It leaves me and Nick alone.

I make my way to the exit as casually as possible. Like he doesn't rattle me. Like I don't want every ounce of his attention.

Nick is right behind me. He stands six inches away. "I'll call a car to take you home."

"I hate cars."

"You never take cabs?"

"If I can help it."

"Then I'll walk with you."

Half of me wants to tell him to get lost. The other half wants to ask him to rip off my clothes.

He wants me too. But this doesn't sound like an invitation to my apartment.

"I don't need an escort. I'm a big girl." I pull my coat tighter. I'm already here. I might as well go for broke. "Unless you're inviting yourself over."

He stops and stares into my eyes. "You don't have any idea what you're getting yourself into."

"Inform me."

Instead of responding, he motions for me to follow him.

I do.

We go straight to the downtown side of the subway station. I tap my toe, trying to feel anything but overwhelmed. Nick is just as imposing outside of the office as in it. He drips power and status.

It's freezing down here. I hug my arms around my chest, a protection from the cold, from Nick's assumption that I can't handle him. Whatever that means.

There's a weight around my shoulders. His coat. I look back to Nick to confirm. Sure enough, he's standing there in his sleek black suit. He's so unreadable. Did it really hurt his feelings when I called him a robot?

It's not a nice thing to say.

I toss his jacket back to him. "If you want to keep me warm, do it with your arms, not your coat."

"Has anyone ever told you that you catch more flies with honey than vinegar?"

"Fruit flies are attracted to vinegar." I shove my hands into my pockets. "And that's a stupid cliché. You're smarter than that."

"Is that what you want?"

"Fruit flies? No thank you."

"Do you really want my arms around you? Can you really handle that?"

I swallow hard. "Yes."

"If that's all it is?"

I nod.

"You're lying."

"Prove it."

A metallic whir echoes through the station. Our train is here. I adopt a patient, calm expression as the doors open.

We step inside.

It's empty. We're the only passengers on this particular car. No one goes downtown on a Friday night.

The doors slide shut. The train picks up.

Nick moves closer. His arms slide around my sides and he pulls me into a deep, tight hug. Heat passes through me. It's instant. My stomach, my chest, my fingers, and my toes are warm.

That ache builds between my legs. Nick's arms are around me. It's not enough. I need all of him, every way I can have him.

He smells so good.

Nick steps back. His eyes meet mine. "Do you really want me to tease you, Lizzy?" He unbuttons my coat. His hand goes to the zipper of my dress. "You'll go home even more frustrated."

I press my lips together. No way I'm relenting now. No matter how right he is. "Try me."

He pulls the zipper to my stomach. He drags his finger-tips over the outline of my bra, from one shoulder to the other.

He does it again.

Again.

Heat surges through my body.

His eyes are glued to mine. His expression is intense. Captivating. Totally in control.

Every touch builds the ache inside me.

How is it possible I need him more?

I bite my lip to keep from moaning. To keep from begging.

"I'm not frustrated." I press my knees together.

"Don't lie to me again."

I swallow hard. "Or?"

"Or I'll punish you."

"What if I want you to punish me?"

His voice is stern. "Do you?"

"What does it matter if you don't fuck interns?"

"I could snap my fingers and destroy your career." He grabs my wrists and pulls my hands behind my back.

I struggle against his grip, but he holds tight. There's no strain in his expression. It's nothing.

"I can overpower you without breaking a sweat." He releases me.

He can. And it makes my sex clench. It makes me hotter.

He stares into my eyes. "What makes you think it's a good idea to challenge me?"

I step backwards and plant in a seat. I uncross my legs, spreading them wide on my way to crossing them again.

His gaze follows my movements. His pupils dilate.

"I can destroy you right back," I say. "Blake Sterling is obsessed with my sister. He'd do anything for her. If I ask, he'll crush your company."

"You won't ask."

"How do you know?"

"I know enough about you."

I stare back at him. "You won't destroy my career."

"How do you know?"

"You're not petty like that."

"Are you sure?"

"Yes. And if not, I don't mind going down as long as I take you with me."

He smiles. "You talking about mutually assured destruction or about oral sex?"

"Either way."

———

AFTER WE GET OFF THE TRAIN, NICK LEADS THE WAY TO my building. We go straight to the elevator.

Its doors slide together. Except for the camera in the ceiling, we're alone.

Nick turns towards me. He unbuttons my coat. His fingertips graze the neckline of the dress, all the way to the still-pulled-down zipper.

I lean into his touch. My eyelids press together. My lips part. I don't have it in me to suppress my moan. His touch is too intoxicating.

Nick shifts. His hands go to my ass. He lifts me and pins me against the wall. His hold is so tight, I can barely breathe.

I stare back at him. "Whatever point you're proving, I like it."

"And when I leave without fucking you?"

"I'm not a fan of that part, but it's probably for the best. I don't have any condoms."

"You have a smart mouth."

"Yeah?"

"It's a defense. It means you're nervous."

I admit nothing.

The elevator dings. My floor. Nick sets me down. His eyes are on fire. He's hard. He wants this as much as I do.

But he's still resisting.

Why?

I pull my coat over my shoulders as I make my way down the hall.

He follows me inside.

With the lights off, the only illumination comes from the moon and the warm blue of the sky.

I toss my purse on my bed and shrug my coat off my shoulders.

His posture is stiff, formal.

"Can I take your coat?" I offer.

"No."

He's still here, still in my apartment.

I weigh all the variables—the desire I saw in his eyes, the heat in my body, the stern tone of his voice, his excitement about teasing me.

This is a risk, but the upside is worth it.

I hold Nick's gaze as I pull the zipper to my stomach. I shift the dress off one shoulder, then the other.

His pupils dilate. "What are you doing?"

"Getting comfortable." I go to push my dress off my hips.

Nick grabs my arm and holds it tightly. "Don't."

"Or?"

"Listen to me."

I press my hands against my sides. "About?"

"Stop rushing into things. You're being foolish."

"Fuck you." I shimmy out of my dress. It falls at my feet. "This is my apartment and I'll take off my fucking clothes if I want to."

His eyes go wide. Something in his expression shifts. It's rougher. "Are you okay with me leaving?"

"Yes."

"You sure?"

"Positive."

Nick wraps his hands around my ass and holds my body against his. He takes two steps forward, pushing me into the wall.

His lips press against my neck. My collarbone. My chin.

I try to kiss him, but he turns his face so my lips make contact with his jawline.

He tugs my bra off my shoulders, one strap at a time. My breasts press against the rough fabric of his suit. It's just enough friction to send a shiver down my spine.

Dammit, he's good at this.

I try to find the meaning in Nick's eyes, but it's not there. When he brings his fingertips to my nipples, I stop caring where this is going. All I know is how badly I want him touching me.

He can't leave. Not yet.

Heat pools between my legs. I reach for Nick's hair, something to contain the sensation, but he pins my hands to the wall. It's as effortless as it was in the subway. He's much stronger than I am. He *can* overpower me without breaking a sweat.

He can do whatever he wants to me.

"Nick," I breathe. "What are you doing?"

He responds by rolling my tights to my knees.

Okay. I don't need conversation. I need him.

His fingers graze the top of my panties.

Yes. Almost.

He pushes my thong aside and strokes me.

My sex clenches. My body is on fire with need. I try to kiss him.

With one hand, he holds my head in place. The other teases me.

Almost.

Almost.

He slides one finger inside me.

My body screams with need. Yes. Whatever he wants, yes, now.

His lips press against my neck. My chest. My cheek. They're an inch from my lips, but they're not connecting.

He's not kissing me.

His thumb makes contact with my clit. I rock my hips to push him deeper.

He rubs me.

Almost. A few more strokes and I'm going to—

Nick pulls his hand away.

What?

His eyes fix on mine. "Are you still okay with me leaving?"

No. My exhale is heavy. The only thing I can feel is the tension in my core. How badly I need his hand. How badly I need to come.

"Lizzy, I asked you a question. I expect an answer."

"You already said that you're not—"

"Put your hands on the desk."

"Are you leaving?"

"Now."

I do.

He runs his fingertips down my back. My legs shake when his fingertips skim my sex. It's almost enough. But not quite.

"Keep your eyes on the wall." His voice is rough.

I do. I can't see him, but I can feel the heat from his body, hear his breath.

"Explain to me why you showed up at that hotel."

"Because I want you to fuck me."

"Do you think I'm that easily manipulated?"

"It's not manipulation. You want this too. Or is that a flashlight in your pocket?"

"Don't be smart. Not about this." He slides two fingers inside me. "What is more important to you—keeping your job or fucking me?"

Our conversation fades to nothing. The only thing I know is how badly I need to come.

He pulls his hand away. I gasp. My legs go slack. No. He can't stop.

Nick grabs onto my hips. He repositions me. "I asked you a question. Answer it."

I can't.

His hand comes down hard on my ass. The smack of flesh on flesh echoes through the tiny room. My skin stings.

"The job," I say.

"Then what the fuck do you think you're doing baiting me?"

He spanks me again. There's something sweet about the sting of pain. It pulls me into the moment. It reminds me that I'm alive.

"Lizzy."

"I don't know. It was an impulse. I've never wanted anyone enough to ignore my judgment before."

He growls, his hand coming down hard on my ass. Harder than the last. It pushes all the way to the brink of tolerable pain.

A groan escapes my lips.

He presses his palm against me. "Right now, what do you want?"

My sex clenches. My legs shake. My entire body is desperate for him.

"You," I breathe.

"How?" He teases my sex with his fingertip.

I shift my hips, trying to push him deeper. "Inside of me. Fucking me. Screaming my name as you come."

He pulls his hand away. Drags his fingertips over the flesh of my ass. "This is a punishment."

"Yes."

"You're not getting fucked."

I bite my tongue.

"You're going to bed dripping and desperate. And when you touch yourself tonight, you're going to think of me, and it's not going to be enough."

It's impossible to breathe. My legs are shaking so hard, I'm sure I'm about to tip over.

He pulls his hand away. "Get dressed."

"What?"

"Now." He steps aside.

I pull my body upright, suddenly feeling much more exposed. "This is my apartment."

"If you don't get dressed, I'm leaving."

He's still hard.

How can he be so calm when he's so fucking hard?

My cheeks flush. I pull my tights up, push past him, and find my robe in the bathroom. I'm sure I look ridiculous with a fluffy purple robe and knee-high stiletto boots, but it's not an immediate concern.

Nick's eyes are on me. His expression is harsh.

I want him so badly I'm aching, and he's ready to leave. How is that possible?

I cinch the robe's tie. "Is that enough?"

"You'll need to compartmentalize at the office. Treat me the same way you'd treat David, Gabriel, or Jasmine."

"And when we're not at the office?"

"I want to fuck you, Lizzy, but only if you're ready to submit. You keep pushing me. I won't tolerate that."

"What does that mean?"

"You do exactly what I say, when I say it. If you don't want that—"

"I do." I want it so fucking badly.

His expression gets serious. "You can't tell anyone. Not your sister. Or your friends."

It's difficult to concentrate on the conversation with the tension between my legs. But I can't admit it to him. Can't prove him right.

He pulls his phone from his pocket and taps something. A moment later, my phone buzzes. It's a text. An address.

"Meet me tomorrow night at eight," he says. "Wear that dress again."

"You liked the zipper?"

"Yes." His eyes bore into me. "I'll send a package in the morning. Wear that under your dress. Only that." He takes a step backwards.

"You're leaving?"

"Yes."

"But we—"

"Push me again, and you'll go to bed alone again."

I bite my tongue so I won't object.

He leans down and plants a kiss on my cheek. "When I see you tomorrow, I don't want to hear anything about Odyssey or the Haley project. You understand?"

"Stop asking if I understand. It's patronizing. I can make terms too, and I'm not doing this if you keep treating me like a child. I know what I want. I want you."

Something flares in his expression. Almost like he's impressed by how I'm standing my ground.

I fold my arms over my chest. "Good night, Nick."

"Good night." He turns and leaves.

In the bathroom, I strip down to nothing and run the shower. The hot water does nothing to cool me down.

I try, hard, to resist touching myself.

But I can't.

One hand presses against the tile wall. The other goes between my legs. With a few strokes, I'm there. My sex clenches and I come.

It's not at all satisfying.

———

ALL NIGHT, I TOSS AND TURN. I'M WOUND UP, DESPERATE for Nick to release me from this tension.

What if he's right and I can't handle him? Our sex in the hotel was nothing compared to this. I've never submitted to anyone before.

Can I really submit to Nick?

I'm not at all rested when I wake. A long session of yoga fails to clear my head. A cold shower fails to temper the heat racing through me.

I need him, need his hands on my skin, his voice in my ears, his body against mine.

But there's so much at stake. My job, my future, my apartment—he can snap his fingers and destroy me.

Sure enough, there's a package waiting for me at the front desk: a white clothing box adorned with a purple bow.

Back in my apartment, with the door firmly locked, I force myself to unwrap the present as slowly as possible. Rolled inside purple tissue paper is a matching lingerie set —black thigh-high stockings, black garter belt, black thong.

They're beautiful, but there's something strange about the thong. It's heavy. I play with the fabric until my fingers hit something hard—a bullet vibrator tucked into a fabric pouch.

Only there's no way to turn it on.

I bang on the toy for a full minute, but it stays off. It's not the smoothest move, but I have to know.

I text Nick.

*Lizzy: How does it work?*

He responds with a picture message—his hand wrapped around a remote control.

Holy shit.

He wants me to wear this in public?

My heartbeat picks up. Someone will know. Someone will see. Can I really risk that?

The picture grabs my attention. His hands are so strong, so expert. I need them on me again.

I need to submit to him.

I need to be his.

Even if it might destroy me.

# Chapter Nine

The restaurant is on the top floor of a nondescript building, all the way at the end of the hall. The lighting is dim —ornate chandeliers and flickering candles.

Nick is in a booth in the corner, his gaze turned towards the entrance.

He motions *come here* as his eyes catch mine. I walk past the hostess stand. I take in none of my surroundings. I'm too fixed on his hands.

One is around his glass of whiskey. The other is under the table, out of sight.

I take a deep breath, bracing myself for the vibrator to suddenly turn on.

It doesn't.

He stands to greet me. One hand goes to my lower back. The other slides to the back of my head.

My eyes flutter closed as he pulls me into a soft, slow kiss. It's the first kiss we've had since San Francisco, and it's every bit as good as it is in my memory.

That hint of whiskey on his lips.

And something else entirely Nick.

Warmth spreads out from every place he touches—my back, my head, my lips—until it fills my entire torso.

He releases the kiss and motions for me to sit.

I nod a *thank you* as we slide into the booth.

I cross and uncross my legs, willing the tension in my lower back to relax. He seems so calm, so in control.

I'm all mixed up. My hands are shaky. My breath is uneven.

Still, I manage to hold Nick's gaze. I have to figure out where I stand. "I have a few questions."

He nods *go on*.

"I'm assuming this relationship is monogamous."

"Yes."

"But what is it? Are we screwing around or—"

"I can't promise anything more than sex."

"Oh." I bite my lip. Before I met Nick, I didn't have any interest in a romantic relationship. Even in dating casually. The guys in my classes didn't interest me.

Nick is so different from anyone else I've known.

So much more appealing.

"Is it that you've never wanted a girlfriend or that you don't see yourself with me?" I tap my fingers against the table. I can't just sit here. I need to move.

"I don't want to hurt you. If you can't handle—"

"Don't do that. All you have to say is that you want a casual relationship, and I understand." It shouldn't bother me this much. It's not like a relationship between us has any chance of working.

"You don't have to be defensive with me."

"You don't have to be condescending to me." I bite my lip. "I've never been particularly interested in having a boyfriend." My stomach twists in an unpleasant way. It's all true though. I've never wanted a boyfriend before. Not since the accident.

I pull my dress over my thighs. No matter how much I like Nick, I can do casual. I'd rather do casual.

It's safer. Less painful when the world figures out how to take him away.

I meet his gaze. "The last guy who wanted to be my boyfriend seemed nice. But he couldn't stand that I was smarter than he was."

Nick smiles. "You're sure you were smarter than he was?"

"Yes." I fold my hands in my lap. "I realize that it's not a concern with you. You're the most intelligent person I've ever met."

"Thank you." His voice is soft. "What happened?"

"He didn't like me when I corrected his grammar, when I fixed his broken computer, when I had an opinion that wasn't the same as his. He only liked me when I was quiet and sweet and exactly who he wanted me to be."

"He was a boy."

"The world is full of boys. Dating isn't worth the trouble. It would be one thing if I didn't have to worry about my back, if I could have casual sex without—"

"Lizzy."

My heartbeat picks up. It's been such a long time since I've been able to be honest with anyone. I love my sister, but she's hopelessly idealistic. There are things she'll never understand.

I play with my dress to calm my nerves. "A lot of people don't like me. In high school, people thought I was bossy, opinionated, whatever. I learned to choose between having friends and being myself. I have Kat and Sarah. That's enough. But that night in San Francisco last year— it didn't matter if you thought I was a hopeless bitch. You were never going to see me again. It was the first time I could be myself in a long time."

"You don't have to worry about that." His voice is warm. "I like you."

I pinch myself to make sure I'm not dreaming. There's no way that Phoenix Marlowe, billionaire CEO, says something as plain as "I like you" when he's sweet-talking.

"You like me? What kind of twenty-seven-year-old guy tells a girl he likes her?" This warmth spreads through my chest. Nick likes me. "You know, the last time a guy told me he liked me was high school."

"A whole ten months ago?"

"Does it bother you that I'm young?"

"I don't enjoy abusing my position of authority." His gaze drifts to the window for a moment. Then it's back to me. "What did you say to the guy who liked you?"

"I let him down easy. He liked sweet Lizzy, not the real one."

"You can always be yourself with me." He leans closer. "Your angry, demanding, strong self."

"You know, I have positive traits."

"Those are positive traits." Nick's lips curl into a smile. "Men will find you appealing, Lizzy. Boys will be scared."

"I don't care what men think. I only care what you think."

"Right now. One day, you'll meet a man who will mean something to you, and you won't care what I think anymore."

"How would you like it if I told you what you'd want in six months or a year?"

"You're young—"

"I've been through enough to know what I want. The only thing you have any say over is sex. Got it?"

"Yes, I do." His gaze goes to my chest.

I flush. He still has that remote somewhere. I'm still

waiting. I latch on to something easy to talk about. "Have you seen *The Matrix*?"

"The first one."

"You haven't seen *Terminator* or *The Matrix*? How can you watch so little sci-fi?"

"I stay busy."

"Sometime, we're going to sit down and have a crazy fictional AI marathon."

He smiles. "I can't remember the last time someone told me what I was going to do."

"Does it toy with your massive ego?"

"No. I like it."

That warmth spreads all the way to my stomach and thighs. The words echo around my head. *I like you.* How can it feel like such a momentous declaration?

I like him too.

Too much, considering how little I know about him.

I try to steer the conversation back to safer waters. "So... when we're together, alone or out of the office, we're fuck buddies, more or less."

He nods.

"What about at Odyssey? Are you going to call me into your office and order me onto my knees?"

"You want the risk of getting caught."

My cheeks flush. My sex clenches. I've never thought about it before, but I do want the thrill. I'm fucking my boss. I want to do it on his desk.

His eyes connect with mine. "When we're alone with the door locked, then it's Lizzy and Nick, and not Miss Wilder and Mr. Marlowe."

There's something about his expression, something dominant and totally appealing. I nod.

"There's minimal soundproofing in my office. Can you manage that?"

"Yes."

And then it happens—there's a buzz between my legs. I gasp, loudly, grabbing onto the bench for relief but finding none. The vibrator is pressed up against my clit, and it's intense.

I lock eyes with Nick, searching for an explanation and finding nothing but that same in-control look.

The buzz stops. I nearly fall over panting.

"What was that?" I ask.

"A test."

"How do I pass?"

"Convince me."

I nod.

His hand moves under the table and there it as again—the toy vibrates against my clit, only the thinnest layer of silk in between it and my painfully sensitive skin.

I bite my lip, trying hard not to make a sound.

Nick's eyes stay on mine. It's like he's transfixed.

Tension builds in my core. I'm close.

But the vibrations stop.

I gasp as quietly as I can manage. "Are you trying to kill me?"

"You want me to stop?"

"No."

His expression is cocky as hell.

It takes me a full minute to catch my breath. My sex is pulsing. I'm desperate for release and he's sitting there patiently, daring me to ask him to finish.

The waitress drops off a water and a fresh glass of whiskey for Nick. "Your appetizers will be out shortly, Mr. Marlowe."

Right on cue, the vibrator turns on. I press my eyelids together, fighting my desire to scream.

Pleasure spreads out to my thighs, my calves, my toes.

When my eyes open, I study our server's expression. There's no sign she knows what we're doing.

How is that possible? It feels like the entire bench is vibrating.

"Thank you." He speaks calmly, like he's not controlling my orgasm with a remote in his pocket.

Oh, God, that vibration is fucking intense. I try to look into Nick's eyes, but I can only manage a few seconds before my lids press together.

The room disappears until I'm nothing but the sounds and the sensations in my body. The faint buzz of the toy, the sharp exhale escaping my lips, the calm inhale filling Nick's lungs.

I'm close.

"Look at me." His voice is commanding. "Or I turn it off."

I force myself to open my eyes. It's so much more intense staring back at Nick.

Without the anonymity of a one-night stand or the inhibition loosening powers of rum and diet, I feel shy and exposed by my ragged breath and flushed cheeks.

I sink my teeth into my lip. Even with my desperate attempts to stay quiet, I moan.

The toy is so much stronger than my hand.

My sex clenches. Almost. I stare back at Nick, at all the desire in his eyes. He has me under his thumb. God help me, the thought makes me want him more.

My eyes close of their own accord. Instantly, the vibrator turns off. I bite my tongue, barely muffling a curse.

"Please don't stop." I look back at him, studying his expression.

When the toy turns back on, I give up on staying silent.

"How do you feel, knowing I can keep you from coming?" he asks.

"Powerless."

"Do you like it?"

Pleasure spreads through my core. "Yes."

"Do you trust me?"

The intensity of the vibration makes it hard to concentrate.

I look into Nick's eyes. They're determined and in control, but they're also earnest.

I nod. Yes. I do trust him.

"Keep your eyes open," he demands.

An orgasm rises up inside me. Almost. It's so intense I can barely breathe. My eyes threaten to close. "I can't."

"You can. Look at me."

The desire in his deep brown eyes pushes me over the edge.

The pressure rises to a fever pitch. It's too much to contain. My lids get heavy, but I fight my impulse to close them.

Instead, I moan. I moan loud enough for the people at the next table to hear.

There. The pressure unravels, spilling through my thighs, spilling all the way to my toes.

Another groan escapes my lips. It's too loud, but I can't stop myself. I have to do something to contain it.

I let my eyelids press together.

The toy shuts off.

It takes a few minutes to catch my breath. When I finally look back at Nick, I feel even more exposed.

How did he get me forget myself like that?

How did he get me to risk so much for him?

I look around the room, certain everyone knows what

we're doing. But no one is looking our away. No one is the wiser.

––––––

WE SPEND THE SOUP AND DINNER COURSES TALKING about TV. Nick only watches mysteries, mostly police procedurals, and only when he can't sleep.

It should be a safe conversation topic, but I keep imagining him alone on a couch in some big empty room, no sound except the low roar of the TV. It must be so lonely living like that.

Dessert is a rich chocolate torte. I'm too wound up to keep eating. We'll be at his place soon. We'll be on to the next part.

Nick licks a crumb off his lip. "I want to take a car home."

I swallow hard. He's watching me, focused on me the way he focuses on his computer.

"Why?" I ask. "We can walk."

"Of course. But I can make better use of the time in the backseat of a limo."

My hand shakes. A limo is the worst of all. No seat belts. Nothing to protect you if it crashes.

He takes the last sip of his coffee then slides the remnants of dessert to the side. "Do you know how to drive?"

"No, and I don't want to learn."

The shaking in my hands spreads to my shoulders. I squeeze my thighs together to keep my legs calm.

I can't learn to drive. It's bad enough suffering in the backseat of a cab.

My heartbeat picks up. My mouth gets dry. I reach for the coffee to wet my throat, but I can barely swallow.

The waitress drops off a sleek black check holder. In one swift movement, Nick pulls his credit card from his wallet and hands it to her. No need to look at the bill. Money doesn't mean anything to him.

It's not enough to distract me from the dread in my gut. I'm still terrified to get in a car.

He sees through me.

I hate that he sees through me.

His voice is a dare. "If you're afraid—"

I stammer some incomprehensible collection of sounds.

"Admitting fear isn't a sign of weakness."

I press my lips together. "Have you ever admitted fear to anyone?"

"I was terrified that night in San Francisco."

"Of what?"

"Losing something important to me."

I take another sip of my coffee, but my mouth is still way too dry. "That's not the same. It's not like you're afraid of bees or spiders or something everyone else is sure won't hurt you."

His voice softens. "I understand if you aren't ready—"

"Stop making it sound like I'm failing to meet some challenge. I don't need to know how to drive. I don't ever need to get in a car again."

"What if you want to go to the airport?"

"I can take the bus."

"If you want to visit a friend who lives upstate?"

"I can take the train."

"And if she lives twenty miles from the nearest train station?"

"I can ride a bike."

"Your knuckles are white."

I pull my hands into my lap. The waitress interrupts

our stare-off. Nick nods a polite "good night" and signs the check.

His attention stays on me, even as his gaze focuses on the paper.

"I'm afraid of losing this project," Nick says.

"Everyone worries about losing their jobs. Their work."

"Not like this. It would be like losing a limb. When I think about it, I stop breathing." He slides his wallet into his slacks as he stands.

Nick offers his hand. I don't take it.

This isn't casual. I rush towards the exit. The tables here are spread out, but it's still hard to move fast. I run into a server with a blonde ponytail and mummer an "excuse me."

Ow. The impact shoots pain up and down my spine. It settles in my mid-back. My muscles tense.

Too much work, too many nights out in heels. I take a deep breath but it doesn't relax my muscles. It's a minor ache. Ibuprofen should send it packing.

I can deal with it when I get home. Even if the tension is getting worse by the second.

My gait steadies as I get closer to the elevator.

Fuck. It hurts. Everything from the back of my neck to the bottom of my shoulder blades is tense and achy.

Nick slides his arms around me.

He holds me against his chest. "Are you okay?"

"Not here."

He takes me into his arms, carrying me like I'm some kind of damsel in distress, and sets me down on a bench at the end of an empty hallway.

I turn away from him, curling my body inward.

He slides my coat off my arms. His fingers trail over my spine. "Where does it hurt?"

"I'm fine."

"You don't have to take a car, but don't lie to me. Where does it hurt?"

"A little lower."

He rubs my back with a gentle touch. When the tension eases, I let out a heavy sigh.

His movements soften. "I know you're strong. You don't have to convince me. I want to know if you aren't okay."

"I panic whenever I'm in a car." I lean into his touch. "I try to keep it to myself, so I won't ruin anyone's good time. It doesn't come up often in the city."

"I understand." He presses his lips against my neck. "I'll walk you home."

"Are you coming in?" My voice is needy.

"No."

"Please. I want to... I want to fuck you. My back is okay. I swear." I turn back to him and stare into his eyes. "I won't lie about that."

He runs his fingertips over my cheek. "It's a fifteen-minute walk to my apartment."

I practically jump to my feet. Ouch. Too fast. I remind myself to slow down as I stretch.

Nick helps me into my coat. He slides his hand to my lower back and guides me to the elevator then to the street.

Our walk is quiet. His hand stays pressed against my back, soft and hard at once.

We stop at a huge apartment building right across from Battery Park.

I shift out of my coat as we walk into the lobby. "You live here? The rent must be a crime."

"It is. I'm making a fortune."

"What?"

"I own the building."

I bite my tongue, attempting to work out the math in my head. Thirty floors plus twenty apartments a floor equals a shit-ton of rent money. Of course money means nothing to him.

He's swimming in it.

"Lizzy." Nick runs his fingertips over my collarbones. "Are you all right?"

I nod as I follow him into the elevator. It's all glass. There are four elevators in the building, and each one is glass.

The reflective surface mocks my inability to hold a poker face.

How can I be nervous about something I want so badly? I'm not a virgin. I've even been with Nick before.

Everything is different now.

He's my boss.

My friend even.

He likes me.

Nick turns to me, his expression intense. "How is your back?"

"Fine."

"Then unzip your dress."

I swallow hard, my gaze going to the glass doors. "Someone will see."

"I'm not going to ask again."

I recognize that look. It's a test. And I'm pretty sure I won't like the consequences of failing.

# Chapter Ten

He wants me to get naked in a glass elevator? Someone will see. Even at this time of night, it's a risk.

His eyes are on fire. There's something about his expression that commands me. My body moves of its own accord. My hands go to my zipper.

I hesitate. Can I really do this?

"I'm not going to ask again."

He's staring back at me.

My nipples tighten, my body answering for me.

I *have* to do this. I have to give myself to him.

I pull the zipper as low as it will go.

Nick pushes the dress off my left shoulder. My breast spills out, on display to anyone in a passing elevator, anyone in the hallway next to the elevator bank.

My sex clenches.

He does the same with the right shoulder. There's nothing covering me above the waist.

I'm exposed.

To him.

To anyone who happens to see.

The thought sends a shiver down my spine. I go to push my dress to my feet but Nick stops me.

"You don't get a say in when you take off your dress." His eyes are on fire. "Not when we're doing this."

I nod.

He runs his fingertips over my collarbones. "Turn around."

He positions me so I'm facing the elevator doors.

We have another ten floors to go. Someone could see me. All of me.

His chest presses against my back. His crotch presses against my ass.

He's hard, but he's so patient about bringing his hands to my stomach and tracing the line of my zipper. His fingers find my nipple and tease mercilessly.

I stare out the glass doors. There isn't a single part of me that wants him to stop. How can I be willing to risk so much for a man? For my sexual release?

There's something about Nick. I want to submit to him. I want to be under his control.

His lips press against my neck. He kisses me as he toys with my nipples. My hips shift of their own accord. My body is desperate for him.

"Put your hands on the wall." He motions to the spot next to the elevator door.

We're almost there. Five floors. There's someone on this floor, at the end of the hallway.

They turn towards us, but there's no way to tell if they can see.

I bring my hands to the wall. They're so clammy that they slide right off the glass.

I wipe them on my dress and try again. Better.

My legs shake as Nick slips his hands under my dress, over my ass. His fingers skim the outside of my panties.

"You're dripping," he groans.

Again, I shift my hips, a desperate attempt to feel more of him.

He pulls his hand away. I sigh from the loss of touch.

"You do what I say, when I say it. Not before. Not after." He drags his fingertips up my thighs, stopping at the top of my stockings to play with the lace.

I fight my desire to press my body against his.

"What if I want you to stop? If something hurts or—"

"We use a code." His palm presses against the outside of my panties. "A traffic light. Red means stop. Yellow means slow down. Green means go."

He pushes my thong out of the way and slips a finger inside me.

I gasp, my hand struggling to keep its hold on the wall.

One floor to the penthouse.

Finally, the elevator stops at the top floor. The doors open but Nick doesn't move.

When his teeth sink into my shoulder, I lose interest in the elevator. In anything except his body against mine.

He slides another finger inside me. Deeper and deeper until it's so much it hurts.

I cry out.

"Yellow?" he asks.

"Yellow."

His touch softens. It's still intense but not painfully so.

I gasp as he pulls his hands away. He rolls my dress over my thighs then pulls my thong to my knees.

I'm completely exposed to him.

My cheeks flush.

He lets out a low groan of approval. "You're beautiful."

"Me or my cunt?"

"Both." He teases me with his fingertip. "I like your wit,

but not when we're doing this. I don't want to feel any defenses. If you're nervous, tell me you're nervous."

"Okay." My stomach flip-flops. Somehow, that promise feels more exposing than having my ass in the air.

"Get smart about sex again and you go to bed wanting again. Understand?"

"Yes."

His teasing is merciless.

Pleasure spreads through my body. He's not touching me properly. I need him to touch me properly.

My hips shift an inch, pushing his finger inside me.

He pulls his hand back. "You like being exposed to me."

"Yes."

"You want to come on my hand?"

My sex clenches. God, yes. "Yes."

"Then stay still."

He teases me again, and again, and again. It takes every ounce of strength I have not to force him deeper.

I'm so wound up, so desperate to feel him properly.

I groan. "Nick. Please."

He scrapes his teeth against my shoulder. "Please what?"

"Fuck me."

"Soon." He slides a finger inside me.

I sigh with relief.

His movements are rough, aggressive. He scrapes his nails against my hips as he goes deeper and harder.

My eyelids press together. My breath goes erratic. Nick is so good at this. He's so precise. And the way he's groaning—

Pressure builds between my legs. I moan in ecstasy. Almost there.

It takes great concentration to stay still. I want so badly to rock my hips so he's deeper inside me.

I need more. I need it faster.

I need to come.

He brings his lips to my neck as he finger-fucks me. His kiss is as hard and aggressive as his hand.

I lean into his body, trying my best to melt. It's not the easiest position. My legs shake. My hands threaten to slip.

But I'm on the edge. I can't do anything that might make him stop.

His strokes push me closer. Almost. I squeeze the glass between my fingers.

There. My sex pulses as I come. Pleasure spreads out through my legs. It's too much to take. My arms fall to my sides. My knees buckle.

Nick catches me, scooping me into his arms. He carries me the way he did in San Francisco.

We move into the penthouse apartment. It's too dark to make out the details. I can only sense the massive size of the place. The living room must be a thousand square feet. There are windows everywhere. They look out on the Hudson River.

Nick lays me on a plush leather couch. He sits next to me, slides my legs into his lap, and gently removes my glasses.

Things get blurry, but he's close enough that I can make out his expression. He's still patient.

"Can I get you anything?" His fingertips trail over the inside of my knee.

"No thank you." My cheeks flush. It's alarming how calm he is.

"I picked up a bottle of rum and another Diet Coke."

My stomach flutters. It's soda, not a love letter. I tell my muscles to relax, but the anticipation makes it impossible. "Okay."

He slides my legs off him as he rises to his feet. My dress is halfway off so I pull it over my head and leave it a heap on the floor.

It served its purpose.

Now, it's useless.

Nick returns with two drinks. He sets them on the coffee table and sits next to me.

I push myself up and turn my body towards his.

He's so close.

Desire spreads over his face as he looks me up and down. He reaches for me and runs his thumb over my lower lip.

My eyes flutter closed. I turn towards the windows, overwhelmed by the intimacy of his touch.

His thumb trails down my chin, his palm resting on my cheek.

He kisses me, sucking on my lower lip with that same precision.

I'm greedy about exploring his mouth. Whiskey and Nick. It's an intoxicating combination. More intimate than him finger-fucking me in an elevator. More intimate than anything I've ever felt.

I sigh into his mouth, melting against his body.

Our kiss breaks. He runs his hand through my hair, his eyes focused intently on me. I shift closer, trailing my hands up his thigh to feel his erection.

How can he be patient when he's this fucking hard?

He grabs my hand and brings it back to my side. "You don't touch me unless I give you permission."

"You don't like it?"

He answers by pinching my nipple. He does it again. Harder. Harder. Then hard enough I cry out.

His touch softens. He draws circles around me with his thumb. "It's flattering that you're eager, but it's not going to get you anywhere."

"Okay." I relax into his touch. My eyes flutter closed as he moves to my other nipple, teasing, then pinching.

Every motion of his hands sends a pang of desire to my core.

I lose track of my breath. My body is humming with pleasure. I'm so desperate it hurts. "Please."

"How is your back?"

"Doesn't hurt at all."

He stands, offering his hand. I follow him in a room adorned with string lights. They cast the room in a soft white glow, almost like candlelight.

He motions for me to sit on the purple sheets. They're nice, silk, soft and sleek like they're new.

"For me?" I ask.

He nods like it's normal to buy a girl sheets in her favorite color.

He shuts the door behind him and turns his attention to me. "Lie on your back and put your hands over your head. I'm going to bind your wrists."

A rush of anticipation passes though me. He's going to tie me up?

Nerves build in my stomach. I shift so I'm all the way on the bed, lie back, and pull my arms over my head.

Nick unknots his tie. He peels off his suit jacket and undoes the top two buttons of his shirt.

It takes everything I have not to pounce and press my hands against his skin.

He pulls something from under the bed. It's a restraint system with silver buckles and supple leather straps. It's anchored somewhere beneath the mattress. It will put me totally at his mercy.

Nick sits next to me. He looks down at me, watching my expression as he teases my nipples. Softly, then harder, then hard enough to make me whimper.

"Nick." I grab his thigh and sink my fingers into it. "Please. Please fuck me."

"Arms over your head."

I follow his command. He buckles the straps of the restraints so they're secure around my wrists.

I flex my forearms to test their strength. Tight enough I can't move but not enough to cut off my circulation. Not enough to make me feel trapped.

He pulls something else from the bed—a wedge-shaped pillow, also purple, about a foot high and two feet wide.

I look at him as if to ask for an explanation.

He responds by lifting my ass and sliding the pillow under it.

It's a sex pillow.

"Is that also for me?" I ask.

"Yes."

He undoes his buttons one at a time then slides his shirt off his shoulders.

Desire overwhelms me. It pushes away my nervous energy.

He stands to slide out of his slacks and boxers. It's almost like he's stripping for me.

I take in the contours of his body the best I can. Those broad shoulders, that strong chest, the narrow waist.

Nick's eyes connect with mine. He stares at me like he knows I'm gawking.

There's no shyness on his face. Only confidence.

He grabs a condom and kneels next to me.

His lips press against mine. There's less softness. His movements are hard. Needy.

I kiss back, exploring his mouth with my tongue.

Nick unwraps the condom and slides it over his cock.

His hands go to my knees and pry them apart. With my ass on the pillow and him kneeling, our bodies are perfectly aligned. He's inches away.

My sex clenches from anticipation.

He pulls out bodies together. His cock strains against my sex, teasing me.

I groan.

He does it again.

My body pulses with anticipation. So close to getting what it wants but not there yet.

Again. Again. Again.

"Nick. Please." I squeeze my knees against his hips.

He adjusts my legs so my feet touch the bed. He's holding me in the air, in bridge pose. The weight of my hips is in his hands.

"You want to come again?" He rakes his nails over my hips.

"Yes."

"Use me."

Use him? He must mean his cock. My sex clenches in anticipation. He's making me work for it. There's something thrilling about that.

I ease my weight into my legs, tilting my hips to test my range of motion. I shift my hips. Again, his cock strains against me. It's not enough.

I arch my hips again. He strains against me.

Almost.

I sigh as he slides inside me. God, that feels good. Like everything in the universe is where it's supposed to be.

He groans. His nails sink into my hips. But his grip doesn't falter. He's still holding me just enough that I can barely move.

It takes a few tries to test where to put my weight. Once

I've got it, I shift my hips as much as I can. It pushes him deep inside me. I do it again. Again. Again.

Sensation overwhelms me. I have to close my eyes to contain it. I forget about any hint of shyness, forget that he's so composed, and I let out a loud moan.

I get louder the deeper and harder I push him. All the muscles in my lower body get tired. My legs are already spent, but I can't stop now.

I go harder. Harder. Until it's just right, then I shift again and again.

His eyes fill with pleasure. His shoulders shake. He's close, too. I want to feel him.

A few more thrusts, and I'm greedy. I'm so achy I can't stand it anymore. I need to come. Screw everything else.

I lose control of my breath, groaning with pleasure as I rock my hips against him.

God dammit, he feels good.

An orgasm rises up inside me. It's so much more intense than the last. Everything in me clenches tight. It releases in a wave of pleasure. So much it knocks me to my ass.

Nick shifts off me. He pushes the pillow aside, lowers me onto the bed, and presses my legs apart.

In one quick movement, he lays his body on mine and thrusts into me.

God yes.

He rocks into me. I open my eyes to watch the pleasure fill his expression. It's a good look on him. It's sexy as hell.

He moves faster. He kisses me, his tongue claiming my mouth, his nails claiming my shoulders. We're locked like that for minutes, his tongue in my mouth, his cock in my sex.

I can feel the orgasm rising up in him. He groans, his thighs shaking, his breaths rapid.

There. Even with the condom, I can feel his cock pulsing.

I shift my hips to hold him deeper.

His groans echo around the room like some kind of beautiful music.

When he's completely drained, Nick shifts off me. He takes care of the condom and gently undoes my restraints.

One at a time, he examines my wrists. His touch is careful. Affectionate.

He plants a kiss on my lips then steps back into his boxers. "Can you move?"

"Doubtful."

He lifts me into his arms and carries me to the couch. This doesn't feel very casual. It's overwhelmingly intimate.

I'm too spent for thoughts like that. I nestle into his body as he turns on the TV and picks out a movie.

It's *The Terminator*.

He's starting our AI marathon.

I rest my head on his chest. I try to keep my eyes open, but I'm out of energy.

I fall asleep in his arms.

————

He's not there when I wake.

The other side of the mattress is cold, like he's been gone for hours.

I get up, brush my teeth, find my glasses on the table in the living room. There's coffee brewing and there's a note on the counter.

Lizzy,

*I'll be out all day. Stay as long as you like. I'll see you tomorrow morning.*

*- Nick*

It's certainly to the point.

I raid the fridge for breakfast. Nothing but milk and condiments. He never eats here. Never entertains beyond a cocktail. It's such a beautiful apartment, and it's so empty.

It must be lonely.

I try to shake the image out of my brain while I get dressed and walk back to my apartment. But it's there during my yoga routine. It's there when I shower.

It's still there when Kat comes over to watch a movie. After a dinner of takeout Indian food—a mix of chicken vindaloo and vegetable curry—we settle on *Ghost World*. It's based on her favorite graphic novel.

She points out every visual detail, only stopping when she falls asleep.

There's a knock on the door. That must be Blake, coming to collect his fiancée. I make my way down the tiny hallway to let him in.

He's standing there with his hands in the pockets of his designer suit.

"How are you?" His voice is warm.

"Good. Tired. Long week." I motion to Kat, asleep on the bed. "Are you going to carry her out of here or would that attract too much attention?"

"I'll wake her." He presses the door shut. "After I speak with you."

"Planning something for Valentine's Day? You must know her tastes as well as I do by now."

"It's not about Kat."

I shift my weight, suddenly in need of an excuse to end this conversation. Kat worrying about me when she should be enjoying her first chance at taking care of herself is bad enough.

I won't be able to stand it if Blake is worrying about me too.

He looks at me, dead serious. "It's about Phoenix Marlowe."

"Oh." I clear my throat, attempting my best poker face.

"It's confidential."

Blake makes eye contact, a look that asks if I'm prepared to be trusted with confidential information.

I nod. "Go on."

"One of Odyssey's lawyers reached out to our acquisitions department with an offer to sell us the Haley Bot project."

My stomach clenches. That doesn't make any sense.

I take a deep breath. "Nick wouldn't sell Haley."

"Nick?"

Fuck me. My silence is an ineffective protest.

"I need you to know something, Lizzy."

"Yes?" I brace myself for a lecture.

"You're my family now. If Marlowe hurts you, I'll destroy him."

"He won't. I trust him."

"I've seen what happens to smart women who fuck their bosses. It ends fine for the bosses—"

"Even at Sterling Tech?"

"It's against policy, but it happens." Blake frowns. "He must be thirty."

"Twenty-seven. And you're five years older than Kat."

His eyes get intense and protective. "Does she know?"

"No, and I appreciate you keeping this between us. She's spent enough of her life taking care of me. Do you know anything else about this offer?"

"No. But I can find out anything you want about Nick."

"Like what?"

"A girlfriend."

"He doesn't have a girlfriend."

He frowns. "Do you have feelings for him?"

"It's just sex."

Blake raises an eyebrow like he's not sure if I can handle a strictly sexual relationship.

Is it all men that think they know better or only the rich ones?

Behind me, Kat stirs with a loud yawn. "What are you two whispering about?"

"Surprise for you. Don't eavesdrop." I lower my voice. "Thank you for the information, but I've got it under control."

All his attention shifts to Kat. He wraps his arms around her, pulling her into a long, deep hug. She sighs, her face lighting up as she smiles.

"I missed you," she whispers.

"I missed you too."

It's a personal moment, and I'm clearly intruding. There's nowhere to get out of the way, so I step into the bathroom with a loud "excuse me" then wash the hints of makeup off my face.

When I return to the main room, they're locked in that same hug.

Kat steps back. "I'm not convincing you to pick more of my movies."

"You can still have the next one." I hug her goodbye then turn my attention to Blake. "Let me handle that thing we discussed."

"If you can't—"

"I can." I walk them to the door. "There's only two months until your wedding. Worry about that."

Kat's eyes light up. She looks at Blake with a wealth of affection. The wall of stone is gone. His expression is caring, loving.

It's sickeningly sweet.

"Goodnight." I wave.

They nod goodnight and walk out the door hand in hand.

I plant in front of my computer and try to dig up more information about Nick's company.

There's nothing useful.

I'll have to ask him.

## Chapter Eleven

Sleep eludes me. I get up early, do an extra-long yoga session, shower, and go straight to the office.

I'm a few minutes early but Nick is here, standing behind his desk, attention on his computer.

"Good morning." His voice is even, like I'm any other coworker.

Like we didn't sleep together.

"Good morning." I fix my cup of coffee and tear my bagel into quarters.

The door to the office is closed but not locked. This is supposed to be professional.

I'm supposed to stand here for two hours, every morning, as if I don't want him to tie me to his bed.

It's impossible.

But it's the only option.

"Is something on your mind, Miss Wilder?" He pulls up our work for the day and motions for me to take a spot behind the computer.

There's so much on my mind. I push Blake's warning

aside. I need to figure out how to handle this before I start bringing up things that will push Nick.

My mind flashes with the memory of him undoing the buttons of his oxford shirt.

He's wearing the same style of shirt today. The same cologne.

I clear my throat. "Nothing interesting." I scan the code on screen. "What are we working on today?"

"Debugging. How much experience do you have?"

A lot. I focus on my expertise, blocking out everything that is not one hundred percent about programming. I still feel a rush of heat when Nick's hand brushes against my side, but otherwise, I'm just an intern, and he's just a mentor.

———

IT'S THE SAME ALL WEEK. I TRY TO TALK MYSELF INTO asking about the sale on my way to work. I chicken out the second I see Nick.

He's strictly business, all calm and aloof like it's easy for him to keep things separate. Not so much for me. I collapse when I get home from work. I can barely manage to make dinner or watch TV.

Friday, I'm antsy. It takes every last ounce of strength to keep my hands to myself.

By ten, I'm out of energy. I gather my things, debating whether I'll drink the shit coffee in the kitchen or take twenty minutes to get a vanilla latte at the place across the street.

Nick's eyes bore into me. There's an intention in his gaze, and it's more than professional.

Vanilla latte wins.

"Are you okay, Miss Wilder?" he asks.

"Do we have to go by last names at the office?"

"It makes it easier to keep things separate." He moves close enough to touch me. "There's something bothering you. Business or personal?"

"Some of each."

"Which is more pressing?"

"Business."

His gaze goes to the clock on the wall. "I have a conference call. Come back here for lunch. I'll schedule our takeout for twelve-thirty, but I want you here at noon."

"To talk?"

"No."

Oh. I consider playing coy, but it's really not my strong suit. "Is half an hour enough time?"

"Not as much as I'd like." His eyes flash with determination. "But I'll make sure you come at least twice."

My cheeks flush. I've got no response to that besides "hell yes." I nod a goodbye and reach for the door. "Of course, Mr. Marlowe. I look forward to it."

Suddenly, I don't need the coffee anymore. I'm wide awake.

———

At five minutes to noon, I walk to Nick's office with all the confidence I can muster.

The door is open enough that I can see inside.

He's sitting behind his desk. No jacket, sleeves rolled up to his elbows.

His eyes connect with mine. He motions *come here*.

I step inside. There's no food on his desk. No plates or silverware.

I can do this. "I have to ask you something."

"After. Lock the door." His eyes flash with desire.

When we're together, alone, with the door locked—

I stare back at him. "It's important."

"We'll talk about it after."

There's something in his expression. Not just desire, but need too. He needs me.

God knows I want him to touch me. It's been agony acting professional all week.

I press the door closed and click the lock shut.

His voice is a command. "Take off your dress."

I unzip my dress and slide it off my shoulders.

It falls at my feet.

His eyes pass over my body slowly, like he's taking in all the details. His pupils dilate. His lips part.

God, desire looks so good on him.

This conversation can wait. I need more of that look. I reach for my bra and unhook it.

Nick's voice gets rough. "Not until I ask." He slides out of his seat, his eyes still glued to me. He moves closer. Close enough to touch. His fingertips skim the side of my hip. They tug at the straps of my garter belt. "You wear this for me?"

I nod. "You haven't touched me all week."

"Did you expect me to undress you?"

I shake my head. "No, I never know what you're going to do. But I hoped you would. I thought about it last night."

"You touched yourself?"

My cheeks flush. I nod.

He drags his hand up my side and traces the outline of my bra. It's the nicest one I own, after the ones he gave me.

He unhooks my bra and peels it off. His eyes go wide as he plays with my nipples. "Did you do it fast or did you take your time?"

"I didn't think about it like that."

His touch gets rougher. "From now on, you make it last as long as possible."

He's telling me how to masturbate? It should bother me that he's trying to command such a private aspect of my life.

But it doesn't.

I want to do what he says. I want to please him.

How can I want so badly to please him?

I meet his gaze. "How will you know?"

He pinches my nipple. The pain shoots straight to my core.

I press my knees together. Dig my heels into the floor.

"I'll know." He brings his hand to my chin. "If you lie to me this is over."

"What if you lie to me?"

"You can end this relationship at any time." He runs his thumb over my lower lip. "But I won't lie to you."

I stare into his eyes. This is important. "Do you promise?"

"Yes." He pulls off my glasses and sets them on his desk. "I care about you. I don't want to hurt you."

His eyes are so honest. I believe him, believe that he'll never lie to me.

I never trust anyone but Kat, and I believe him.

The question bubbles up in my gut. It's this wall between us and I can't stand it. I know him better than I did a month ago, but it's not enough to trust him this deeply.

To think about him this often.

Nick runs his hand through my hair and undoes my bun. "What are you thinking?"

I bite my tongue. Nick doesn't get to know every thought in my brain, but I want us to be on the same page here. "I care about you too. It scares me how much I care about you."

"Lizzy, I can't offer you—"

"I know. I don't expect you to... I don't want a boyfriend." But I do want him. As much of him as I can get.

I swallow the thought. I can't get mixed up over Nick. This is casual. It will end sooner rather than later. I'll lose him sooner rather than later.

He stares back into my eyes, running his fingers through my hair.

His mouth opens like he's going to speak but he says nothing.

Nick leans closer. Six inches. Close enough to kiss me.

My eyes flutter closed.

I wait.

Our lips connect.

It's fast, rough, electric. His tongue slides into my mouth. His hands dig into my ass, pulling my body into his.

He's hard. I shift my hips for a better feel. God, he's so fucking hard.

His touch kindles a fire inside me. Heat spreads through my torso, to my limbs.

My legs go weak.

My knees buckle.

Nick slides both hands under my ass. He lifts me. I wrap my legs around his hips, my arms around his shoulders.

He sets me down on the couch. No thud. His movements are precise.

His hands go to my hips and he pulls my panties to my knees, my calves, my feet.

Then they're gone. On the floor somewhere. His pupils

dilate as he wraps his hands around my ankles and pries my legs apart.

I'm practically on display for him.

It sends a pang straight to my core.

Nick undoes the knot of his tie. "Put your hands over your head. Palms together."

I do.

He pulls the tie around my wrists and cinches a snug knot.

I'm on my boss's couch, tied up and nearly naked. The rest of the office is on the other side of that wall. If we're too loud someone will hear.

We can get caught.

The heat raging through me collects between my legs. I press my palms together. I squeeze the couch with my toes.

He's not touching me yet.

I need him touching me.

Nick's eyes meet mine. "You have to keep your voice down."

I nod.

He drags his hand down my stomach. Lower and lower. His thumb presses against my clit. Soft. Then hard.

"Nick," I groan. Pleasure surges through me. "How loud is too loud?"

"Not a single decibel more."

He rubs circles with his thumb. More pressure. More. It's too much. I gasp. He pulls his hand away.

I look back at him. His eyes are wide with ecstasy. His cheeks are flushed.

He really does get off on being in control.

God, how I like him getting off.

I nod. "I'll be quiet."

He brings his thumb to my clit, rubbing me until he finds just the right spot. I groan as quietly as I can.

His fingers curl around me. They tease my sex. Almost where they need to be but not quite there.

I make eye contact. He's fixed on me, studying my reactions like his life depends on it.

I relax into the couch, pressing my eyelids together, sinking my teeth into my lip to keep myself from screaming.

He slides one finger inside me. Then two. He rubs me as he pushes his fingers deeper. I gasp. I can't help it. His touch is fucking intense.

An orgasm builds inside me. I'm powerless to do anything but feel it. Tension knots in my core. There's more with every brush of his thumb.

My lips part. A groan escapes. "Nick, I can't keep quiet. I have to scream."

"You can."

I moan. "How?"

"Do you trust me?"

I barely manage to nod.

"Look at me." His voice is in control.

I do. God, the pleasure on his face. It's commanding. That knot cinches tight. With his next touch, it unravels. A wave of pleasure spreads out to my fingers and toes.

I see white, nothing but the blinding light of bliss as an orgasm rocks through me.

A groan rises up in my throat. There's no way to contain it. As soon as I'm moaning, his hand is covering my mouth, muffling me.

Nick reaches for something on the bookshelf. A condom. He unzips his slacks and rolls it on.

A groan escapes his lips as he grabs my knees and lifts my ass into the air. He brings our bodies together. The rubber tugs for a moment, then he's inside me.

I gasp. He feels damn good.

Pleasure spreads across Nick's face. He keeps his hands wrapped around my legs, using them for leverage to push himself deeper.

His movements aren't as forceful as they were in his bed. They're softer, like they're designed to be quiet.

He thrusts just enough to keep the couch from shaking. He digs his nails into my skin just enough to push me to the brink of screaming.

My eyes flutter closed. I focus all my attention on the sensations in my body. The sting of pain as his nails scrape against the delicate flesh of my inner thighs. The pulse of pleasure as he thrusts into me.

I want to groan, to pant, to scream. But I can't. I don't even care that we can get caught. Only that he'll stop.

He drags his hands to my ankles and presses my legs against his chest. My ankles hook around his shoulders. He leans into me, pinning me to the couch and thrusting deep.

I fight my urge to scream. It's too much pressure. It's too intense.

"Nick," I groan.

He slides his fingers into my mouth. It's strange at first, how they taste like me. But they're inviting. Soft and hard at once.

I suck on him to keep my volume down.

Harder and harder as he goes deeper and deeper.

His groans get louder. Almost too loud. His shoulders tense. His free hand sinks into the flesh of my ass.

I'm almost there. I thrust my hips, desperate for every inch of him I can get. The tension winds up again. So tight I want to scream.

Instead, I bite him.

He groans. His breath gets heavy.

His next thrust sends me over the edge. I come, my sex clenching around him.

For a second I forget how good ecstasy looks on him, and I feel nothing but the intense pulsing of my orgasm.

When I finally regain my senses, he's there—shaking, groaning, clawing at my skin. He brings his mouth to my neck and sinks his teeth into my flesh.

He groans as he comes.

It reverberates down my neck, all the way to my toes.

Nick pushes himself up. He takes care of the condom, tucks his cock back into his slacks, zips up.

He's going to smell like sex all day.

Like me.

He sits back on the couch next to me, undoes the knot of his tie, and fastens it around his neck. Except for ruffled hair and a not quite wrinkle-free shirt, he looks normal.

He leans down to press his lips to mine. "Our lunch is due in a few minutes. Ms. Lee is going to bring it when it's here."

So I need to get dressed. Nick helps me into my clothes. He slides my glasses onto my face with a gentle touch.

There's something sweetly intimate about it. I can almost imagine him as my doting husband, assisting with my zipper before a special occasion.

What's wrong with me? A relationship with Nick is already off the table. If I keep thinking like that, I'll scare him off, and I'm not ready to be alone again.

"I should clean up." I reach for the door and unlock it slowly. "Excuse me." I step into the main room. It's quiet. Only three or four people here and they're all in the opposite corner.

No way they heard us.

I clean up in the bathroom. My makeup isn't a total travesty. My hair, on the other hand—I pull it into a messy ponytail. There. It's not terrible.

Now there's nothing left to do except ask him.

———

WHEN I GET BACK TO NICK'S OFFICE, IT'S CLEAN AND neat, like nothing happened. He rearranges his desk so his stuff is on one side and our takeout is on the other.

"Green curry or red?" He motions for me to sit.

I do. "Green."

He hands me a plastic container. I pull of the lid and the smells of galangal, lime, and chili peppers waft into my nose. My stomach rumbles. This looks amazing.

Still, I wait until Nick is sitting across from me, everything scooped neatly onto paper plates.

He hands me a plastic fork. "What do you need to talk about?"

I rack my brain to figure out a way to explain it without revealing my source or lying. "I heard something. You could call it a rumor."

"From who?"

"I can't say. I promised to keep it a secret."

"Then you shouldn't ask me about it."

His expression is hard, business again.

I play with my food. "Don't you want to know what it is?"

"There's a weight to other people's secrets. It catches up with you."

"Oh."

"You can ask me, but I can't promise to keep it confidential."

I stab a pepper. "I heard a rumor that someone from the company is trying to sell the Haley project."

Concern spreads over his face. "Where?"

"Nick. I can't say."

His brow furrows.

"It didn't sound right. That project means everything to you. But you're very—" I turn away from Nick's gaze. "—enigmatic. I thought I'd ask."

Even without looking at him, I can tell he's staring through me.

"Lizzy, who told you that?" His voice gets rough.

"I can't say."

"I can only guess the source of your information. Was it Blake Sterling?"

I say nothing.

Nick sighs. "I can't discuss it with you."

"Because I won't give up my source?"

"No. Your source is obvious. There's no one else who would share this kind of information with you."

"Maybe there's another tech CEO who wants to fuck me. You're the one who said that men will find me irresistible."

He brushes off my comment. "You shouldn't be so careless with your questions."

I push my chair back. "I asked you because I trust you."

"It was careless."

"So I shouldn't trust you?" I press my hands together. "I want to help you."

"You can't."

"But—"

"Don't be stubborn. This is none of your business. You shouldn't have asked."

"But Nick. You're upset. You don't have to talk to me as your co-worker, but we are friends... Aren't we?"

"Yes."

Somehow, it sounds like *no*. Like *go away*. Like *this is my burden to carry and I don't want your help.*

There's so much pain in his expression, but he's locking me out. Every impulse in my body is begging me to wipe that pain away. To kiss him, or stroke his hair, or whisper in his ear that it's going to be okay.

I never want to do that. I don't even know how to comfort someone. I tried and failed a few times when Kat was upset.

But I do know how to resist another person's comfort. I know how it looks. And right now, Nick is resisting help.

Which should be fine. If this relationship really is casual. If we really are fuck buddies.

I tap my fingers against my skirt. I take a few bites of my food, but it doesn't have any taste. I don't want it anymore.

It's not fine.

He's next to me, but he's not here. He's off somewhere in his head.

I've been through that with so many other people. But not with him. Not anymore.

Sitting next to him and feeling alone is too hard.

I stand and smooth my skirt. "Excuse me. I have to make a call. I should go. Thank you for lunch, but I'm not feeling very hungry."

"Lizzy—"

"You want to be alone. I'm not going to intrude."

He stares back at me, a wall of stone again. "I'll see you at seven to check your work."

I give him ten seconds to tell me I'm wrong, to ask me to stay.

He doesn't.

## Chapter Twelve

I make a lunch out of the snacks in the break room and throw myself into programming. There's plenty to do. It holds my attention.

At seven on the dot, Nick arrives at my desk to check my work. We're the only people here. The lights are off.

He's calm and aloof. "Are you all right?"

"Nothing I won't get over." Eventually. I clear my throat. "Do you need me here for this?"

"Yes." His posture hardens. He turns to the screen and points out half a dozen errors. "This part is good. You can finish it tomorrow."

"Thank you. Have a great night." I find my coat hanging off the back of my chair and go to put it on.

Nick helps me into it. His eyes meet mine, but he doesn't say anything.

———

At home, I shove my furniture aside, roll out my yoga mat, and stream an extra fast vinyasa video. I push myself too hard. My back will pay for it soon. I can't help it. I need the release from my thoughts.

It hurts seeing Nick in pain.

Much more than it should.

There's a knock on my door. Must be a neighbor who needs something.

I wipe the sweat from my brow and make my way to the door. "Yes?"

"I'd like to speak with you."

Nick.

I pull the door open. "Why?"

His eyes go to my exposed stomach. They scan my body slowly.

Nerves build in my stomach. I love the way he's looking at me. I can't help it.

"Can I come in?" His voice is even.

"Sure." I motion for him to follow and plant on my bed.

Nick makes eye contact. "I'm sorry."

I swallow hard. "You are?"

"Yes. I appreciate that you want to help."

"Really?"

He nods. "But there's nothing anyone can do. I have a one-third stake in the company. The other owners don't need my permission to sell. I should have explained that."

I pat the spot on the bed next to me. "You really hate losing control, huh?"

"Yes." He sits next to me.

"Is that why you're into BDSM?"

"I'd rather not discuss it right now."

"I'm glad I'm not your girlfriend. I bet I'd hear those words every single day."

"Probably." He pulls me into his lap. "I'd like to make it up to you. To take you somewhere tomorrow night."

"Where?"

"It's a surprise."

"You have to give me a hint if you want me to agree."

"You'll get a chance to test your life philosophy."

"That's the worst hint I've ever heard."

He wraps his arms around my waist. "You'll have the chance to take a risk."

"That's ten percent better."

He smiles. "I should let you get on with your night."

But he doesn't leave. He pulls me closer. He presses his lips against my neck. My cheek. My lips.

God, he tastes good.

When the kiss breaks, I stare into his eyes. There's that same loneliness, like it hurt him that he couldn't talk to me.

It hits somewhere deep. I don't like seeing him lonely. It's too familiar. Too painful.

"Why don't you stay?" I ask. "We can have dinner and watch the second Terminator movie. It's better than the first one."

He looks around my room like he's afraid of intruding. Nick's never loved anyone. Is it possible he's never spent the night in a woman's apartment doing anything besides fucking?

"I have to shower," I say. "But otherwise, you're welcome."

"Okay."

"Okay." I smile much wider than I mean to. "Do you want to order dinner or do you want a cheese sandwich?"

"I'll order something spicy."

———

WE FEAST ON EXTRA-SPICY CHINESE FOOD ON MY FLOOR. Hot and sour soup, Kung pao chicken, stir-fried green beans. It's authentic—just the right amount of oil and salt. Not like the rich people, healthy takeout food my sister likes.

After dinner, we watch *Terminator 2: Judgment Day*. There's nowhere to sit except my bed.

Nick places his body behind mine, his legs around my hips, his chest against my back.

There are way more car crashes in the movie than I remembered. I close my eyes and lean into his body. He pulls me closer. He strokes my hair.

He's so warm.

Soft and hard at once.

Even though he's in his suit, he's not stiff or awkward. He's comfortable. It's been so long since anything has felt this comfortable, this safe.

I keep my eyes closed as I melt into his arms. I shouldn't fall asleep like this, but I can't bring myself to resist it...

I wake up in the dark. There's a weight shifting on the bed. Nick. He's leaving. The TV is off.

"Did you finish the movie?" I ask.

"Yes."

"Wasn't it sweet, at the end?"

He nods.

"I'm sorry I called you a robot. You didn't deserve that."

"Yes, I did." He kisses me. "Good night, Lizzy."

"Good night, Nick."

# Chapter Thirteen

I wake up to a text message from Nick.

*Nick: I left a package at the front desk of your building. I'll pick you up at 8:00. We leave at 8:30.*

*Lizzy: What do we do with those thirty minutes?*

*Nick: You're not subtle.*

*Lizzy: Give me a break. I just woke up. Let me try again. Are you going to spend those thirty minutes fucking me?*

*Nick: No.*

I send him a frowning-face emoji.

*Nick: Do you know what my mom said whenever she saw me frowning?*

*Lizzy: "Don't cry. One day you'll be a billionaire."*

*Nick: "Don't pout. You'll get wrinkles."*

*Lizzy: Didn't work. You frown all the time.*

*Nick: I will fuck you tonight. After.*

That earns him one smiley-face emoji. I leave my phone on my desk and hightail it downstairs. Sure enough, there's a package for me. The doorman hands it over with a knowing smile.

I smile back despite my urge to tell him to mind his own business.

It's hard to feel upset when my head is dreaming up all sorts of beautiful images to go with Nick's promise.

There are so many possibilities. He could fuck me here, or in his apartment, or in the office, or wherever it is we're going.

The package is not the most helpful clue. It's a purple cocktail dress and a lingerie set in the same shade of amethyst. Seamless bra and skimpy thong panties. Both are soft silk.

It's sexy.

But what the hell does it mean?

————

THERE'S A KNOCK ON THE DOOR AT EXACTLY 8 PM.

Nick.

"Just a minute." I throw off my lounging clothes, slip into the matching purple bra and panty set, and answer the door.

Nick looks damn handsome in his sleek black suit. Better with his eyes wide.

Somehow, there's no surprise in his expression. He's cool, collected.

He steps inside, shutting the door behind him.

His hands go to my ass. He lifts me and presses me against the wall. All that heat of his body melts into mine.

We're close, and he's staring into my eyes with this expression I can't place.

"You trying to tease me?" His nails dig into my skin.

The burst of pain wakes up all my senses. I run my hands through his hair.

For once, I can touch him. It feels damn good to touch him.

"Are you mad I answered the door in lingerie?" I press my body against his. "Lingerie you sent me?"

"No." His teeth scrape against my neck.

"You seem mad."

He shifts his hips, pinning me against the wall. "Put your hands on my shoulders."

I do.

Nick pulls my bra cup down so my nipple pops out. He kisses his way down my neck and chest, until his mouth is around my nipple.

He bites me.

Fuck.

My sex clenches. It hurts in such a good way.

He does it again, a little harder.

"Nick." I squeeze my thighs around his hips. "I don't know what you're doing, but please keep doing it."

He bites me again and again, harder and harder. Every time, my flesh stings with pain.

I tug at his suit jacket. Squeeze my legs around his body.

His palm presses against my sex, over my panties. It winds me up. God, I want him touching me.

With his next bite, I yelp. He doesn't stop. Only goes harder. I close my eyes to focus on the hurt, the way my body screams out for him. It's intense, but I can manage it.

Harder.

Harder.

"Ow." It's too much. I tug at his jacket. "Yellow."

He softens then moves to my other nipple and teases it mercilessly. His palm rubs against my panties, pressing the silk against my skin.

I give up on figuring out his intentions and surrender to the sting of pain, the pulse of anticipation in my core.

I want him so badly I can barely breathe.

He bites me until I cry out. His eyes meet mine. They're full of desire but he's still so calm and collected.

No relenting, he bites me again.

Fuck. It's too much. "Red."

Nick shifts, unpinning me and setting me on the ground. He's hard. He's hard but he's effortlessly collected.

He brushes his fingertips against my cheek, looking into my eyes like he's trying to make sure I'm okay.

"What was that supposed to be?" I ask.

"You teased me. I teased you back."

Okay. That makes sense. More or less. Maybe a little less. I try to find a clue in his expression. It's almost like he's frustrated.

My gaze goes to the bulge in his slacks. That looks like a frustrating problem.

Hell, it's torture just looking at him without having him in my hands or my mouth or my cunt.

"You wanted to fuck me," I say.

He's unblinking.

"You almost did." I can't help but smile. "It pissed you off that you wanted to go against your edict. That you wanted me that badly."

"No one likes a sore winner."

My smile is smug as hell. "We have twenty-five minutes. No reason why we can't use them."

"After." He moves to my desk. "How well do you know Texas Hold 'Em?"

"Okay, I guess. I made that bot a year ago. Played a few times since. Why? If I knew, would you fuck me?"

"Yes."

Damn. What a time to be ignorant of a poker variant.

I study Nick's expression. It's not steel, but it's determined. He's going to get his way. I might as well get into my clothes.

I slide into my cocktail dress and present my back to him. "Zip me."

He does. His fingers linger on my exposed skin. It sends a pang of lust straight to my core. It's torture knowing he won't touch me properly until later.

Is it torture for him too?

He pulls a deck of cards from his jacket pocket and motions to my desk.

I sit. "It wasn't hard to teach the bot the statistics. The hard part was teaching it when to bluff."

"Your program was the most ambitious poker AI I've even seen."

"Really?"

He nods.

I beam. There's affection in his expression. It does something to me, makes me warm everywhere. "Why are we talking about poker?"

"You're playing in a tournament tonight."

"That's not possible, because that would mean you entered me in a tournament without my permission." I fold my arms. "I can't play for money. And certainly not—Nick, did you pay an entry fee for me?"

"It's not a high-stakes game."

"I'm pretty sure we have different ideas of high-stakes."

"The pot is about a hundred thousand dollars. Most serious games are two or three times that."

My ability to breathe falters. A hundred thousand dollars. Chump change to Nick. A fortune to me. To any reasonable person.

He brushes my hair behind my ear. "The entry fee was about four thousand dollars. There are thirty players. The top seven places come out ahead. Anything after eighth and you go home with nothing."

I take his cards and press them against his chest. "You cannot pay for my entry fee. Uh-uh. No fucking way."

"Consider it an investment. We split your winnings, fifty-fifty."

What a load. "You'll find some loophole to force me to keep all the money."

He shuffles the deck and places it on my desk. "I won't. I promise. We each keep half." He extends his hand to shake.

I don't take it. "Gambling is illegal."

"Don't tell me you're afraid of risk."

"It's your money."

"It's paid."

He deals the cards. Three face up. Two to each of us. "You know the rules?"

"Yes." I stare into his deep brown eyes. "You're going to do some BS thing like spend all your winnings on lingerie for me."

"Lingerie is a gift for me as much as it is for you."

I motion to the door. "Didn't seem like it."

"You didn't enjoy that?"

My cheeks flush. "Then why were you—"

"You like being teased. You liked me teasing you. What's to explain?"

"But you didn't... you didn't seem like you liked it."

"I do. I like you desperate and wanting."

That explains a lot.

He runs his fingertips over the neckline of my dress.

"Nick..."

He presses his lips to my neck. "I want to throw you on that bed, rip off those panties, and fuck you until you're screaming my name."

God, he's good at teasing. He's on a whole other level.

"You're evil," I groan.

He releases me and kneels next to the desk. His eyes meet mine. "Once upon a time, a wise woman told me that it's good to want things. It makes you know you're alive."

"Wise, huh? You sure she wasn't trying to manipulate you?"

"She was flirting. In her way." He smiles and runs his fingertips over my cheek.

The touch is so sweet, so intimate. It sends a shiver down my spine. Makes me want him on a whole other level.

His voice gets harder. "You wear that lingerie for me."

It's not a question. I nod anyway.

"That gets me off. Knowing you're mine. Knowing you want my attention."

How can this relationship be casual if I'm his? I swallow the question. I have to worry about losing four grand. I can't deal with any distractions.

He drags his fingertips over the back of my neck as he takes me through a dozen sample games. I remember the rules, the statistics, the strategies. Sure, I can bluff well, and I know enough about reading other people to figure out when to call and when to fold, but there's no way I can compete with anyone who takes poker seriously.

Nick might as well kiss that entry fee goodbye.

———

WE TAKE THE SUBWAY TO A FANCY BUILDING ACROSS from the Hudson. A password to the doorman grants us access to the penthouse floor.

The den of sin is a gorgeous apartment with an amazing view. The main room has a wet bar, lounge chairs, and a smattering of gambling offerings. Not just poker tonight—there's roulette, craps, blackjack.

Nick nods to a back room. It's bright yellow from the fluorescent lights, somehow ominous and sterile and the same time. Most of the room is hidden from view but I can see a poker table and a circle of chairs.

"This is the first tournament. The stakes get higher as the night goes on." He takes my coat and hangs it on a rack. His hands return to my shoulders, his touch gentle. "You ready?"

I nod. "You're such a bad boy, breaking the law like this. Maybe I should punish you."

He smiles. "You don't want to."

I admit nothing.

He knows he's right though. I can see it in his cocky smile. I like it.

I like the way he smiles, the way his eyes light up and his cheeks get wide.

There's this lightness in my body. All from Nick's smile.

He checks his watch and motions to the back room. I follow him.

The room is just big enough for three tables. There are about thirty people here. Mostly men. Most of them do double takes when they see me.

Their eyes go to my chest, their tongues slide over their lips. The cleavage is a shrewd distraction. Never thought Nick would encourage such a cheap tactic.

Maybe I'm wrong about him being honorable.

The tournament manager directs our attention to a white board with seating arrangements. It's time to get started.

Nick squeezes me so tightly I can barely breathe. God, he feels good like this too. I hug him back, then shift all my focus to the game.

Maybe four thousand dollars is nothing to him, but it's a lot to me. I have to try my best to double his money. I don't want to owe him anything else.

I find my seat and take in my opponents. There are seven other players. Five are typical business guys in their forties. One is more of a cocky playboy type, younger. One is an older woman.

At first, I hold back, following the energy of the table. By the fourth round, I have a feel for my opponents. Cocky playboy is, in fact, overly confident. The older woman taps her nose when she has a good hand. Of the five typical business guys, only one is hard to read. The other four wear their cards in their eyes.

My bets get more aggressive. I call three bluffs and end up with more than half the pot. Players go out one at a time, until it's just me and the older woman.

The tournament master rearranges everything. What started as four tables is down to two. I have new opponents. Five this time. I take my time to read them then I get aggressive, bluffing when I have a decent chance, calling anyone who falters or bites his lip a little too long.

Nick is on the sidelines with another dozen or so people. He pulls out his phone, looks at it closely, and frowns. Did his mom really tell him not to frown? He's a chronic frowner. So much weight on his shoulders. I hate that. I hate it when he frowns. I want him to smile, to wrap his arms around me and—

Fuck.

The betting is to me and I have no idea what's happening at the table. My hand is so-so, but it's just me and another business guy. He bets big.

I fold. Not worth risking.

My attention goes back to the game, but it's there, in the back of my mind, trying to distract me. Something is bothering Nick. I don't like that something is bothering him.

Somehow, I play well half-distracted. No one can tell if I'm bluffing. After a dozen rounds, we're down to six players and one table.

I've already placed.

No matter what I do, I'm not losing Nick's money. Which means all the risk is mine.

I give myself more leeway to play aggressively. The men at the table look at me like I amuse them. Whatever. I'm used to people underestimating me.

I delight in calling their bluffs. It's less wonderful when someone's full house beats my two pair, but what are you gonna do? It's poker.

The table knocks down to four.

Three.

Me and two men. The older one looks at me like he thinks I'm an idiot. He raises, doubling the pot. The other guy folds.

It's just the two of us.

My hand is good. Two kings with a third on the table. I call.

Next card is a queen, also a heart, but the odds of a straight are low. A straight flush is practically nonexistent.

I bet high. He calls.

Last card is the ten. Also a heart.

He bets high enough I have to fold or go all in. It's a fuck-you play. One that dares me to call him.

I study his expression. It's a bluff. I know it is.

Time to go big or go home. I call.

There's nothing left to do but to turn over our cards. I go first. He nods, giving nothing away.

Then him.

Fuck me.

He's got the straight flush.

"Good game." I nod and make my way back to Nick. I was sure that guy was bluffing, but my hand didn't justify such a high bet. That's what I get for trusting my gut.

Nick rubs my shoulders. His mouth hovers over my ear. "Don't pout. You'll get wrinkles."

I laugh.

"You just won twenty thousand dollars. Ten thousand if you're only counting your half."

No. That can't be right. I look at his face for a sign he's kidding, but it's not there.

He nods.

I shake my head.

"Third place takes eighteen percent of the pot."

I do the math in my head. He's right. Nerves rise up in my stomach. "What am I supposed to do with all that cash?"

"Spend it."

"On what?"

"There's a safe in your apartment if you want to save it."

"You're not going to offer to help me launder it?"

"No."

"When do I get it?"

Nick runs his hand through my hair. "When did you get so impatient?"

"Phoenix Marlowe, don't play games with me."

He smiles. No more anguish, no more frustration. He's smiling.

"We can collect it before we leave or I can have someone bring it to the office." He runs his fingertips over my neck. "I'm not walking home with a briefcase of cash. If you want it now, we're taking a car."

Fuck. I didn't think about that. It's late enough that the subway is only running every hour or so.

"Are you okay taking a car?" he asks.

I swallow hard. My impulse tells me to play strong. To say yes. But the way he's touching me... he feels safe.

"I don't know," I whisper. "Can we revisit the topic after we have sex?"

He laughs. "I hope you never change, Lizzy. You're perfect the way you are."

The words are sweet, but they're confusing too.

I nod like his affection isn't rattling me.

## Chapter Fourteen

I follow Nick through the makeshift casino's lounge area. My gaze is drawn to any place with potential. The booths are too visible. The bathroom gets too much traffic. Every room is in use.

Nick leads me to the stairs in the corner.

Oh. The penthouse has a second story.

The staircase is gorgeous. Marble floors, stainless steel railing. The big glass windows look out on two dozen midtown skyscrapers.

My attention goes straight to the top of the Empire State Building. It's lit up in purple today. I'm sure it's for NYU, but it feels like it's for me.

For us.

The door clicks shut behind us. There's no one here, but there's nothing preventing anyone from following us.

From catching us.

Nick slides his arm around my waist. "You played well."

"I was cocky."

His fingers trail over the low back of my dress until they find my zipper. "Do you regret your bet?"

"No. It was worth the risk."

"Is this?" He pulls the zipper down. Then the left strap. The right strap.

I step back until I'm pressed against the wall. I'm facing the door. If anyone walks in, they'll see me. I'm half-dressed at the moment, but soon I'll be naked.

My sex clenches.

"Lizzy, I asked you a question." Nick pulls my bra aside so my breast spills out. His fingertips toy with my nipple.

Every touch sends a pang of need to my core. I'm exposed to him. To anyone who walks in. It's scary but it's exhilarating.

I nod. "Yes, it's worth the risk." Of getting caught. Of falling fast and hard for someone I'm going to lose.

His dark eyes fill with anticipation.

My thoughts slip away.

I arch my back and press my eyelids together as he teases me.

My lips part. No more thinking. Just this.

"Nick," I groan. "Please."

He pulls the other strap of the bra aside, so I'm as good as topless.

His lips find mine as he cups my breasts. He kisses me deeply, slowly. It's not the kiss of two people fucking frantically in a staircase. It's one steeped in affection.

Casual. This is casual. I try to remind myself of his terms, but there's so much feeling in his kiss.

His body presses against mine, pinning me to the wall. He's hard. I shift my hips a few inches to grind against him.

He presses his lips into my neck. "Beg me."

I don't hesitate. "Please fuck me."

"Keep going."

"Please, Nick. I need you. I've been desperate since you got to my apartment. Since you told me you'd fuck me this morning."

He slides my dress off my hips. It tumbles to the floor. Instead of removing my thong, he pushes it aside. His finger teases me again and again.

I kiss him harder. I need more of him. I need to touch him. I reach for his belt.

In an instant, he removes his hands from my body and steps back. His eyes cloud like he's getting pulled somewhere else.

"You don't want me to touch you?" I ask.

His hands wrap around my wrists. "I can only do this on my terms."

His posture hardens. It's an all-or-nothing proposition. All his way or nothing.

I look into his eyes. "It's okay if you don't want me to touch you. I just want to know."

"I do want that." He presses his palm against my sex. "But not yet." He pushes my thong aside and rubs my clit.

He doesn't want to talk about it.

I can respect that, even if I'm desperate to get my hands around him.

Even if I hate the hint of pain in his eyes.

I press my nails into my palm. "Okay. Your terms. Whatever you want, but please fuck me. I need you inside me. I need to feel you come."

Nick pulls his hand away. "Turn around."

I turn so my back is to him.

He pushes my thong to my knees. "Put your hands against the wall."

His voice commands me. I press my palms against the

wall. A shudder passes from my head to my toes. I try to push my concerns aside. I like his terms.

I crave them.

Nick slides two fingers inside me. I gasp from the shock of it. There's no more teasing. He goes deep and hard.

His hand digs into my hair. He pulls my head back, pulling my body against his.

There are footsteps outside the door. Voices. They're close.

Nick does nothing to slow down. He shifts his weight. There's a zipper coming undone, a condom unwrapping. His hands go to my hips as he positions me.

No one opens the door.

We're still alone.

With one swift thrust, he enters me. It's deep. Hard.

I gasp. Fuck it. I can't stand keeping my volume down. I do nothing to temper my moans.

One of his arms slides around my pelvis to hold me in place. The other plays with my nipples, one at a time.

There's no more teasing. Nick thrusts into me. His movements are hard and fast, like he's letting down his guard.

I do the same, rocking my hips to meet his, pressing my fingers against the wall.

He groans. His nails rake down my back. It's a hard, violent motion. Sure to leave a mark, especially in my backless dress.

He's marking me.

God, I love him marking me.

I turn my head to press my neck against his mouth. He bites me. The pain is so intense it pulls my attention away from the orgasm building in my core.

I don't care. I need to feel his release, his desperation.

He bites harder.

I groan.

Harder.

I scream.

I take a deep breath, relaxing my body into his, focusing on every sensation.

Nick is here. In this moment, he's mine, and I'm his. In this moment, we only exist to fulfill each other.

He bites me again.

It's too much. I can't take it. "Red."

He stops instantly. His mouth goes to my ear and he sucks on the lobe. His fingers dig into my thighs.

His breath is heavy. Erratic.

There are more footsteps. They get closer. Closer. The handle turns.

The door opens an inch or two. It closes. No telling if the person saw and ran off, or if they changed their mind.

We almost got caught.

We can still get caught.

The thought makes my sex clench. I let my eyes close and I surrender to the pleasure building in my body.

Nick's hands go to my hips. He guides my movements.

Almost. I groan. There must be someone on the other side of that door.

Still, I groan as loudly as I can.

He does the same. The sound of his bliss pushes me all the way to the edge. With his next thrust, I tumble into an orgasm.

My world is bright, and warm, the most beautiful shade of purple. My sex clenches around him as I come.

A few more moments and he's there, digging his nails into my thighs, sinking his teeth into my neck. He's here, with me, in this moment.

I never want to lose track of him again.

I never want to lose him.

I shake my head to regain my senses. It's just sex. It makes you feel things sometimes. Clouds your judgment.

But I can't shake the thought.

It's like something is missing when he pulls out and adjusts his clothes instead of wrapping his arms around me.

It makes sense. We can't exactly linger here.

But I hate it.

He brings his mouth to my ear. "I'll be back in a minute."

He climbs the stairs and pulls open the door to the second floor. Like he knows something I don't about an empty place to clean up. Like I'm not the first girl he's fucked in this particular stairwell.

I focus on the noises outside the door as I slip into my clothes. There are voices, glasses clinking, footsteps, laughter. But it feels far away.

I'm so caught up in the sounds of the room that I don't notice Nick's return until he's wrapping his arms around me.

I don't feel cold anymore. Nothing is missing.

It must be the sex messing with my judgment. I take a deep breath as Nick slides his arm around my waist and leads me back to the main room.

It's just sex.

No big deal.

A dozen people look at us. All of them know we were fucking in the stairwell.

My cheeks flush, but the risk of embarrassment feels like nothing compared to the risk of my feelings.

He smiles as he fills out some form to collect my winnings. I melt. All I ever want is to see him smile again.

"Are you sure about the car?" he asks.

I nod. Even that seems less scary.

———

OUR RIDE IS A SLEEK BLACK TOWN CAR. THE DRIVER opens the door for me with a polite nod. I step inside and slide to the end of the bench.

I was wrong. This is too hard. Too terrifying.

I try to reason with myself.

It's only a ten-minute drive to his apartment. Speeds in the city are low. The chance of a crash bad enough to hurt us is almost nothing.

My hands are shaking as I buckle my seat belt. I can't back out now. I'll disappoint Nick.

He slides in after me. Despite his considerable height, he sits in the middle seat, fastens the belt, and takes my hand.

It's sweaty as hell but he doesn't complain.

The driver slides into the car. "Where to?"

Nick gives him my address. So I'm not invited over. It means something, but my thoughts are in messy squiggles.

Nick runs his fingers through my hair. Leans in close. "If it's too much, tell me. We can walk."

"But what about—" I nod to the briefcase.

"I'll figure something out." He stares into my eyes. "Promise you won't suffer in silence."

I can't lie to him. I have to mean it. Deep breath. "I promise."

The car turns on.

I've been stuck in a car a dozen times or so since the accident, but it's been a while. The movements feel jerky.

We pull onto the main street. I take a deep breath.

We're going a reasonable speed. We haven't died yet.

The driver slams on the brakes. I squeeze my eyelids together. Nine minutes to go, give or take. That's too many. I can't do it.

"Lizzy." Nick runs his fingers through my hair. "It's okay."

"Right. No big deal."

"Don't bullshit me." He presses his lips against my forehead. "I won't let anything hurt you."

I shake my head. "You can't protect me from another car." My body tenses. We're still here. I go to reach for the door handle. I can't be in here anymore, but I can't roll onto the road. We're going thirty miles an hour.

"It's okay." He wraps his arms around me, holding me close. "I've got you."

His touch is so comforting. Not enough to counter being in a car. But enough to keep me from jumping out of the fucking door.

It's the best thing I've ever felt, his arms. His lips. His voice, when it's like this, soft and sweet.

Again, the car jerks to a stop. There are horns honking.

All my muscles tense at once.

"I can't do it. I'm not strong enough." I squeeze Nick's arm until his skin turns white.

"You are." He runs his hands through my hair. "You're the strongest person I know."

"You don't mean that."

He pulls me closer. "I only say things I mean."

His words are confusing. No more talking. I tug at his jacket. Not close enough. I tug at his shirt instead.

He runs his fingers over my skin with a gentle touch. It calms me just enough to make this bearable.

I lean into his comfort. We'll be done soon. I can manage a few more minutes. Even if I have to do it with my eyelids squeezed together.

Deep breath. I try to forget about everything except Nick's touch, but I can still feel the motion of the car, still hear the whir of the motor.

"We're almost there." His fingertips trail over my neck.

I lean into the gesture. It soothes me. I manage to pry my eyelids apart. We are close. Just a few more blocks on Broadway. The street is empty.

It's going to be okay.

Still, I close my eyes for the rest of the ride. Finally, we park in front of my building. Nick helps me out of the car with a soft touch.

His hand slides around my waist as he leads me into the building. Into the elevator.

It's just us, alone. He looks into my eyes like he sees through me.

He does. He sees too much.

The elevator arrives at my floor. Nick leads the way. He digs into my purse to find my key, unlocks the door for me.

I grab the purse back as I step inside. He saw too much of me. I can't let him see any more. Not with the terms of this relationship. It's already going to hurt so much when I lose him. If I get any closer...

It will be unbearable.

He steps inside after me. Closes the door.

"I should get to bed. I'm tired. And I'm meeting Kat for brunch early." I go straight to the bathroom, strip to my underwear, wash my face, brush my teeth.

He's standing there in the hallway, all strong and untouchable.

"Thank you for the poker. And the rest." I adjust my bra and underwear in the hopes of feeling less exposed. It doesn't work.

Nick's eyes scan my body for a moment. Then they're back to mine. "Of course." He motions to the briefcase. "I am a man of my word."

"Oh, right. Take your half."

He opens the briefcase, slips a few stacks of hundred-dollar bills in his slacks, then nods to me. "Do you want this here or in the safe?"

"There is fine. I'm really tired, so I'll see you tomorrow." I find the bed, get under the covers, and lose the underwear.

He's still standing there.

"Nick, I'm not going to be able to sleep if you're standing there watching me. It's strange."

He doesn't leave.

He locks the door, strips to his boxers, and gets in bed next to me.

I say nothing. I'm speechless over how good his body feels against mine.

How much calmer I feel with his arms around me.

How much warmer the bed is with him here.

## Chapter Fifteen

In the morning, he's gone.

I spend the day with Kat, but my thoughts are with Nick.

She asks me what's wrong a dozen times.

Every time, I lie and say it's nothing.

I hate lying to her.

Monday, I arrive at work at eight on the dot. There are bagels and coffee on Nick's desk, like everything is normal.

Our two hours together are intense and they're focused exclusively on programming. When we're finished, he leaves for a meeting.

I stay busy. I drown my thoughts in work.

There's a change in the atmosphere today. People are talking about something juicy.

Sitting in the break room listening to Gabriel and David whisper does nothing to make my homemade sandwich more appealing. I pull the crust off my bread while I eavesdrop.

"Second month in a row he's flown to SFO. What else

could he be doing on those trips?" Gabriel talks with his mouth full.

"I'm sure it's a woman."

"Nah, Marlowe would fly the girl to a hotel here. He's got plenty of pussy in New York. Why would he go three thousand miles for more?" Gabriel looks past me, to Jasmine's desk.

I drop my sandwich.

They glance at me then turn back to their conversation with knowing smiles. I'm next to Jasmine on the list of women in New York who Nick can fuck.

Which means they don't know that I am fucking him.

That's a good thing.

But the rest of their conversation is far from reassuring.

David's voice breaks my concentration. "I hope Tech Edge is right. I've been trying to find an excuse to move to San Jose."

I load the Tech Edge homepage on my phone. It's right there—*Google Poised to Buy the Next Siri*.

The article is conjecture. There's only one decent fact in it—the owners of Odyssey Industries are fielding offers for their AI virtual assistant software.

Rushed footsteps break my concentration. A woman's high heels and a man's dress shoes.

I turn and there are Nick and Jasmine, whispering on their way to his office. I wait until they pass then duck behind a desk to listen.

"I'll call a meeting, but I'm not lying to anyone here." She folds her arms over her chest, not shy about confronting him. "The story broke two hours ago."

"Are you gossiping?"

"Phoenix, you'll know if I'm gossiping. You'll feel the stares on your back as everyone wonders how many—"

"You made your point."

She leans in, lowering her voice. "He's left three messages already. If you meet with him, apologize about last year—"

"Out of the question."

"You have no control over this. You know what he's like."

His voice is soft. "You don't need to—"

"This is my job. I shouldn't have taken it if I can't handle corresponding with one of the co-owners." She adjusts her cardigan. "Prepare a statement for the staff. I'll set a meeting for two o'clock."

"Thank you."

"Nick, I..."

My stomach twists. I don't like their familiarity.

"He flew in today." She bites her lip. "I'm sorry. I should have forwarded the call to you, but you were with Miss Wilder and I know... how much those mornings mean to you."

"It's fine."

They share a look of understanding. I hate it. I hate everything about it.

Jasmine turns back to her desk. Her eyes connect with mine then go to the floor.

"Miss Wilder." Nick's voice booms. "Can I speak with you?"

His eyes bore into me. His brow is furrowed. His jaw is clenched. He's angry, but that can't all be directed at me. Not for something as trivial as eavesdropping.

"Now."

I press my hands to my sides. "Of course." Five steps and I'm in Nick's office, the door closed behind me.

He stands three feet away from me. His expression gets intense. "Lock the door."

"What?"

"Do I need to explain?"

His intention is right there in his eyes.

He stares back at me, challenging me. I take a deep breath, willing my judgment to kick in.

Maybe he does need to explain. I don't know what he wants from me.

But whatever it is, I want it too.

I lock the door.

Nick points to the couch. "Sit down."

I do.

"Unbutton your blouse."

"What are you—"

"Now."

I undo my buttons one at a time.

His expression is half-frustration, half-desire.

"Are you going to explain what's going on here?" I ask. "With the company?"

"Soon."

"To me?"

"Yes." He sits on the couch next to me. He's not patient today. He cups my breast over my bra. The lace fabric rubs against my nipples, rough and soft all at once.

"You keep wearing the lingerie I bought you." His touch hardens. "Is this what you were hoping would happen?" He brings his lips to my neck.

My eyes flutter closed and the rest of the room fades away. My world is Nick–his teeth, his hands, his breath.

"I asked you a question," he groans.

"Yes."

Nick removes my glasses. He sets them on the arm of the couch and grabs my knees.

He pulls me over his lap, so I'm on my stomach, my face pressed against the couch cushion. His fingers trail over the backs of my tights.

"Nick," I breathe. "What are you doing?"

He rolls my skirt to my waist. "If you want me to stop, say the word."

My skin buzzes from his touch. I'm already keyed up, but there are too many different feelings whirring around my brain. "Is this a punishment?"

"No."

"Then what is it?"

"I need to feel you submitting." He peels the tops of my tights over my ass and down my thighs. "If you want something else, tell me to stop."

My sex clenches.

No. He can't stop. Not now.

I press my hands into the cushion. "Are you going to fuck me?"

"Tonight."

"Am I going to come?"

"If you're quiet."

Nick drags his fingers over my thighs. He adjusts me so my ass is hanging off his legs, like I'm waiting to be spanked.

Fuck. I am waiting to be spanked.

Desire collects between my legs. He has such a hold on me. How is that possible?

He teases me, dragging his fingertips over my skin. They trace the outline of my thong from one hip to the other then back again.

He presses his palm against my sex, over my panties. "God dammit, Lizzy. You're dripping."

I swallow hard.

"You like being spanked?"

"Yes."

He lets out a low groan.

Nick brings one hand to my lips. He drags his thumb

over my lower lip, that same gentle, tender movement that really makes me believe he cares about me.

I press my eyelids together. How can it feel so caring, him bending me over his knee to spank me?

He slides his fingers into my mouth. "Suck on me if you want to scream."

He's teasing me again.

God, how he teases.

Without warning, his hand makes contact with my flesh. It's more of a tap than a smack. I suck on his fingers to keep from begging.

He hits me again. Harder. The sting of pain reverberates all the way to my mouth. I suck harder. When that's not enough, I bite him.

He groans as he hits me again.

His hand is inches above my sex and I'm throbbing, desperate for him to touch me.

Tonight. Not now. Not soon, but tonight.

How am I supposed to wait that long?

A knock on the door interrupts.

Jasmine's voice is muffled by the door. "Mr. Marlowe, I need to speak with you. Whenever you're... finished. Take your time. Sorry about the intrusion."

There's this awkward tone to her voice.

She knows what we're doing.

She knows I'm fucking Nick.

I push myself off the couch, landing on the floor with a very unpleasant thud.

My mid-back tenses. It will be trouble later, but right now my main concern is putting my clothes back on before I completely throw away my judgment.

I pull my tights to my waist, fix my skirt, and reach for the door. No. I still need my glasses. I grab them off the couch.

Nick grabs my wrist, stopping me. "Your shirt is unbuttoned." He pulls me into his lap, his grip tightening. "I didn't tell you to leave."

"Red." I break free of his grasp and fumble over my buttons. "What the fuck happened to this relationship being a secret?"

He says nothing.

"Any other secrets you share with Jasmine?"

"Yes."

I grab onto the door, but I can't turn it yet. I'm too unsettled.

"Lizzy, it's not personal."

"No, how could it be personal? You don't even trust me enough to let me touch you."

"Let's talk tonight. I'll take you to dinner."

Right on cue, my stomach growls. "How come you get to make all the terms? Do you know how hard it is for me to keep things from my sister?"

"Yes."

"And you tell your fucking secretary?"

"She's not my secretary. We have a history."

"Do you think I'm stupid or just naive?"

"Lizzy."

With a deep breath, I open the door and walk back to my desk. I'm acutely aware of eyes on me.

I try to work, but I can't think. I lock myself in the handicapped stall of the women's bathroom so no one can disrupt me.

My phone is no solace. There's a new text from Nick. Instead of reading it, I turn the damn device off.

Once I've calmed down, I leave the office in favor of the coffee shop across the street. I don't return until well after the meeting is over.

## Chapter Sixteen

The office clears at five, but I'm too behind schedule to go home. I focus on my work, only stopping to get water or use the restroom.

The lights turn off around eight. All but the one streaming out from Nick's office. The door opens and he steps into the main room.

It's not fair that he's so handsome. It makes it harder to resist him.

His eyes meet mine. "I ordered you shrimp scampi. I have sriracha in my office."

"You've been hoarding hot sauce?"

He nods.

"I should probably finish this."

"It's your decision." He steps into the elevator.

My work no longer holds my attention. I'm too tired and too drained to think straight. I might as well take solace in spicy noodles.

The elevator doors ding open. Nick steps into the main room holding a paper bag. He motions for me to follow him into his office.

I do.

He leaves the door open. "We are alone, so—"

"Planning to make good on your promise to fuck me tonight?"

He passes a takeout container and a fork to me. "Would you really want that?"

"I don't know." I consider it. "Yes. I would. I understand you when we're having sex. Other times..." Not as much.

The smells of garlic, tomatoes, and shrimp waft into my nostrils as I pull off the lid. It's just like the last time we tried to eat a meal in his office. There's still a wall between us. He still has all the cards.

He hands me a bottle of sriracha. "Jasmine was my brother's high school sweetheart. She helped me whenever I had a problem with him. She was always trustworthy."

"How did she end up working for you?"

"I offered her a job after they broke up. He was planning on staying in the Bay and working at another startup, and I was set on Odyssey being in New York."

"Why?"

"People are serious here. They don't spend their weeknights slamming shots. They don't come to work in hoodies and t-shirts."

"You don't like the laidback Silicon Valley thing?"

"Do you?"

"No. There's a word for it, you know, 'brogrammer,' like a bro programmer. Those guys crash Stanford parties on the weekends and pick up college girls by bragging about their six-figure salaries. They're all assholes." I stir hot sauce into my pasta. My mid-back tenses. No amount of wiggling or stretching helps. "Thanks for dinner." I stuff pasta in my mouth so I won't have to respond.

"Jasmine asked if we were sleeping together a few weeks ago. I could tell she knew the answer."

"You must be close to know her expressions that well."

"I'm not interested in her."

"But she's your friend. You trust her."

"I trust you."

There's regret in his eyes. He's barely touching his food.

I take another bite so I won't say something stupid.

Once again, all I want to do is wrap my arms around him, to wipe the pain from his expression.

I can't keep doing this. I can't care about him this much. Not if he's going to withhold things from me. Not if this really is casual.

After my next bite, I push my food aside. Wipe my face. My eyes meet Nick's. "You don't have to explain. Your company is your first priority. You want casual. And this isn't feeling very casual anymore." My eyes go to the table. "It's better if we end things before we get too invested."

"Is that really what you want?"

No. But I'm not seeing another choice. I open my mouth to speak, but I can't bring myself to add to the hurt look in his eyes.

If I'm wrong, tell me I'm wrong.

Please, Nick. Please tell me I'm wrong.

He doesn't.

"You said that you didn't want to hurt me." I play with my hands. "If that's really true—"

A knock on the door interrupts me.

Dammit, this is getting to be an annoying trend.

The person, whoever he is, doesn't wait for a response.

A man in a navy suit steps inside. He looks a lot like Nick. Just as tall and broad. Just as handsome. Same dark hair, but his eyes are blue.

He looks from me to Nick with an amused expression. "Where is Jasmine?"

"I sent her home," Nick says.

"Shepard Marlowe." He extends his hand to me.

I only barely manage to shake it. "Lizzy Wilder." My gaze goes to Nick. Shepard Marlowe. No way his last name is a coincidence.

And he called Jasmine by her first name.

Shepard makes eye contact with Nick. Frowns. "You're still pretending like I don't exist?"

"You were on a leave of absence until last month." Nick grits his teeth. "Miss Wilder, this is my brother, Shepard."

"CFO of Odyssey." Shepard takes a step backwards.

"So you're the person trying to sell the company?" I ask.

"Yes." He taps his toe impatiently. "I hate to be rude, but could you give us a minute?" He looks at Nick. "I doubt you want your girlfriend to hear this."

"I'm not his girlfriend," I say.

"Whatever you'd like to call it." Shepard folds his arms, waiting. "Did you get tired of Jasmine or did you inherent Dad's philandering streak?"

Nick's brow furrows. "Lizzy, give us a minute."

I don't like the frustration on his face. I want to stay, to do whatever I can to protect him.

"Now," Nick says.

"Of course, Mr. Marlowe." I leave the door open a few inches on my way into the main room.

I stay close enough to eavesdrop. The tension in my back spreads up and down my spine. I need to lie down with a heating pad and a heavy dose of ibuprofen. Even that might not be enough.

I should go now. Before it gets really bad.

But I can't go until I hear this.

"Jesus, I thought Jasmine was young for you. How old is that girl?" Shepard asks.

"I never touched Jasmine."

"Sell whatever story you want. I don't have any interest in listening to you lie about fucking the only woman I've ever loved." Shepard clears his throat. "I'm flying back to the Bay tomorrow. I need a number or I can't negotiate." There's a pause, like he's waiting for a response. "How much is Odyssey worth right now?"

"A tenth what it will be worth in three years."

"How much is it worth today?"

"If you want out, I'll buy your share."

"I don't want your money."

There's a pause. I can't see them, but I can feel the tension all the way over here.

Nick breaks the silence. "If you want to hurt me—"

"My life doesn't revolve around you." Shepard's voice gets irritated. "Give me a number so you can get back to your plaything."

"Don't talk about her like that."

"I'm sure the two of you are in love and you're going to live happily ever after. It's not like you're her boss and she's what–your intern? I thought you were better than that asshole Mom married." Shepard scoffs. "You should thank me for selling this company before she sues you for everything it's worth."

"Don't talk about Lizzy like that."

"Nick, I'm not interested in hearing about your sex life."

"I never slept with Jasmine."

"Don't lie to my face. She always confided in you. Always trusted you. Do you expect me to believe you wouldn't take advantage of that the way you're taking advantage of this poor kid?"

"Shep-"

"Tell me how much the IP is worth so I can leave."

Nick sighs. "Thirty million to most companies. A hundred million to the right company."

"I'll get two hundred."

There's silence for a moment.

Shepard breaks it. "You're going to get wrinkles frowning so much."

The door opens, and Shepard steps out. He and Nick are both staring at me. I'm sure that with my eyes wide and my mouth hanging open, I'm giving away that I heard everything.

Shepard looks at me. "Be careful. Nick doesn't love anyone but Haley."

My eyes catch Nick's. There's so much frustration in them.

I can't stay here, desperate to comfort him. I need to get away now before I'm in too deep.

I take a step towards my desk. My heels are not helping my back feel better. I'm not supposed to wear heels, but I get tired of not being allowed to do things.

I grab my coat and go straight to the elevator.

Its doors open with a ding.

"Lizzy, wait." Nick takes a step towards me.

Not happening. I get into the elevator and press the "close" button. Mercifully, the doors slide together just in time.

I grab onto the railing, leaning into the wall to rest my back. It's getting worse by the second.

Ten blocks to my apartment. They're city blocks. Short.

A deep breath does nothing to dampen the pain. It's

already bad. It's going to be a full-blown spasm soon. I brace myself for a miserable night.

The elevator dings at the lobby. Every step on the tile floor is hard. The concrete is worse. I only make it one block before I'm resting against the side of a building.

Nine more blocks. I can manage that.

Once the chill sinks through my coat, I push myself off the wall.

Every step hurts more than the last. The knot clenches until it hurts so badly I can't breathe. I know I've been careless, but did my back really have to pick today to give up?

I slink to the ground and pull my knees into my chest. The stretch helps, but not enough. Tears sting my eyes. It hurts. Everything hurts.

There are footsteps. No doubt someone thinks I'm passed out from too many drinks. This is a nice neighborhood but it's still New York City. It's not safe being so defenseless.

I go to look up at the footsteps but my neck tugs. It hurts too much.

"Lizzy."

It's Nick.

He came after me.

His brother is trying to take away his company. He won't tell me the truth about anything until his hand is forced. There's all this pain in his eyes that he's desperate to keep to himself.

But he came after me.

Again, my back tenses. Shocks of pain bring tears to my eyes. I'll worry about Nick's intentions later. Right now, I don't have a choice but to accept his help.

Whatever that means.

He kneels next to me, no doubt dragging his several-thousand-dollar suit through a puddle. His fingertips skim my chin. "Your back?"

"Yes." His touch is comforting. I'm desperate to close my eyes and drink in everything about it.

"Do you keep muscle relaxants with you?"

"No. And I don't have any at home. Just a heating pad and a bottle of ibuprofen."

"I'm going to take you back to my apartment." He peels my hands from my knees and slides one arm under my legs. "I can carry you the twenty blocks, but it will take a while."

Fuck.

"There's a cab waiting." He slides his other arm around my back, pulling my body into his, cradling me against him. "Is that okay?"

I bite my lip, trying to argue myself out of my fear. I managed Saturday but only barely.

Of course it's not okay.

But I don't have much of a choice.

I cling to Nick, digging my nails into the fabric of his suit. I can smell that same cologne. I can feel all the warmth of his body.

There's no way I can survive twenty blocks cradled in his arms. My heart will explode.

I exhale slowly. "It's okay."

How the hell am I supposed to survive the drive?

How the hell am I supposed to survive falling in love with him?

# Chapter Seventeen

My back is still murder and I have to get into a car.

It's easier in Nick's arms but easier isn't enough to keep tears from rolling down my cheeks.

Nick carries me ten or fifteen feet. He's careful about setting me back on the ground.

My feet make contact, but I'm not really standing upright. I'm pressed against him. The cab is parked on the street, two feet away. Same yellow color as always. Same white sign on its roof.

I reach for the car door and pull it open with a weak grip.

It's only five minutes. It can't be that bad.

The lie only makes my backache worse. It's like my muscles know they're confronting the source of their pain.

I lean down just enough to slide into the car.

Nick sits next to me, reaching over me to buckle my seat belt. He holds me against his chest, running his fingertips over the back of my neck.

"It's going to be okay," he whispers.

I don't do anything but breathe. Even that is hard. Every inhale strains against my tight muscles.

My eyelids press together. I pretend as if I'm anywhere else. At some point I should get a handle on my fear, but not today.

Nick gives his address to the cabbie. He holds me close, stroking my skin with that same gentle touch. "I'm sorry about Shepard. He has this idea that Jasmine left him for me."

"Did she?"

"No. She left because he wouldn't stop drinking. She's a lovely woman, but I have no interest in her." Nick presses his fingers against my neck like he's taking my pulse. "There are lots of reasons why he could want to hurt me. Or it could be he needs the money for some other project. I have no idea what his intentions are."

His body tenses. That must mean that my pulse is totally erratic. It certainly feels like my heart is beating hard enough to jump out of my chest.

"Lizzy." His tone changes, more like everything is okay. "When is your sister getting married?"

An easy thing to talk about. Perfect. "April. At the Brooklyn Botanicals Gardens. She has a thing for cherry blossom trees. I guess it's a family obsession. Our parents always loved them. We went to DC every year until—" Until that car crash took away everything.

It's not easy to talk anymore.

It's not easy to breathe.

Nick's voice stays calm. "Does she know about your tattoo?"

"No, she'd die. I went with my friend, Sarah. The one with the hot-pink dress."

"What happens if you go to the beach?"

"Don't you keep up the styles, Nick? Retro is in. I wear a halter one-piece or a longline that covers it."

"I'd like to see that." He runs his fingers over my neck. "Though I'd prefer to take it off."

My cheeks flush. It's a very effective distraction. I barely notice when the cabbie slams on the breaks again.

There's another car about three inches in front of us but it's a normal red light.

"Are you in the wedding party?" Nick holds me close.

"Maid of honor. I am the only bridesmaid, but I'm sure I'd be maid of honor even if there was any competition. She's not exactly a social butterfly. She mostly stays home to draw or read."

"What does she read?"

"Stuff about angst and feelings. I tried to get her into shōnen manga, but says she doesn't care about things aimed at fourteen-year-old boys. The one time we read one together, she pointed out all the anatomical mistakes."

"You love her a lot."

"Of course. She's my best friend. I'd do anything for her." I take a deep breath. It's not quite as difficult. "Why does your brother hate you so much?"

"We'll talk about it later." He runs his hands through my hair. "I want to know what makes you happy."

"I like to get lost in the city. There's so much possibility here. You go one mile and everything is different."

"What else?"

"I like to move." I let out a very painful laugh. "Not at the moment, but usually."

I keep my eyes closed, my head buried against his chest. Despite my throbbing back, I'm managing to breathe okay.

Not great but okay.

The quiet brings my mind back to that awful morning.

The brakes skidding, the screech of the metal, that moment when everything went white.

"What would you do if you weren't studying computer science?" he asks.

"I didn't love working retail, but I like fashion, the way clothes can transform someone from a femme fatale to an innocent librarian. What about you?"

"There's nothing else I want to do."

"Except swimming and poker and mysteries."

"Yes."

"*Law & Order*?"

"Yes." His voice is shy. "Though it's not my favorite."

"Can you believe I've lived in New York for my whole life and never stumbled on a dead body? I need to work on my snappy banter."

He laughs. "You really are charming, Lizzy."

"What if I had found a dead body? Would that be more charming?"

He lets out a sigh of pleasure.

I blink my eyes open, very much aware that I'm in a horrible automobile. It feels like the city is whirring by us even though we're only going thirty miles an hour.

"I would like to teach you to drive," he says. "One day. When you're ready."

No way in hell. My pulse picks up. I'm not sure if he's testing me or if he's earnest, and I don't care. I only want to think about something else.

I dig my hands into the soft fabric of Nick's suit jacket. At this point, it's familiar. There's something so calming about that.

The car slows. I blink my eyes open. Almost there. I sit up as straight as my back will allow. Turns out that's curled like a question mark.

We stop in front of Nick's building. He pays the cabbie

and helps me out of the car. One arm goes around my waist, the other around my knees. He carries me into the building, then the elevator.

I'm sure we're making a scene, but I can't bring myself to care. I hook one arm around his neck and hold on as tightly as I can.

In his apartment, Nick lays me down on the couch.

My mind flashes with the memory of the last time we were on this couch. Such a nice memory.

"Stay here." He presses his lips to my forehead and goes to another room. A few minutes later, he returns with a pill and a glass of water. "A muscle relaxant. It will make you drowsy. You'll need to spend the night."

"Okay." I swallow the pill and drink half the water.

Nick sets the glass on the table. It's half empty. That's supposed to mean something, that I see the glass as half empty.

"I'll put something on. *The Matrix* or *The Terminator*?" He smiles, teasing me.

It really is a nice smile. I take a deep breath. I can't blame the car for the awful feeling in my stomach. "I just want to lie down. In your bed if that's okay."

He nods. Again, he lifts me, carries me into the other room, and sets me on the bed. Nick sits next to me. He removes my shoes one at a time then slides my tights off my feet.

His fingertips skim the waistband of my thong. "Do you sleep in that?"

"No."

Slowly, he pulls my underwear to my ankles. I manage to kick it off my feet as I roll over to my side.

"I suppose it would be too much trouble to ask you to get the bra too?" I let out something half-laugh, half-groan.

Being on my side isn't helping matters. I close my eyes, willing the drugs to work faster.

Nick rolls my dress off my shoulder. He drags his fingertips to my back to undo my bra.

Like it's easy as pie, he gets the bra off one shoulder.

I fall flat on my back, my dress halfway off, my breast exposed.

He leans down and presses his lips to mine. There's heat in the kiss, but it's more tender than demanding.

My body buzzes, desperate to latch onto a pleasant sensation.

Before I get the chance, Nick releases me. He slides my dress off my other shoulder, then the bra, then the bra is on the floor.

I lie still with my dress at my waist, my gaze on the ceiling.

I try to relax as Nick pulls my sleeves back to my shoulders. There. My dress is back in its proper place, nothing under it.

His hand lingers on my collarbone. "I'll let you rest."

"Will you stay with me?" I bite my lip, cursing the neediness in my voice. It still hurts and he's being so comforting.

"For a few minutes." He strips to his boxers and lies on the bed behind me.

All that warmth returns to my body. Nick pulls a soft comforter over us. Then he takes me into his arms.

I block out every conscious thought in my brain, especially the ones about how good his body feels next to mine.

The drugs work their magic. One by one, my muscles soften. My jaw relaxes. My eyelids grow heavy. After a few deep breaths, I relax.

I fall asleep in his arms.

# Chapter Eighteen

It's two in the morning when I wake. I'm still in Nick's bed with his arms around me.

Without the magic of the muscle relaxants, my back is stiff. It's tolerable.

Nick stirs. He slides his arm around my waist and pulls me closer.

Warmth spreads through my body, tensing and relaxing me at once

I take a deep breath. I'm in Nick's bed, in his arms. This is dangerous territory.

"How are you feeling?" he asks.

Overwhelmed. "A little tense."

"I can run a bath." He drags his hand down my stomach. "Or I can release some of that tension."

I play dumb. "What do you mean?"

He shifts, bringing his other hand above my head. "You can't pull off coy."

"I'm not sure what you're referring to."

Nick slides his hand over my thigh and just under the hem of my dress. His fingertips slide between my legs to stroke my clit. "God dammit, Lizzy. You're going to kill me."

"I think you have that backwards."

His fingers skim my sex. "Your body is so responsive."

"Only because it's you."

He shifts, pressing his crotch against my ass so I can feel his erection. "I'm not going to tie you up tonight."

I fight a frown. How is it possible I'm already craving releasing control?

"What feels better—arms above your head or at your sides?"

That sounds a lot better. I pull them over my head, shifting until I'm comfortable. It stretches my chest muscles, but it's in a pleasant way. "This."

"Tell me if your back hurts."

"Not if it means you'll stop."

"I'll make sure you finish." He pulls his hand away from my sex. "Do you want to come?"

"Yes."

"Then promise you'll tell me if your back hurts."

"I promise."

With one hand, Nick holds my wrists against the pillow. The other strokes my inner thighs. Up, up, up.

His touch is light as he drags his fingertips over my sex. It feels like he's teasing for minutes. I stop breathing, and all my muscles clench. I need his hands on me.

I arch my back to break up the tension in my muscles. It's enough to relax them. Nick's touch is so light. It's driving me out of my mind.

I close my eyes, soaking in the sensation. I'm not tied up, but I'm still at his mercy.

He rubs my clit. The shock of the pressure sends pangs to my sex. I don't think. I don't resist. I breathe, and I feel.

My orgasm builds quickly. I arch my body into his,

pressing my ass against his cock. His boxers are in the way, but they do little to contain him.

I want that hardness against me, inside me, mine.

Not yet.

I focus on the bliss building inside me. A few more strokes, and I'm about to go into freefall. I climb higher and higher.

Then I'm soaring.

"Nick," I moan. "God, Nick."

Pleasure rushes through me. It starts at my core and works its way up my stomach and down my legs. The stiffness in my back and neck relaxes. My legs and arms are jelly, his to move or not.

He presses his lips to my neck, holding me close for a moment. Then he shifts, pulling something from the dresser drawer. A condom.

Lust returns to my body with great force. I'm greedy, I know, but I can't help it. He's fucking irresistible.

"Nick." I reach back and run my hands over his well-defined stomach. "I want to touch you."

"Not tonight."

"Soon?"

"Yes. I promise." He unwraps the condom and slides it on. "Put your hands back over your head."

His cock strains against my sex. The tease is horrible and wonderful at the same time. I'm aching for him inside me. I groan, my arms shaking.

His fingers dig into my hips. "Tell me what you want."

"I want you inside me. So deep inside me I can't breathe."

"Close your eyes."

I do.

He holds my body against his. "I want you to feel this. Every second. No rushing to get to the next part."

Nick slides inside me slowly. It's a hint then he pulls out.

He does it again.

Again.

He teases me until I'm panting so hard I forget to breathe.

Again.

I resist my impulse to rock my hips into him. Every second is agony and ecstasy at the same time.

I focus on the ecstasy, the pleasure spreading through my thighs, the tension collecting in my core.

Again.

My sex clenches. I bite my lip, shifting my arms to keep my hips steady. Almost. Almost.

There. He shifts inside me. All the way. No more teasing. My body relaxes. I let out a low sigh.

Nick's groan reverberates against my neck. He keeps his movements slow as he thrusts into me. Every impulse begs me to push him deeper.

Instead, I melt into him.

The ache inside me builds slowly. Every time he thrusts into me, every time he groans, I'm closer. I can feel his pleasure in the shaking of his chest, the way his fingers dig into my skin. I turn my head to press my neck against his mouth. He sucks hard.

My impatience melts away. The buildup is too good to rush. I never want it to end. Everything in my world is beautiful—the string lights on the walls, the soft purple sheets, the feeling of his hands on my skin.

It can't be much more than a few minutes, but it's so intense it feels like hours.

His lips stay on my skin.

His motions stay controlled. All the pressure in my sex builds until I'm at the edge again.

This time, I'm not rushing into free fall. I'm soaking in every second of bliss.

His next thrust sends me over the edge. My eyelids squeeze together. My hips shake of their own accord, desperate to feel him a little deeper.

He groans like he's just as desperate.

This orgasm is more intense.

"Nick." My breath is ragged as I come down. My thoughts are incoherent.

"Come here." He shifts our positions so he's on top of me. His hand stays around my wrists as he thrusts into me.

Faster. Harder. Deeper.

My sex pulses from the wealth of sensation.

His groans fill me with a different kind of need. It's as good as my orgasm. Better even.

I soak in every bit of his pleasure as he comes. His lips part, and they go to my neck. His kiss is soft. Tender.

"Nick." I arch my hips to feel the pulsing of his orgasm.

One last thrust and he's finished. He collapses next to me. His lips go to my forehead.

We haven't kissed. Morning breath. Well, middle of the night breath.

Nick discards the condom and returns to the bed. He plops next to me and runs his fingertips along the neckline of my dress. "Join me in the shower."

My nod fails to express my enthusiasm. I take his hand and follow him into the bathroom. I didn't notice the room last time I was here. It's huge with a glass shower the size of my apartment.

"How many people fit in here?" I pull my dress over my head and leave it on the floor.

Nick looks at the mess with faux outrage. "I've only tried myself."

"Really?"

"I don't bring women home."

"Where do you bring them?"

"I used to keep a place."

"You kept an apartment just for sex?"

He nods. His fingers skim my cheek. "I didn't want to invite anyone into my home."

"But you invited me?"

"Yes."

"Why?"

"Because I want you here."

I clear my throat, willing my thoughts to stay planted in the lust section of my brain. "Do you have a toothbrush? I want to kiss you but I'm afraid of the garlic in the shrimp scampi."

His hand on my lower back, he leads me to a marble sink. There's an extra toothbrush, still in its package, on the counter. It's purple.

*Get a grip, girl. It's a toothbrush, not a declaration of undying love.*

Nick watches as I pull off the packaging.

I hand him the paper so as not to further mess up his perfect bathroom.

He tosses it into some equally clean, modern trashcan then his attention is back on me.

"Don't watch me. It's weird." I squeeze toothpaste.

"We just had sex."

"Brushing your teeth is a lot more intimate than sex." I motion for him to turn around.

He doesn't. Instead, he pulls out his toothbrush.

I stare at him, waiting for him to avert his gaze.

It's not going to happen.

Fine. I focus on the mirror as I brush my teeth. After a few moments, my attention shifts to his reflection. I've never watched a man brush his teeth before. It's so domestic.

For a split second, I imagine a life with someone—getting ready for bed, brushing our teeth, falling asleep in each other's arms.

The someone shifts into focus. He's tall with black hair and deep brown eyes. He's unmistakably Nick.

I'm uneasy when I'm finished. I force the feeling away by rising to my tiptoes to kiss Nick. His tongue is aggressive, like he's been waiting as desperately as I have.

We stand there for minutes, his hands on my lower back, mine around his neck, making out like desperate teenagers.

When the kiss breaks, he leads me into the shower. There are buttons on the wall. One heats the floor. Another turns on the water. Yet another turns on the water —there are three faucets in here.

Of all the things to spend money on, why would anyone pick a shower?

Nick brings his body behind mine. The skin-to-skin contact makes me sizzle. His body feels damn good against mine.

He drags his fingertips between my breasts, all the way to my belly button.

"I'm not going to stop you from going again, but if you do, I'll need a note to my boss about why I'm coming in to work late." I place my hand under the nearest showerhead. The water is tolerably hot.

"You should take the day off. See a doctor for your back."

"It feels okay now. Something melted away the tension." I step under the shower to wet my hair. It occurs to me that my makeup isn't waterproof.

Fuck it. I throw my head back and rub my face.

Nick runs his thumb against the top of my cheeks like he's wiping off my liner. It's strangely intimate.

He reaches for the shower caddy in the corner and pumps shampoo into his hands. "Turn around."

I do.

He runs his hands through my hair, dispensing the shampoo. His touch is soft and delicate. I can't believe I mocked Kat for liking this. It's amazing.

A groan escapes my lips as he massages my scalp. Water runs over my front. I'm too hot to think anything but yes.

When he's done, Nick turns me and tilts me under the water. His hand slides around the back of my neck, supporting my head as he rinses my hair.

He does the same with conditioner. I'm so hot I want to scream.

His eyes are wide, his expression attentive.

Nick leans close enough to whisper. "The other shower head is detachable."

The thought makes me groan.

"Next time." He rubs me down with soap and rinses me.

Once I'm deemed clean, I shampoo and condition his hair.

He's so tall that I can't reach him on my tiptoes. He brings his chin to his chest so I can run my hands through his messy brown hair. I'm of no help with rinsing off his hair, but I certainly enjoy watching the muscles of his chest contract and relax as he throws his neck back. We do the same with conditioner, then I take my sweet, sweet time soaping him down.

It's my first chance to really explore his body. I run my fingers over the lines of his back and around the contours of his chest. His ass and thighs are just as muscular and they feel just as good against my hands.

He groans as I drag my hand up his thigh, but I don't stray past his quads. Not tonight. But soon.

It's like I can feel it in my bones.

I trust Nick to give me what I want.

But at 3 AM, I'm not about to contemplate just how much I trust him. Or just how much I want him.

# Chapter Nineteen

There's a purple pajama set in Nick's dresser drawer. It's new, still in the tags, a cozy flannel blend that prioritizes comfort over sex appeal.

It's mine.

I towel dry and change into my new outfit. It's strange that he keeps buying me clothing. I'm tempted to refuse— I'm not a doll, and I don't need gifts—but there's something so Nick about all his selections. Classic, beautiful, understated.

He pulls on boxers and pajama pants. "Come on. I'll make you something to eat."

My stomach rumbles. I ran out well before I finished dinner. I nod. "You cook?"

"Yes."

He presses his palm into my lower back to lead me to the kitchen.

I lean against the counter and watch him scour the fridge. It's mostly empty. I don't imagine Nick gets many chances to cook, working from 8 AM to 8 PM every day.

I'm exhausted and I've only been doing it for a few weeks. How does he keep that up constantly?

He's seamless in the kitchen, heating a pan as he chops and dices. The smell of fresh red peppers fills the room.

"Do you cook a lot?" I ask.

He slides a row of chopped vegetables into a sizzling skillet pan. "I cooked when my mom got sick, but I've never been motivated to cook for myself."

I pour myself a glass of water and attempt to sort out my thoughts. "Did you cook for Shepard?"

"Until he left for college." Nick focuses intently on the food.

I study his expression, what I can see with him turned away from me. His lips are curled down. His shoulders are slumped. He's upset.

I press my palm into my empty glass. "Do you want to talk about it?"

"When we sit down." He cracks half a dozen eggs into a shiny silver bowl. "Do you want something to drink?"

"If we're having eggs, this is breakfast. So coffee." My gaze goes to the coffee maker on the counter. The same as the one in my apartment. "I can do it."

"Thank you."

There's a defensive edge to his voice. I bite my lip, trying to focus on my coffee-making at the expense of everything else.

One drop at a time, the carafe fills. After a few minutes, the room smells like coffee. I fix two mugs and bring them to the thick wood table in the corner.

The sky is pitch black. The only light coming through the windows is from the apartment complex next door and the streetlights lining Battery Park.

I watch the smooth current of the river as Nick brings over two plates of scrambled eggs.

And sriracha.

"Thanks for breakfast." I draw a question mark on my eggs with the hot sauce then stir them quickly enough he won't see.

"Thank you for the coffee." He looks out to the river, staring like he's deep in thought. "The truth is I don't know why Shepard is trying to sell the company. But he has every reason to hate me."

I take a bite, chewing slowly to buy myself time to think. My brain isn't working too well with the lack of sleep.

"He's always coped with excess. Drinking before Jasmine left him. Other women once she was gone. For a while he was high-functioning, but last September, I forced him into rehab."

"You can't force someone into rehab."

"I used some fine print in the Odyssey contract. He didn't want to go, but he knew how much Odyssey could be worth. He wasn't about to lose that."

"That was the problem you handled the night we met?"

"Yes. I shouldn't have started a company with my brother. Too personal. But he was good with business. Too good, actually. Our main investor is wrapped around his finger."

"Oh."

"Shepard got out of rehab last month. We didn't talk while he was in treatment. His counselor specifically asked me not to visit."

"Is that the usual policy or just for you?"

"For me."

I swallow hard.

"It would have got in the way of his treatment." Nick looks at the table. "He drank to forget his demons. Once he stopped, they came back full force."

I don't like where this is going. I take a long sip of coffee to wet my throat, but it's not any easier to talk. "Remembered what?"

"Our father left when I was about ten. My mother was broken. When she met our stepfather, it was like she came alive again. She was happy. I didn't know much about love, but I knew that she was in love with him."

I play with the handle of my mug.

"I was fourteen when they married. Shepard was eleven. He graduated high school early and did college in three years. He's only twenty-four." Nick focuses on the table. "Our stepfather, he was kind at first. My mother was so happy he took an interest. But there was too much interest. I should have realized."

Oh God. He needs to be in control. He doesn't trust anyone. It must be...

I don't want it to be true.

I offer Nick my hand. He doesn't take it. He's half here, half in that memory.

He forces the words out. "I was fifteen the first time he touched me. I wrote it off as him being drunk, confused, but he kept doing it."

My stomach drops. I reach for him. Even though his eyes are on the floor, he pulls away. Like it's a reflex.

"I was as strong as he was. I could have stopped him. I could have killed him. But even so, I was scared of him." Nick clenches his fist. "I didn't say anything. I thought that was better. It would have destroyed my mother."

I force myself not to use a euphemism. "He raped you?"

Nick nods.

I can't breathe. I bite my tongue. When people hear about my accident, they say all sorts of stupid things. I won't do that to Nick.

196

"I'm sorry you went through that." I fold my hands in my lap. "Is there... what happened with your brother?"

"I thought I could protect Shepard if I stayed home, but I was wrong. My brother, he was so ashamed he never told anyone. I caught him. I went to the police, but it was too late. Shep was never the same." His eyes fill with sadness.

"You're not the one who hurt your brother. It's not your fault."

"I let that monster stay in our house."

I move closer. Touching him might startle him, so I offer my hand. This time, he takes it and squeezes hard.

"I'm so sorry, Nick. No one should ever have to go through that."

"I could have protected him."

"He blames you?"

"It was my fault."

My heart breaks for him. He really believes it was his fault. No wonder he walks around like he has the weight of the world on his shoulders.

I bring my other hand to his arm, brushing lightly against it to test his response.

He leans in to my touch instead of flinching.

I move closer. I run my fingers over his arm, his neck, his hair. I have to comfort him the way he comforted me.

I have to help him.

It's the only thing in the world I know.

We stay like that for the better part of an hour. When we break, Nick plants a soft kiss on my lips.

He stares into my eyes. "I was in therapy a long time, but I still—"

"It's okay. I don't have to touch you."

"I want you to. I don't want that to have been the last time someone—"

"You've gone, what, eight years without a woman touching you?"

"More or less." He runs his fingertips over my cheek. "It will have to be on my terms."

I nod. I wrap my arms around him and squeeze tight. "This isn't casual anymore, is it?"

"No, it's not."

I squeeze tighter. I need to make him feel better and there's only one way to do it with words. "You think we're at business casual or all the way at black tie?"

His laugh breaks up the tension in the room. "Thank you. I needed that."

It makes me warm, his laugh. Even with all this darkness around us, it makes the world feel light.

# Chapter Twenty

Nick leaves for work around seven. He arranges a house call. I wait dutifully in front of the TV, all of my attention on Nick's past and none of it on the screen.

He's suffered deeply. Maybe he doesn't have to hurt that much anymore.

I don't know what it means to be more than casual. I've never been serious with anyone, never been in love. But there's something about Nick. Every molecule in my body wants to be around him, wants him to be happy.

The doctor arrives around ten. He checks my vitals, asks me to perform all sorts of exercises, and writes a prescription for more physical therapy.

There's a change of clothes for me in the bedroom. Jeans, a sweater, flat boots, wool socks. I have no clue how Nick got these here so fast. Or when. But they're perfect.

I have plans to meet Kat for lunch-break dress shopping. I change into my new outfit and hightail it to the pastel pink boutique.

I'm ten minutes early, so I sit on one of the benches

and pore over Kat's list of sample dresses on my phone. Only two are decent. The rest are totally wrong for her.

"That is one serious hickey." Kat slides her arm around me in a sideways hug then turns to face me. "And those don't look like work clothes."

"You know you're supposed to buy a wedding dress six months before the day. You're going to have to buy something off the rack."

"I'll manage." She moves my hair to inspect my neck. "I can't remember the last time you had a hickey. Had to be Robert. Whatever happened to him?"

"We broke up after the accident."

"Oh yeah. What a jerk." She slides her purse off her shoulders to take off her coat. "You want to get coffee before we start looking?"

"I always want to get coffee, but we'll stain the dresses." I push myself to my feet and find the sales counter.

"You want to tell me how you got that love mark?"

"A man used his mouth to apply pressure to my neck. I'm sure you and Blake have tried it, but if not, I can explain the process step by step."

The salesgirl waves at us, clearly taking her dear time making her way to the counter. Kat's eyes are laser-focused on me like I need protection.

"Elizabeth Marie Wilder." Kat taps her toe. "You have something to fess up. I can tell."

Mercifully, the salesgirl steps up to the counter.

"We're here for a one o'clock appointment. She wants something with sleeves, lots of lace, no train. Mermaid, a-line, or sheath. It's a garden wedding, so simple." I turn back to Kat with a smile. "I had sex last night. Do you want any additional information?"

The salesgirl does nothing to hide her eavesdropping.

"Right this way, Miss Wilder." She looks at me. "Are you the maid of honor?"

"Yes." I follow her to the left side of the store.

"We have a great selection of bridesmaid dresses in the back of the store." She points to a rack of dresses in every color of the rainbow then to the rack of dresses in every shade of ivory. "These are a great independent label. There are more designers as you go clockwise." She hands Kat a dozen clothespins. "If you see any dresses you want to try on, mark them and I'll start a room for you."

"Thank you." Kat waits until the salesgirl leaves then turns back to me. "With whom did you have sex?"

"Some guy at a club."

"What was his name?" She examines a chiffon ball gown.

I point her to a more subdued dress—an ivory lace sheath. "I didn't ask for his name."

Kat feels the fabric, deems it unacceptable, and moves to the next rack. "And what did he look like?"

Out of all the dresses, only one fits her style. I point to it. "It was dark."

Kat turns to me with folded arms. "What about his body? Not something you could miss during some crazy hot sex."

"It was good."

"Specifically?"

"What are you hoping to prove here?"

"I'm not sure." She looks at the dress with interest. "It concerns me that you're lying."

I take a clothespin and mark the dress.

"Blake told me about your company, how the owners might sell. That must be stressful." She shifts through the dresses, one eye on me. "Do you want to talk about it?"

"No. Shit happens at start-ups. Nick is trying to prevent the sale."

"Nick?"

"That's his name."

"You're blushing." Her gaze goes to my neck. "Do you have a crush on him, or is it more than that?"

An out, a perfect out. I have a crush on Nick, and I hooked up with some guy to get him out of my head. I can erase her questions with one little lie. But I can't stand any more lies.

"You do realize that we're shopping for your wedding dress?" I ask. "Maybe we should focus on that."

"Whatever happens with Odyssey and Nick, you're always welcome with me and Blake."

"Thank you."

"If you tell me you're having sex with him, I won't freak out. I swear I won't. Even though it's so stupid to have sex with your boss."

"That's very encouraging. Thanks, sis. You really make me feel like I'm not an idiot." I play with my coat.

"These dresses are too showy. Let's blow them off and get coffee."

"You're getting married next month. You need to find a dress."

"We'll come back after the coffee. The store is dead. What's she going to do?"

"God, if I was working here, I'd hate you."

"Please. She's looking at me like I'm a dollar sign. It's all about the commission."

"Not everyone has a billionaire fiancé."

"Or a CEO... who gives her hickeys." Kat nods to the salesgirl. "We're going to grab espressos. We'll be back soon."

The salesgirl frowns. "We can't hold the dresses."

"That's fine. Should be half an hour." Kat links arms with me and leads me towards the exit.

I yell back at the salesgirl as we walk out the door. "Just find something classy with lace. She'll buy anything pretty. She has no taste."

Kat play-smacks my arm. The street is bustling with people on their lunch breaks. We stop into the nearest coffee shop that isn't a Starbucks and wait in line.

"So..." Kat taps her toe against the tile. "How is your internship going? Besides the hickeys and the owners trying to sell the company?"

"Amazing. Nick is a programming and AI genius. I'm learning a lot under him."

"And you're learning a lot *under* him?"

I clear my throat, praying for the customer in line in front of us to be quick.

He isn't and Kat is staring at me with laser beams of concern.

Finally, he finishes. We step to the register and order vanilla lattes.

She quick draws her credit card, waving away my objections. "You're helping with my dress. Coffee is the least I owe you."

"You never owe me anything for helping you."

"Okay. Then I just want to buy my sister a coffee. You can get the next one."

We move to a table against the wall.

Kat sits up straight, her hands folded in her lap, her eyes focused on me. "What's up with Nick? I won't judge or try to help or do anything but listen."

"You swear? Especially the middle part."

"I swear on my ability to draw."

I want to tell her the truth, but I'm not so sure about

her ability to stay uninvolved. When the barista calls our order, I excuse myself.

Kat's eyes are wide. She bites her lip like she's trying not to show how worried she is. There's more control and confidence to it than there was this time last year.

She's in charge of her life. She's going after what she wants.

Maybe it's possible that she won't put my problems ahead of hers.

I set the drinks on the table as I slide into my seat. The sweet, creamy beverage fills me with warmth.

Risking my desires is one thing. Risking Kat's well-being is totally out of the question.

"You're not doing me a favor by keeping whatever this is a secret." She plays with her sweater. "You're only making me more worried."

Damn, she's a mind reader.

I take a deep breath. I can do this. I can admit how reckless and headstrong I've been. "I slept with him."

Her eyes go wide and her jaw drops. She pulls it up quickly, pursing her lips like she's trying to hide her shock. "Just the one time or more?"

"It's an ongoing thing."

"Oh."

"You're freaking out."

"Not at all." She takes a long sip, worry spreading all over her face. "So are you two fucking or is it more serious than that?"

"I'm not sure. I like him. More than I've ever liked anyone." I soak in the warmth of my drink. "It's confusing."

"What about it?"

"It was supposed to be casual. My head is telling me it's a bad idea, but my heart—"

Her voice is soft and sweet, not teasing anymore, just concerned. "It's love. Listen to your heart."

"But that's going to get me hurt."

"No risk, no reward." She studies my expression. "Do you want to like him?"

I nod.

"Do you want to trust him?"

"Yeah." I do. I want to find out everything about him. I nod.

"Then, whatever you decide, I'm behind you one hundred percent."

"Thanks."

"Though he's probably behind you, huh?" She smirks.

"Did you just make a sex joke?"

"I'm not totally uncool."

"Only mostly."

———

WHEN WE RETURN, THE BOUTIQUE IS EMPTY AND THE salesgirl has a custom rack of half a dozen dresses. I help Kat into them, one at a time, *oohing* and *ahhing* as she steps onto the platform.

Kat scrutinizes her reflection with confusion. After three dresses, she's slow and tired.

"I should have made that a triple shot latte." She slides out of a ball gown and hangs it up. She turns to me, not at all shy about wearing nothing but bikini underwear. "Why does this have to be such an ordeal?"

"It doesn't. You can show up just like that. Well, with pasties. Maybe a 'B' and an 'S' to show your love."

She smirks. "I forgot my strapless bra. You don't mind, do you?"

"Just surprised. You used to run into your room and lock the door to change."

She shrugs. "I guess I'm used to being on display."

"Gross." I examine the dresses on the "try" hook.

One is pretty but too poufy and showy for Kat. I move it to the "no" hook.

Another is too big. There's not enough time for that level of alterations.

The last is beautiful—a lace sheath with elbow-length sleeves and an illusion neckline and back.

I glance at my sister again. She's smaller and thinner than she is in my head. Almost like she's the one who needs my protection.

I slide the dress off its hanger.

"Last one?" she asks.

"Last one. Then we get more coffee."

"How much money do you spend on coffee a week? It must be in the three figures."

"I plead the fifth." I unzip the dress and help her into it. It's a little tight in the bust and loose in the waist (a nice problem to have). Otherwise, it fits perfectly.

Kat takes a deep breath. She shakes her shoulders like she's trying to relax. "You're not saying anything."

Warmth spreads through my chest and stomach. "Let's look at it in the main room."

"That good?"

"Better."

She steps into the main room, her gaze going to the three-panel mirror. Her jaw drops.

She looks gorgeous. The dress hangs off her curves with a slight flare below the knees. It's much simpler and straighter than the other styles, and it's so her. The lace is feminine and sensual and beautiful. It's Kat.

A tear rolls down my cheek. My sister is really going to do this. She's really getting married.

"I'm pretty sure that means you like it." She turns back to me. "You're going to make me cry."

"It's perfect. You have to get it." I wipe my tears. "If you like it."

She turns back to the mirror, examining her reflection. Her eyes fill with wonder. It's the same look she gets when she's lost in thought about her comic. "I love it."

"You look happy." I nearly choke on the words. That warm feeling in my stomach spreads out to my toes. I never thought I'd see her so happy. I never thought either of us had a chance for that.

I certainly never expected love to bring tears to my eyes. It's not bullshit. It's fucking real.

It's possible. Real love is possible.

Kat blinks back a tear. She wipes her eyes. "You got me started."

"You look so beautiful."

She steps off the platform to hug me. I turn my neck to avoid getting any makeup I failed to wash away on her dress. All the lingering tension in my muscles relaxes as my sister squeezes me.

I'll always have Kat. I'll always trust her. Not everyone is so lucky.

———

KAT BUYS THE SEVERAL-THOUSAND-DOLLAR DRESS AND arranges an appointment for rush alterations. We celebrate with a long lunch and a matinee.

I use the dark, empty space of the theater to take a half nap. What I catch of the movie—some sort of mother/daughter indie drama—isn't half bad.

After, Kat heads home to work on her latest comic. I'm about two miles from my apartment, and the weather is high forties and sunny. I unbutton my coat and check my phone as I start my walk down Broadway.

I have a text from Nick. It's a few hours old.

*Nick: How are you feeling?*

*Lizzy: Good. Doctor says I'm clear for "any physical activity."*

*Nick: How did he say it?*

*Lizzy: With a wink and a riding crop. Are you afraid of competition?*

*Nick: No. I can snap my fingers and get you out of your clothes.*

*Lizzy: Go on.*

*Nick: I'll be distracted during my meeting. Did he flirt with you?*

*Lizzy: I'm going home to get into bed all by myself. I could stand to be distracted.*

*Nick: You're teasing.*

*Lizzy: You like it. What if he did? Flirting is normal. I used to flirt with every male customer at Pixie Dust. And any woman who showed interest.*

*Nick: Didn't that make you feel cheap?*

*Lizzy: I couldn't afford to care. I needed the commission.*

Someone bumps into me, making me acutely aware that I am standing on the corner with a walk sign in front of me.

I press the phone against my chest as I cross the street. It buzzes with the next text message but I force myself to walk another three blocks before I look at it.

*Lizzy: I should go. I'm walking home, and I'm going to walk straight into a pole. Plus, you have that meeting.*

*Nick: Did your sister pick out a dress?*

*Lizzy: It's beautiful. Perfect for her. I cried when I saw it.*

*Nick: You're sweet.*

*Lizzy: Agree to disagree.*

*Nick: Meet me tonight. For dinner and a movie. The Matrix is playing at a theater in Brooklyn.*

*Lizzy: And you didn't lead with that? Damn, Marlowe, I thought you were good at getting what you want. Just so you know, there will be no funny business during The Matrix.*

*Nick: Funny business?*

*Lizzy: Yes, funny business. You were a teenager once. I'm sure you at least made out in a movie theater.*

*Nick: At least?*

*Lizzy: You never did anything at a movie? Did you even have girlfriends in high school after everything that happened?*

*Nick: I'm not broken. You don't have to be careful with me.*

*Lizzy: Did you?*

*Nick: One. I moved so slowly that she told all her friends I was gay.*

*Lizzy: Get out.*

*Nick: It's true.*

*Lizzy: Did that bother you?*

*Nick: I didn't have anything to prove.*

*Lizzy: Did you ever tie her up or anything? I know that being dominant isn't caused by abuse or anything, but it seems like it helps you.*

*Nick: I didn't try that until I was older. At first, it was the only thing that could relax me enough to make it possible for me to enjoy sex. Then I started to like it. There's power when someone gives themselves to you willingly. The trust is intoxicating.*

*Lizzy: Are you trying to tease me, Marlowe?*

*Nick: Yes.*

*Lizzy: I should let you go. You have that meeting. I don't want to distract you with the mental image of me in your lap, my panties at my knees, your tie around my wrists.*

*Nick: Meet me for dinner at seven. Movie starts at eight.*

*Lizzy: Are you distracted?*

*Nick: Thoroughly.*

# Chapter Twenty-One

I meet Nick at a hole-in-the-wall Thai restaurant.

He's sitting in a booth in jeans and a purple t-shirt. It's so normal. He still looks handsome, of course, but like any especially attractive twentysomething guy in Brooklyn.

I sit across from him. "You own normal clothes."

"You need to work on your compliments."

I shrug.

"You look nice tonight."

"Thank you." I steal a sip of his whiskey. "How'd you get here so early? You usually work until eight."

"I was motivated." He pulls his drink to his side of the table. His eyes scan my neckline, stopping on the same spot that intrigued Kat.

The damn hickey.

Nick laughs. It's a big laugh, the biggest once I've heard from him.

"What is funny about this?" I ask.

"Nothing."

"You know how awkward it was when my sister asked how I got a hickey?"

"What did you tell her?"

I bite my tongue. Dammit. Our relationship is supposed to be a secret.

His eyes meet mine. "I wanted to keep this from Shepard. It doesn't matter who else knows."

"Good. I told her everything."

"Everything?" He raises an eyebrow.

"Not that part." I give the menu a cursory scan, but my heart is set on green curry shrimp. "Why do you want to keep this from Shepard?"

"I don't trust him not to hurt you."

"Have you considered trying to reconcile with him? Maybe he's mad about the rehab and not... everything else."

Nick's expression steels. "It won't matter. Once he has his mind set on something, he won't stop until he gets it."

"You don't begrudge his hatred?"

"I deserve worse."

"What if it is about Jasmine? If he really believes you stole her and he's really doing this to win her back?" There's almost something romantic about it—that Shepard is willing to do anything to win back the woman he loves.

Nick's eyes turn to the table. "Lizzy, I'm sure you have good intentions, but I didn't invite you out to talk about my brother." His cheeks flush with a hint of red. Like he's nervous. "I need a break from this."

"And I'm a convenient distraction?"

"No." He takes a long sip of his drink. "I need you."

He's blushing. Full-on blushing.

It makes me all warm and gooey inside. Phoenix Marlowe, billionaire programming genius, needs me.

"How do you need me?" I ask.

"Tied up with your legs spread."

Now I'm the one blushing. I stammer something incomprehensible. "I hope that was to prove a point."

He nods. "I care about you. More, even."

More even. Like that he loves me. He didn't say it, so I don't have to say it.

That warm feeling spreads through my belly. "I care about you too. Maybe even—"

The waitress, an Asian woman in her twenties, saves me from finishing my sentence. She drops off a Diet Coke and we order dinner.

My gaze goes to Nick. There are dark circles under his deep brown eyes. His shoulders are slumped. His scruff goes beyond five-o'clock shadow. He's tired.

We need the same thing—each other.

The thought engulfs me. I do need him. He's the only person, besides my sister, who understands me. Who sees the real me.

I slurp the last sip of my soda. "Let's play a game. I ask you a question, and you have to answer honestly. Then you ask me a question, and I have to answer honestly."

"How do you win?"

"Winning isn't the point."

He shakes his drink. "Then it isn't a game."

"Ugh. What a nerd." I curse his technical correctness. "It's like Tetris. You can't win. You can only lose."

He perks up, interested.

"You lose if you refuse to answer a question."

"Is anything off-limits?"

"Anything about Odyssey or Shepard, I guess."

Nick takes a sip and sets his drink to the side. He sits up straight, his eyes focused on me. "I'll give you the advantage. You can start."

"You're so generous." I rack my brain for a question. "Have you ever been in love with anyone?"

"No. Have you?"

"No. I liked my high school boyfriend, but I never felt like I could be myself with him. It was like my personality was too much—too aggressive or intense or something like that." I look into his deep brown eyes. "Why is it you don't trust anyone? Because of your step-dad or something else?"

"I trust you."

"With anything?"

He looks off towards the window like he's deep in thought. "Almost anything."

That warmth spreads all the way to my fingers and toes. I don't know anything about falling in love, but I do know trust.

And I can feel the intensity of our trust.

"I trust you too." I stammer the words. "With almost anything."

He stares into my eyes. It's like he's looking into my head.

Usually, that kind of thing would make me feel exposed.

But I like the way he does it. I like him knowing what's in my head, in my heart.

I want him to be happy.

I want to be around him.

Maybe I do love him.

His voice pulls me back to the table. I can contemplate my feelings for him later. Right now, he's here, and he's mine.

"You gave up on the world after that accident, didn't you?" he asks.

I nod. "I was never Miss Congeniality, but I trusted people before the accident. I trusted the world not to take everything I cared about." My gaze goes to the street outside. I don't talk about this with anyone, not even Kat. "At first, when I came out of the ICU, people were really supportive, visiting and bringing flowers, crying they were so happy I was okay. But it was all for show. The second things got hard, they were gone. Is that how it was when your mom died?"

He nods. "A lot of people promised to make her time worthwhile. But none of them stuck around past a hello and a cup of coffee. Not even her brother. They couldn't stand seeing her sick."

"What was her name?"

"Olivia."

"What was she like?"

"Loving. But her work always came first."

"And your stepfather. Was he still around then?"

"Yes. I waited until after she was gone to press charges."

"She never knew?"

"She knew something was wrong, but never what it was."

"You were trying to protect her?"

"Yes."

"Do you try to protect everyone, even when it comes at the cost of your well-being, your happiness?"

"It's my turn to ask a question."

"But you do."

"Yes." His eyes bore into mine. "Did you think you were going to die?"

I nod. "I still remember the moment the other car hit ours. It was an undivided road, a head-on collision. That's why my parents... the front seat was worse."

He sets his hand on the table. I squeeze tightly. It's different than the last time he offered me this. Harder.

My eyelids press together. "The car was coming

towards us. I knew it was bad. Then everything went white. I still remember hoping that my sister got the news after she finished her cross-country meet, so she'd win her race."

Nick smiles. "Did you really?"

"Yeah. I woke up a few days later. I was in a coma, supposedly. I don't remember anything but the sensation of morphine-dulled pain. They waited to tell me my parents died. They didn't want to traumatize me when I was already so weak. Really, it made it worse, not knowing what was going on, having my hope crushed like that."

"Do you miss them?"

I nod. "We fought a lot, but I always knew they loved me. They were teachers, and they were sure they were going to change the world, or at least their underfunded school. They did so much good. It's not fair they're gone."

"What was it you told me in San Francisco?" He quotes me. "Life doesn't give a fuck about what you want."

"Something like that. You don't like the sentiment or the vulgarity?"

"I love both."

I swallow hard. That word, love, it sounds good on his lips.

I shake my head so I'll focus on the moment. After all, life doesn't give a fuck about anything I want. I need to grab onto what I have while it's in front of me.

I make eye contact with Nick. "What was it like, your mom putting work first?"

"Lonely. I thought I could take care of the family, but..."

"I'm so sorry you went through that. It hurts me to think about it. I can't imagine how much it hurt you."

"Don't feel sorry for me. I'm a very lucky person."

"It's not pity. Just that... I hurt when you hurt."

The waitress interrupts with our food. We order another round of drinks.

I bury my face in my shrimp curry to buy myself time to sort out my thoughts.

It's not quite as fresh as the expensive Thai place downtown, but the spices are stronger. Ginger, galangal, Thai basil, and the salty kick of fish sauce.

Is this what love feels like? It's intense.

"I think it's your turn," I say.

He pulls out his phone and shows me a picture. It's a photo of an STD test. He's totally clean.

"Are you on birth control?" he asks.

"Yes, I have an IUD." I look back at him. "I'm clean. I had a test last year. I haven't been with anyone but you since September."

"I trust you." He shifts his phone into his pocket. "It's your decision, if you want to use a condom."

"Is that your question?"

He nods.

God, what a question.

It's an easy decision. I've never had sex without a condom before. I absolutely want to feel Nick, all of him.

I nod. "I don't. I trust you."

He smiles.

I'm going to fuck Nick bareback.

Do I really need to stay for the movie?

## Chapter Twenty-Two

Even in the packed theater, Nick and I are in our own world. It's a bubble free of all the stress of Odyssey or family or accidents that take everything away.

After the credits roll, I try to pull my thoughts together in the women's restroom. The question presses at me. Do I love Nick?

It's possible.

Likely even.

I let lust take over my brain. It's easier to understand.

I'm going to have sex with Nick without a condom. It's so personal, so intimate—

So fucking hot.

I'm distracted on the subway ride. When we're finally at our stop, he wraps his hand around my wrist and pulls me to my feet.

My legs are jelly. The walk to his apartment only takes five minutes, but it feels like fifty.

Finally, we step into the lobby. The elevator's ding announces its arrival. Nick punches in some code for the penthouse floor as he pulls me inside.

In one swift movement, he presses me against the wall and presses his lips to mine.

He's not wasting any time. Thank God.

My tongue slides into his mouth. It's different with so much on the table. Knowing how deep my feelings go. How I need him.

How he needs me.

Nick needs me. It makes me warm all over.

He pushes my coat off my shoulders. Groans against my neck then sinks his teeth into it.

It sends a pang straight to my core.

I need to touch him today, to show him how good that can feel.

My hands go to his shoulders. I tug at his coat but it doesn't budge.

Okay. It's not like we need to do this in the glass elevator. He'll feel safer in his apartment.

For the rest of the ride, I run my hands through his hair and kiss him back with as much feeling as I can muster. Words are so complicated. I can never use them to explain myself.

But this—

His lips on mine, his hands on my skin—

This I understand.

I nearly jump when the elevator doors slide open. Almost. I kick my coat into the penthouse and move inside. He follows with a curious look. Like he knows I've got my mind set on something.

Nick hangs our coats on the rack. He takes my purse. Kneels to undo my shoes. His hands trace a line up my legs, over the seam of my jeans, then over the soft fabric of my t-shirt. They stop to trace my neckline.

His touch is soft as his fingers skim my collarbones. My cheeks. My lower lip.

He pulls my t-shirt over my head. Unhooks my bra and flings it aside.

He's quick today. Like he's desperate.

Nick pins me against the wall as he kisses me.

I need him so much more than I've ever needed anything.

Want his pleasure more than I've ever wanted anything.

His lips go to my neck. I shift to my tiptoes so my mouth hovers over his ear.

Here goes nothing. "I want to touch you. Please."

"That might not end well."

He presses his body against mine, every hard inch of it, like he's warning me I might not get my prize.

Worth the risk. "I know."

He pulls back to look into my eyes. I stare back. Those deep brown eyes. It's like they go for miles.

He runs his fingertips over my stomach. "I'm in charge. You can't do anything until I ask."

I nod.

He brings his hand to my chest, his fingertip millimeters from my nipple but not touching yet.

I look for meaning in his eyes.

He's testing me.

I have to pass.

Every part of me wants to arch my back, to press my chest into my hands, but I have to be patient. Nick will get me there.

He brushes his fingertip over my nipple with the faintest hint of pressure. I bite my tongue and stare back into his eyes.

His other hand goes to my jeans, to my inner thigh. An inch from where they need to be. Then half an inch. Then so fucking close it takes every bit of strength I have not to rub my body against his.

"Nick, please." I'm not sure what I'm requesting, only that I need it.

The man has no mercy. He rubs my inner thigh as he sinks his teeth into my neck.

He bites his way to my ear, then it's just his breath. The warmth of it sends a buzz of pleasure down my spine.

"Give me your left hand." He presses his lips against my neck.

I do.

He brings it over my head and presses it against the wall. He takes my right hand and places his palm behind it. He's guiding me.

It's hard not to push things forward. I manage it by staring into his eyes. They have to be wide with desire. Nothing else.

He presses my palm against his jeans so I'm cupping his erection. That's Nick under all that denim. Never thought I'd hate such a utilitarian fabric so deeply, but I do.

"Unzip my jeans then your hand goes to your side." He pulls his hand from mine.

I fumble over the button and the zipper. There. It's so tempting to touch him, but I follow his orders exactly.

There's vulnerability in his eyes. This is a big deal. I can't push him.

Nick pulls his t-shirt over his head. He slides out of his shoes and pushes his jeans to his knees. They fall to a heap on the floor.

Just boxers now.

He pins my hands to the wall as he kisses me. The sizzle of his bare chest against mine sends waves of need to my core.

We'll get to me later. Right now, I need him feeling

good.

Nick releases my right hand. He leads me again. Brings my hand to his boxers so there's nothing but thin cotton fabric between my fingers and his cock. God, he feels good.

He pins my other hand to the wall and brings his mouth to my ear. "Take off my boxers."

God yes. I push his boxers to his knees. They fall on top of his jeans.

He brings my hand to his cock. My palm brushes against him. Then my fingers.

A sigh falls off his lips as I touch him. He feels good. He wants this.

I surrender to his guidance. My hand wraps around him. I stroke him. Then I'm going harder, faster.

His body shakes. He sinks his teeth into my neck.

It does something to me. Makes me even more desperate.

He pulls his hand to my wrist then all the way to his side. "Keep going."

Hell yes. I pump him with steady strokes. He pulls his lips away from my neck so he can stare into my eyes.

God, the desire in his eyes. I need more.

I watch his reactions as I go faster. Harder.

His hand goes to the back of my head. It pulls my lips into his. He kisses me hard, deep, sucking on my tongue.

When the kiss breaks, he stares back at me. "Get on your knees."

God yes. I lower myself much faster than I should. Ow. They call it hardwood for a reason.

I press my hands against my sides, awaiting instruction.

Nick takes my left hand and presses it against his hip. He presses against the back of my head, guiding me closer. Closer.

"Tease me." He tugs at my hair.

It's been a while since I've done this, but I can make up for my inexperience with enthusiasm.

My lips brush against his cock. Just a touch. Again and again. I flick my tongue against him.

He tastes good. I want more. I want all of him in my mouth. But I have to keep teasing.

I do it again and again. Until he's groaning. Until he's shaking.

His hand presses against the back of my head. "Wrap your lips around me."

I do.

"Look at me."

My eyes connect with his. There's no apprehension in his expression. Just desire.

"Suck me off." His voice is a command.

Good thing I want to obey. I take him deeper. The hand in my hair tugs. The other goes to my nipple and toys with me.

I swirl my tongue around his head until his eyes flutter closed. There. I focus on the spot driving him insane and flick my tongue against it until he groans loud enough to wake the people on the floor below us.

I take him as deep as I can. When I can't go any farther, I wrap my hand around his cock and stroke. Nick groans, pinching my nipple so I'm forced to moan against him.

Lust collects between my legs. It's the most exhilarating feeling, bringing him to the edge, making him desperate.

He presses his hand against the back of my head, guiding me over his cock. He's still in charge, and I'm still surrendering.

Nick shifts his hips, thrusting into my mouth. I relax my throat to take him deeper. I'm a vessel for him, for whatever he needs.

I lose track of everything except the sounds of his groans, the feeling of him in my mouth. He tugs at my hair. Toys with my nipples.

My body pulses with desire. Not yet. First, I need to feel him come.

His hands go to the back of my head. There's the most delicious look of pleasure on his face, and I can't bear to do anything but build it.

His fingers dig into my scalp. His eyes flutter closed. "Fuck, Lizzy."

Hell yes. I slide my tongue around him.

"I'm going to come." He holds my head in place as he thrusts into my mouth.

The beautiful agony of an orgasm spreads over his face. His lips part. He groans.

Hell yes.

I surrender to his guidance, sucking as his cock pulses, as he fills my mouth.

When he's finished, I swallow hard.

My thighs are shaking, from desperation or fatigue or some mix of both.

Nick reaches down to take my hands and pulls me to my feet. He presses me against the wall and kisses me hard.

When he pulls back, he strokes my cheek. "That was amazing."

My cheeks flush. "Thank you."

"Can you take more?"

"Can you—" I clear my throat. "Again?"

He brushes his palm against my breast. "I'm not Superman. I do need a few minutes." He steps back and pulls his boxers to his waist.

"How few are we talking?"

Nick smiles. "Are you trying to kill me?"

I nod.

# Chapter Twenty-Three

Something cold and wet presses against my neck. A mixed drink in a glass. Then Nick's hand is on my shoulder.

I turn and take the drink from his hands.

He presses his lips to mine. His hand slides around my side to my lower back, and he leads me to the couch.

His drink is sitting on the coffee table. Whiskey on the rocks from the looks of it. I sip from my glass. Rum and diet. I need the caffeine. It's late.

Nick pulls a blanket from under the couch and drapes it over my shoulders. "You're shivering."

I pull the blanket tighter. It is cold in here. "Could you turn up the heat?"

Nick gets up and taps a few commands into the thermostat. A moment later, the heat kicks in. It's warmer already.

He sits next to me and pulls me into his lap. I shift so I'm looking into his deep brown eyes.

The way he's staring at me, with all that affection, builds a flutter in my belly. It's different than wanting to touch him. Less and more demanding at once.

"What are you thinking?" he asks.

I take a deep breath. "There's something I want."

He runs his fingertips over my collarbone, his gaze locked with mine. "Besides coming in my bed?"

My cheeks burn. "You're a very distracting man."

He nods.

"Do you use this skill in negotiations?"

"Not in the same way." He drags his fingertips down my chest until they're against my nipples. "Let's not talk about work."

"We're talking about something?"

He draws a circle around me. "You want something."

"Yes." Something important. I shift to break his touch. It's awful, but it's the only way I can concentrate. "I don't want to keep this relationship a secret anymore. It's too hard to make up lies about what I'm doing."

He stares back at me like he's figuring something out. "Not while we're working together. People will think you got the internship on your knees."

"I can deal with that."

"I can't."

"Is this about my reputation or yours?" I ask.

"I'm not going to listen to people call you a slut behind your back."

"People will still say that if we wait until we stop working together. There will be rumors. If you think this will end before we even have to worry about it..." I play with the fabric of the blanket. "Your life is full. If there's no room for me, I understand." My stomach tenses. I understand, but it will break me into a million little pieces.

"I want you here." He runs his fingers through my hair. "After the sale settles down, I'll figure something out."

"You promise?"

He nods. "I don't like hiding it either."

"Really?"

"Really."

"I'll be busy the next few weeks. I won't be able to see you much."

"I'll miss you. Miss this."

"Me too." Nick presses his palm against my back. "You're sweeter than you let on."

"Don't tell anyone." I rest my head on his shoulder. "It will ruin my image."

He lets out a sigh of pleasure. His arm slides around my waist, and he holds my body against his. "I trust your judgment. More than you realize."

"You made me sign an NDA that covered our personal relationship."

"And I've yet to sue you for breaking it."

I laugh, shifting to check his expression. He's smiling.

"I like it when you joke. And when you laugh." I bring my head back to his shoulders. "Unless you are planning on suing me."

He shrugs. "Who knows?"

My laugh hurts as much as it feels good. He's doing something to me. Something exhilarating and terrifying all at once.

"I'll be super pissed at you if you sue me," I say. "I'll have to countersue you for sexual harassment."

"Nothing like lawyers to encourage two people to trust each other."

This laugh melts away everything else.

I nestle into Nick's arms. My eyes flutter closed. Fifteen minutes until the caffeine takes its full effect in my blood stream. I only need a few of those to rest.

Only a few minutes, and we can go to his bed.

Only a few minutes...

———

I am not on the couch. I am in Nick's bed, covered in a comforter, stripped out of my jeans and underwear.

According to the sleek black alarm clock on the bedside table, it's almost morning. Nick is fast asleep next to me. There's a sheet wrapped around his waist. Otherwise, he's naked.

Dammit, what a time to fall asleep.

Somehow, I'm not upset. My pulse is normal. My breath is even. If anything, I'm calm. Happy even.

Nick looks so peaceful in his sleep, like he's finally not carrying the weight of the world around on his shoulders.

I run my fingers through his hair. There's so much going on in that beautiful head of his. I want to know everything about it.

I want to know him, really know him.

That's entirely unsettling. I plant a kiss on his cheek and move to the living room, away from the source of my confusion.

My clothes and purse are in a neat pile on the coffee table. There's a box next to them. It's wrapped in a purple bow. I find my glasses in the pile and read the card.

*I was going to give this to your last night. Wear it whenever you want to cash in.*

There's another note on the back of the card.

*Rain check.*

*- Nick*

A smile spreads across my lips. He left me a fucking rain check. I fold it neatly and slide it into my purse.

I unwrap the present without a hint of patience. It's another lingerie set. This one is racy. A sheer bra and a matching thong in black lace.

I dress and look for some way to leave Nick a note. There's nothing, so I send him a text message.

*Lizzy: Went to change for work. See you at eight. You bring the coffee.*

There's something awfully impersonal about texting a man who is sleeping in the next room, but if I stay here I'm not sure I'll be able to leave. I make my way to the lobby and walk the ten blocks to my apartment.

The doorman, that same grey-haired, portly man, shoots me that *good for you for getting laid* look. I shrug like I have no idea what his expression means.

---

WE ARE ALL BUSINESS FOR OUR TWO HOURS TOGETHER. Then Nick disappears into his work, and I do my best to disappear into mine. It's past eight o'clock when he checks my code and sends me home with a soft goodbye.

He's more affectionate in front of other people. It's nothing obvious. He doesn't kiss me or hold me, but he smiles, and he laughs, and he brushes his hand against my lower back.

It's difficult going home alone, knowing he'll be working until dawn, but I manage it by going out with Sarah or burying myself in sci-fi movies.

Thursday night, he walks me to the elevator. "I'm sorry I've been so busy. I'll make it up to you tomorrow." He presses his lips to mine. "Wear that lingerie."

Hell yes.

---

THE LACY LINGERIE SET IS GORGEOUS. IT GIVES MY breasts enough shape that, save for the outline of my nipples poking through my blouse, it looks like I'm wearing a proper bra.

I cinch a blazer tight so I won't show off to anyone but Nick.

In my black suit and purple blouse, I'm the picture of a professional businesswoman. Especially with my glasses on and my hair in a bun. There's no way to tell that I'm wearing something sexy under my getup.

No one knows but us.

Nick is unbearably professional during our lesson. Our work is intense. There's a lot to do.

At ten, he leans in close. "You're having lunch with me today. Be here at one." He nods to the door, all business.

"I'll see you then, Mr. Marlowe."

I set an alarm so I'll get sucked into work. When it beeps, at five to one, I make my way to Nick's office. He and Jasmine are standing outside his door, deep in conversation about something.

Their voices are low, but not low enough to be out of range.

Jasmine hands Nick a neat brown folder. "OmniTech faxed their offer. Are you going to read it?"

His voice is stern. "No."

"It's a fair offer. Fifty percent more than Google's."

"I'm aware."

"If you're so against it—"

"Save it." Nick pushes the folder into her hands. "I'm sure you have work to do."

"This is my work. If you want to keep Shepard from selling, you're going to have to do something besides pout."

He stares at her with anger. "Do you honestly believe it's possible to change his mind?"

She frowns. "He's not a bad person. He loves you. If you would just—"

"Would I ask you to make up with him?"

Jasmine steps back. "You might. If you were desperate enough."

"Do you really believe that?"

She bites her lip. "Yes. But I understand. This company is everything to you." Her voice drops. "Nick, I don't like seeing him like this either. But I can't go back to him. Not after the way he hurt me."

"I would never ask you to do that." Nick's voice gets stern. "This is not your job."

"No, this is my job." She pushes the folder against his chest. "Mr. Marlowe, here is the offer. Please review it and forward your thoughts to our CFO, Shepard Marlowe. You should know him. He's your brother and your business partner. And if you want to keep acting like it's impossible for you to reach out to him, then accept that the company is being sold and stop pouting about it." She spins and walks back to her desk.

Nick's expression flares with frustration. He clenches his fist as he checks his watch. His eyes meet mine, and he motions *come here*. I follow him into his office, closing the door behind me.

The office feels smaller than it did this morning. Nick looks taller. Broader. More imposing.

I press my back against the door. Press my lips together. "Are you going to look at that?"

"I don't want to talk about work." He drops the folder on the desk. His breath is steady. His expression is stoic.

"Is it a fair offer?"

"Lizzy, stop. This is not something I want to discuss. And not with you."

He doesn't want my help. I try to reason my way out of how much that hurts. He's a CEO, seasoned in business, and I'm an intern. I can't give him any advice. There's no way I can help him with his company.

But he looks so hurt. I have to do something.

I nod. "Tell me what I can do to make you feel better."

"There's nothing. You should get back to work."

"But Nick." I take a step towards him. I swallow hard. This is quite the offer, but it's the right move. "Use me to feel better. Use me to feel in control again."

He stares at me like he can't believe what I'm asking.

"Please." I hold my breath waiting for his response.

# Chapter Twenty-Four

His expression is weary.

This is the way I can help him. The only way, maybe.

I slide my blazer off my shoulders. "Please."

His eyes go to my chest. His lips part. His pupils dilate. "You don't know what you're asking."

"Yes I do. I want you to use me to feel better. Whatever that means."

His brow furrows like he's working through something. He nods. "Lock the door."

I do.

Nick stares deep into my eyes. "Come here."

Three steps and I'm inches from Nick. His fingers skim my chin, his touch gentle.

He pulls my glasses off and places them on his desk.

His hands go to my blouse. He undoes the top button. The second. The third. My shirt spills open.

My bra is completely see-through. It's like my breasts are being presented to him. On display just for him.

Nick lets out a low sigh of pleasure. Something in his expression relaxes. This really is what he needs.

My body buzzes from the proximity. His hands are millimeters from my skin but he's not touching me. Not yet.

He undoes my fourth button, the last that isn't tucked into my skirt, and pries the sides of my shirt apart.

Heat spreads out from my core. I wish I could drink in the look in his eyes. I wish I could feel this desirable all the fucking time.

His eyes fix on me. He watches my reactions as he cups my breast and rubs his thumb over my nipple. It presses the lace of my bra against my tender bud.

The friction is fucking divine.

I stare back at him, watching him the way he's watching me. His pupils dilate. His lips part. He increases the pressure until I'm groaning. My eyes flutter closed. I can't watch him anymore. I can't do anything but feel.

His lips go to my neck. His teeth scrape against my skin.

The sting of pain tightens the knot between my legs.

Fuck yes. I melt into his movements, panting and tugging at his suit jacket so I won't make a sound.

He kisses his way to my collarbone, then down my chest. He's three inches from my nipple. Then two.

He undoes my bra and tosses it aside.

His mouth closes around my nipple.

I moan as softly as I can.

The pressure of his mouth sends pangs of lust straight to my core. My sex clenches. My knees buckle. It's impossible to stay quiet, so I press my palm against my lips and use it to muffle my groans.

When his teeth scrape against my nipple, I can't muffle it anymore. The burst of pain makes everything better. "Nick." My voice is loud. Loud enough someone might hear.

He doesn't stop me. He only bites me harder. "What do you want?"

"To make you feel good."

He slides his hands under my ass and carries me to the couch. He arranges us so I'm kneeling over him, my knees planted outside his thighs, my hands planted on his shoulders.

He rolls my stocking to my ankle. His fingertips slide over the sides of my patent black flat.

One flick of his fingers and the shoe is on the floor. The stocking joins it.

I dig my hands into the couch to contain the anticipation coursing through my veins. Nick drags his fingertips up my inner thigh, under my skirt, closer and closer. He's almost touching me when he moves to my other leg. He rolls off my stocking, flicks off my shoe.

He pushes my skirt to my waist. I'm on display for him. It does something to me. My sex clenches. Pleasure spreads all the way to my toes.

He pushes my panties to my knees.

He presses his palm against the back of my hand and he drags it up my thigh. Until I'm almost there.

Nick looks up at me. "Have you been lonely this week, without me?"

I nod.

"Because you miss this—" he brings my hand between my legs so my fingertips skim my clit "—or because you miss me?"

"Both."

He moves my hand to my thigh. "Pick one."

Huh? I stare into his eyes. "I don't understand the question."

"You miss getting off or you miss me?"

"You. I can come whenever I want. I came ten times this week from my hand."

"Did you think about me?"

"Every time. I can't stop thinking about you. Worrying about you. I fall asleep wishing you were next to me. Not to fuck me, though I certainly wouldn't turn it down, but to hold me."

"Then why are you letting me use you?"

Damn. He's blunt.

I hold his gaze. "Because you need it. And because I want to feel close to you, and I'm not sure how else I can do it."

"I don't deserve you."

My stomach clenches. "Don't say that. It hurts." I press my hand against his shoulder. "You've already done so much for me, made me realize the world isn't a total shit-hole. If you say things like that..." I swallow hard. "Please, Nick, I can't keep thinking about this or I'm going to lose it. I want you to use me. I want you to feel better after."

He stares deep into my eyes. Nods. "Put your hand between your legs."

I do.

"Show me how you touch yourself."

That flush in my cheeks spreads all the way to my toes. Show him how I touch myself? Somehow, it's more inti- mate than anything we're done. More like I'm giving some part of myself away.

He slides his hands around my hips, holding me in place.

I press my eyes closed and drag my finger over my clit. I'm already sensitive, already desperate. A few strokes and the pressure builds to a fever pitch. I'm almost there. It's too fast. I need more of him.

I blink my eyes open to stare into Nick's. He's fixed on

me, watching me like I'm his favorite movie. His grip around my hips tightens.

His fingers feel good against my skin.

He drags one hand up my side and around my breast. His thumb rubs against my nipple. "Close your eyes."

I do.

His hand slides back to my hip. "Hand on your inner thigh."

With my left hand planted on his shoulder for support, I bring my right hand to my inner thigh.

"Soft. Like you can barely take any pressure."

I *can* barely take any pressure. I drag my fingertips up my thigh as lightly as possible.

Desire overwhelms any lingering awkwardness. It's too soft. I can't take that. I need more. I need harder. I need to come.

"Go slow. Tease yourself."

Fuck me. I'm too keyed up to stand any teasing.

I try my best to keep things soft. I drag my fingertips over my outer lips. My hand skims my clit. The pressure is so light I can barely feel it. Somehow, that makes it more intense.

My sex clenches. I tug at his jacket.

Nick takes my hand from his shoulder and brings it to my mouth. His grip tightens around my hips. "I've got you."

I slide my fingers into my mouth, sucking hard so I won't scream.

My eyes flutter open and lock with his. I don't want to touch myself the way I do when I think of him.

I want to do it for him.

I want to show him how desperately I need him.

I spread my legs wider. No more teasing. I rub myself with greedy strokes.

He stares back at me like he's transfixed. "You get this wet just thinking about me?"

I nod, sinking my teeth into my skin so I won't scream. The knot inside me tightens. I'm close. Very close. But I'm not ready yet. I slide two fingers into my sex.

A sigh escapes my lips. Not as good as him inside me, but still damn good. I tease myself until biting my fingers isn't enough to keep me from groaning.

That look in Nick's eyes is perfection. I focus on him as I bring my fingers back to my clit. No more teasing. No more waiting. I need to show him how good he makes me feel.

I rub myself until the pressure is just right. He holds onto my hips, his eyes fixed on mine, his lips parted like he's in awe.

That knot tightens until it's too much to take. I pull my hand from my mouth and dig into his hair. "Nick, I can't... I have to scream."

He pulls his hand from my side and drags it over my bottom lip. "Here." His fingers slide into my mouth.

It's so much better than sucking on my own fingers. I press my tongue against the fleshy pads of his fingertips as I stroke myself.

The pressure builds until I'm at the edge. I suck hard on his fingers as I come. All that pressure unravels in a wave of bliss. My legs and arms go slack. I only stay upright by virtue of his firm grip.

Nick brings his hands to my ass and pulls me into his lap. He presses his lips to mine, his tongue plunging into my mouth.

His hand goes to the back of my head. He finds the band keeping my bun together and pulls it out. My hair spills onto my shoulders, messy in the best possible way.

He unknots his tie and pulls it from his neck. "Back on your knees."

I adjust myself so I'm in the same position, knees planted outside his thighs, hands on his shoulders.

"Hands behind your back."

"How?"

"Trust me."

I pull one hand behind my back. My knees sink into the firm fabric of the couch, but I manage to keep my balance. The next hand is more difficult. I slip, landing in his lap, my face pressed against his chest.

"I've got you." He grabs my ass and slides me into his lap, so I'm straddling him.

I can feel his erection through his slacks. Desire rages through my body. I need that. I need him.

Nick brings his tie around my wrists, loops twice, and cinches with a knot.

I move my arms to test the binding. It's tight. My shoulders are pulled back, my chest thrust into his face. I'm on top, but I'm not in control.

His hands go to my ass. He lifts me, adjusting my legs so I'm kneeling. "You want me to get a condom?"

"No."

How does he make asking me about going bareback with my arms tied behind my back feel like the most caring thing in the history of the universe?

With one hand, Nick holds me in place. The other goes to his slacks. He unbuttons, unzips, shifts his boxers and slacks to his knees.

My gaze goes between his legs. Today, he's all mine. There's nothing to dampen the sensation of our bodies joining as one.

His hands go back to my hips. I relax into his grip as he pulls me closer. We're inches from joining.

My breath speeds up. Heat collects between my legs. I stare into his eyes, desperate for some way to contain my anticipation.

There are over twenty people on the other side of this wall. If I scream, they'll hear. They'll know what we're doing.

The risk is more thrilling than anything. I shift my hips to press against him. In response, he lifts my hips, moving our bodies farther apart. The look in his eyes says "patience."

It feels like an eternity passes. It can't be more than thirty seconds. His fingers dig into my skin as he pulls my body onto his. His cock strains against me.

Hell yes. I surrender to his movements, to his grip.

Pleasure spreads through my torso and thighs. It's torture and perfection all at once. Slowly, he brings my body onto his, shifting deeper and deeper inside me.

I can't do anything more than moan softly. My eyelids press together, something to contain my bliss. God, he feels good inside me.

With his hands on my hips, he pulls me up, until his cock is teasing me again. He drags me down, so he's deep inside me. It's damn intense, the feeling of him entering me again and again. How the hell am I supposed to keep quiet like this?

"Nick." It's a whisper. "I can't..." My sex clenches around him. "I can't stay quiet. It feels too good."

"You can." He thrusts deep into me.

I can? No. I cannot. I squeeze my thighs against him. I rub my wrists against the tie. Neither helps contain the ecstasy growing inside me. I need to groan. I need his name on my tongue.

He does it again, harder and deeper this time. I let out a much too loud gasp.

Nick digs his nails into my hips. The burst of pain is too much. I bite my tongue until it's numb.

"Nick..." I groan.

"Say it like that." He thrusts into me again. Rakes his nails against me again.

It takes every ounce of concentration I have, but I manage to keep my voice level.

"Nick," I groan.

He thrusts into me, his grip tight around my hips as he holds me in place. I relax my thighs and wrists, soaking in every ounce of sensation, in every ounce of his control.

"Nick."

He goes harder. Deeper. I lose track of everything except the pleasure coursing through me.

"Nick."

His breath gets faster. His eyes press together. He's getting there.

"Nick."

A few more thrusts and an orgasm rises up inside me. No screaming. Nothing to contain it. Nothing to do but feel.

The pressure is almost too much to take. I only manage by biting my tongue. With his next thrust, I go over the edge. My sex pulses, releasing as I come. Bliss spreads through my torso and limbs. It's better looking into his eyes, seeing the relief there.

He does need this. Need me.

I collapse into his arms. He holds me for a moment, his lips meeting mine in a desperate, needy kiss. I thrust my tongue into his mouth, exploring it like I'll never get another chance to kiss him.

He scratches me so hard I'm sure I'm bleeding. I groan into his mouth to contain the burst of pain. That's how good he feels. How desperate he is to contain himself.

I can feel his orgasm in the movements of his body. The way his tongue claims my mouth. The way his nails dig into my skin. The way he thrusts faster and harder.

Then I can feel him, pulsing inside me, filling me. It's the first time I've ever had sex without a condom, and it's fucking amazing.

When he's finished, Nick undoes the binding. He shifts so I'm next to him on the couch. He rubs my wrists. Then he drags his fingers over my hips, inspecting my deep, red scratch marks.

"Come here." He pulls me into his lap, holding against him and stroking my hair.

God, he feels good like this too. I allow myself a few minutes with my eyes closed and my head pressed against his chest.

My breath and heartbeat return to normal.

I shift off him, onto the other side of the couch. "What are the odds that no one heard us?"

"Not as good as I'd like."

"Was it worth it?"

His gaze goes to the floor. "It won't matter soon." He shifts back into his boxers and slacks. Then he pulls a towel from his desk drawer and hands it to me. "To clean up."

"Oh, yeah. It's a lot messier without a condom."

I wipe off and put my clothes back into position. Even without a mirror, I can tell that I'm not fooling anyone.

My hair is a mess. My makeup is smeared. My neck is throbbing like I have an impending hickey.

Maybe it doesn't matter. It will be easier for us to be together, whatever this is, if the company sells. It's not the end of the world. Even if there's a deep well of pain in his eyes.

I do one last adjustment of my clothes and reach for the door.

Nick stops me. His gaze goes to the clock on the wall. "Our delivery should be at Jasmine's desk."

"Is waiting for you to finish lunchtime quickies another part of her job description?"

"Maybe I'll add it." He smiles. "I'll get it. You look like you just got fucked."

"Wonder why."

"It looks good on you." He pulls open the door.

"I'm going to do some damage control in the bathroom."

He nods. Either he's ready to take our relationship public or he really believes his company is doomed.

God, I hope it's the first.

The women's bathroom is a respite from all the questions swirling around my brain. I have one task and that's looking like I didn't just have sex on the couch in Nick's office. Only my glasses are still on his desk. I can manage okay without them.

I wash my hands, fix my hair and makeup, change back into my bra and underwear. It's about twenty percent better. Not going to fool anyone who's paying attention, but the people around here don't pay much attention.

Nick is waiting outside the bathroom holding a plastic takeout bag in one hand and my glasses in the other.

He slides my glasses on with a soft touch. It's affectionate in a way obvious to anyone looking at us. No one is looking at us, but this isn't like him. He doesn't take unnecessary risks.

He presses his hand against my lower back. "Let's eat this in the conference room."

I nod and follow him to the glass-walled conference room. Anyone who walks by this side of the building can see us.

He passes me a Diet Coke and sets up the plates. It's Thai food again, curry. It smells good.

I stir hot sauce into my green curry. "Thank you."

"Of course." His eyes meet mine. "I want to take you somewhere tomorrow."

"Where?"

"It's a surprise."

"Can I have a clue?"

He shakes his head.

"Doesn't sound like there's any reason why I should agree."

"I'll pick you up at 8 AM."

"How do you know I'll go with you?"

"I know."

## Chapter Twenty-Five

Nick is at my door at exactly 8 AM.

I invite him in while I finish getting dressed, making a show of pulling on the lacy purple lingerie set.

He sits at my desk chair with his eyes wide and his lips zipped.

"Are you really going to deprive me of clues?" I check the weather on my phone—forties and sunny—and pull on a pair of comfortable canvas sneakers.

"Really." He stands and hands me my coffee.

Once we're on the street, Nick points to a food cart. "Did you eat breakfast?"

I shake my head.

We order egg sandwiches and another round of coffee. There's still something incredibly endearing about seeing Nick in normal clothes. Or seeing him do normal things.

He's every bit as handsome in jeans and a fitted t-shirt.

And every bit as effortlessly in control.

It really isn't fair.

I finish the sandwich by the time we get to the subway.

We're heading towards Queens. I look to Nick for a clue, but he's silent.

We spend the ride in plastic seats, my head on his chest, his arm around my waist. We get off way into Queens.

I squeeze his hand as he leads me out of the station and onto the street. We walk for ten minutes, stopping in front of a massive building. It's the entrance to some kind of arena. But it's totally empty.

I squint so I have a better view.

It's a racetrack.

I pull my hand to my side.

No.

No fucking way.

"Lizzy." He grabs my wrist, turning my body towards his. "Think about it before you run away."

"What the fuck is this supposed to be?"

"A safe way to try driving."

"Safe? Have you ever seen a NASCAR race? People crash into the wall at a hundred miles per hour. Their cars burst into flames. I've seen all the clips on YouTube, and I'm not going to die in a fucking explosion."

"You won't be going a hundred miles per hour."

"No." I step backwards until I feel the curb under my heel.

"Look at it for one minute. If you want to leave, we'll leave."

I meet his gaze. It's sincere. Caring. But he... But this...

I can't breathe. I can't think.

I shake my head.

Nick moves closer. He wraps his arms around me.

It's calming.

Fuck him for that.

For all of this.

I inhale everything about him. "Why are you trying to fix me? I live in the city. I don't need to drive."

"You're not broken. I can't fix you." He pulls me closer. "This weighs on you. I don't want you to live with that burden."

"You have a lot of fucking nerve throwing this at me without a warning."

"You wouldn't have come if you knew what we were doing."

"Because I don't want to do it." I release the hug and look into his eyes. "Why can't you surprise me with a weekend in the Caribbean or something?"

"You want to go to the Caribbean, we'll go to the Caribbean."

"Really?"

"It will be a few weeks before I can get away, but really."

"Okay." I nod. "We'll go after Kat's wedding. Did you... there are going to be a lot of people who follow tech swirling around to take pictures. I know you still want to keep this a secret. But... you could come with me. As my date."

"I'd love to." His voice is soft, sweet.

I look into his eyes. They're sincere. "Are you sure?"

"Positive."

I beam. Nick is going to be my wedding date. It's damn normal.

It's not enough to distract me from the horrible possibility of circling a track like a suicidal NASCAR driver, but it is nice.

Really nice.

Even if he's a fucking asshole for this.

I suck a breath through my teeth.

We're so far from casual. Even without a label, I know

he's mine, and I'm his. That anything else would be madness.

"Kat will ask if you're my boyfriend," I say.

"You want to make this official?"

"I do."

He smiles. "Then it's official."

My whole body is warm, gooey, the way it gets when I haven't seen my sister for ages.

Nick is my boyfriend, and he's going to be my wedding date.

He's got this crazy idea that I'm going to drive a car, but that's a minor imperfection when everything else about him is so intoxicating.

Okay.

It's a major imperfection.

But maybe he does have a point.

This does weigh on me.

It forces me to stay in the city. I love the city, but I want to travel too. To go places only accessible by car without crumbling into a pile of nerves or downing a Xanax.

I meet his gaze. "I will look at the track, but that's all I'm going to do. You're going to hate yourself for wasting the morning taking the subway to Queens."

He nods, then unlocks the gate with a key from his pocket.

He holds the door open for me, his expression totally inscrutable.

I take a deep breath as I look around the track. It's big, maybe three-quarters of a mile in one long oval shape.

The gray asphalt is worn with tire marks. The stands go all the way around it. There are enough seats for a few hundred people. A few thousand even.

It's no NASCAR track, but it's plenty.

Dirty Boss

There's a car parked in the middle of the roadway. A black luxury sedan.

I swallow hard. "Should I even ask how you made this happen?"

"I made a few phone calls."

"How much did it cost?"

"Less than it's worth." He pulls keys from the pocket of his jeans and hands them to me. "It's your choice."

There's no one else here. No people I can run over, no cars I can hit. The worst I can do is run into a wall or divider.

I run my fingers over the metal edge of the key. "I'll try sitting in the car, but I'm not promising more than that."

"I have a limo reserved for the day." He looks me in the eyes. "In case you get comfortable being in the car."

"What's the limo for?"

He traces the neckline of my t-shirt. "Motivation." He smiles. "So we only waste fifteen minutes getting back to the apartment."

"Are you implying that I was snippy?"

"I deserved it."

"Fuck yes, you did."

He smiles. "No one stands up to me like this."

"No one stands up to rich, white men. Especially when they're handsome." I take his hand. "I appreciate that you want to help, but next time warn me. Okay?"

"Okay."

I nod. I can do this. In theory.

I squeeze Nick's hand as we walk out onto the track.

The car has an electronic lock. I press the button and it makes that beep-beep sound. The locks click open. I grab onto the door handle and pull it open.

Easy. Totally easy.

My dad let me drive a few times when I was a kid.

When we were visiting family outside of the city. It was exciting then, all that power in my hands.

I slide into the driver's seat and fasten the buckle tight.

Nick settles into the passenger seat and closes the door.

Yes, the door. I need to close that. I reach over and slam it shut.

Easy. Totally easy.

My hands are shaking so hard I can't get the key into the ignition. I close my eyes and channel my yoga breathing. Deep inhale to fill up my lungs. Deep exhale to release everything.

I look down at my hand. It's not shaking quite as hard. It's manageable.

I slide the key into the ignition, but I don't turn it. Not yet.

"You okay?" Nick reaches over to offer his hand.

"So far." I dig my fingers into the steering wheel. "Is it even legal for me to drive here without a permit?"

"No."

I look at him. "Who are you and what did you do with the Phoenix Marlowe who interviewed me in January?"

"You do something to me." He places his hand over mine.

"What is it I do?"

"You make me forget my priorities."

I stare into his eyes. "What does that mean?"

He breaks eye contact to look at the track. "Are you ready?"

"Yeah." I bring my hand to the key. I remember how this goes. I press my foot against the brake as I turn the ignition.

The engine kicks with a roar. The dash lights turn on. Cool air blows from the vents.

"Want me to walk you through it?" he asks.

"Please."

"Foot on the brake."

I press against the brake as hard as I can.

"Right hand here." He taps a button on the center console. "Press this as you take the car from park to drive."

"Is this your car?"

"Yes."

"What if I crash it? Your insurance won't cover that."

He laughs. "Are you really worried about my insurance?"

I shake my head. Okay. Hand on the center console, finger on the button. I put the car in drive.

We're at one end of the track. There are about five hundred feet before I have to turn. I can drive in a straight line at ten miles per hour. That should be doable.

Even if my hands are shaking like a goddamn earthquake.

"Take your foot off the brake." His voice is calm, even. "The car will start to move forward, so keep your hands on the steering wheel."

"Okay." My breath races. I can do this. I can drive this fucking car.

I take my foot off the brake. Sure enough, the car rolls forward. My hands dig into the steering wheel. I move it too far right then too far left. After a moment, I'm mostly steady.

"Put your foot on the gas. Softly. Don't press down yet."

I don't quite have the hang of hovering over the pedal. I tap it and the car lurches forward. According to the dash, it's only about eight miles per hour. It feels like a million.

Nerves flutter in my stomach. I'm in a car, and it's rolling forward. I know that I'm not going fast enough to do any real damage, but that does nothing to slow my breathing.

My fingers dig into the steering wheel. For a quick second, I glance at Nick. His eyes are on me. There's some mixture of affection and pride on his face.

I focus on the road.

"Keep one eye on the dash and stay under twenty miles per hour."

As if I would drive any faster than that. I press on the gas as lightly as I can.

The car lurches forward. Slows. Lurches forward. My neck jerks. My muscles tense.

Steady. I need to apply a steady pressure. With one eye on the track and one on the dash, I press down harder.

The car speeds. Ten miles per hour. Fifteen. Twenty.

I manage to steer mostly straight.

My heart thuds against my chest as we get closer to the curve.

Nick places one hand on the steering wheel. "Try to turn. I'll keep you steady."

His voice does something to me. Makes me forget about things I've held onto for a long, long time.

Driving isn't the worst thing in the world. Not on this empty track.

I turn the wheel to the left, leaning into the curve. I'm going too steep. It's no good. I lose control of my breath, my hands clutching the wheel so hard my knuckles turn white.

Nick evens out the car. We don't crash. We make it all the way through the curve without crashing and exploding in flames.

Of course I know the car isn't going to explode, but that doesn't keep my head free of the image of NASCAR drivers running from their cars with their suits on fire.

How do I have such a vast reserve of terrifying mental images?

The straight part of the track isn't bad. I keep the car at an even twenty miles per hour. My breath isn't normal but it's not quite so strained.

I manage the next turn. The next straightway.

I go around the track half a dozen times. I'm doing it. I'm driving. I'm driving and I'm not crashing.

By the time I reach a dozen laps, I'm too anxious to take anymore. I press on the brake much harder than I mean to. The car screeches to a halt, jerking out bodies forward and back.

I look over at Nick as I take a deep breath.

He's smiling.

His eyes are filled with deep affection. He takes my hand, leading me through putting the car in park. Then he leans over and wraps his arms around me.

His lips hover over my ear. "I'm so proud of you."

"Can we be done with this now?"

"Yes." He shifts back into his seat. "The track is reserved for the rest of the day if you want more."

I shake my head. "That's not happening." I press my foot against the brake as I turn the car off.

My back and neck relax as the engine shuts off. I survived driving, but I'm in no rush to prove I can survive it again.

I undo my seat belt and get out of the car as fast as possible.

Nick slides out of the passenger seat. He moves to me and wraps his arms around me. The hug is so tight it takes my breath away.

I squeeze his waist over his coat. "Can we get a cup of coffee or something before we head home?"

He presses his lips to my forehead. "You don't need more coffee."

"Because I'm shaking or because I'm an anxious mess?"

Nick slides his fingers under my chin, tilting me so we're face to face. "You're not a mess, Lizzy. You're the bravest person I know."

A lightness passes through my chest and stomach. I believe him.

It hardly seems possible that, out of the hundreds of successful people Phoenix Marlowe, tech CEO, knows, I am the bravest.

"You are—" he kisses my cheek "—a bit anxious."

"I'm still having coffee."

———

WE FIND A DINER AND RELAX FOR A LONG LUNCH AND A conversation about nothing. The sandwiches and coffee are so-so, but it's the nicest meal I've ever had.

It feels so good being around him.

Seeing him happy.

I want it more than I want anything.

After Nick signs the check, he turns his attention to me. "It's your call—should we take a limo home or take the subway?"

A limo with Nick is awfully tempting, especially when the subway ride takes an hour. Driving around the track wasn't so bad. This should be okay.

I look into his eyes. "The limo. But you have to promise to distract me."

He nods. "You won't even know what planet you're on."

# Chapter Twenty-Six

The limo is nice. Leather bench seats, tinted windows, soft lighting. And seat belts. Plenty of seat belts.

The tightness in my chest relaxes. After driving in circles, I can survive a short ride in the backseat of a car with the belt fastened tight.

I shift out of my coat, press my back against the seat, and stretch my legs.

Nick sits next to me. We're alone back here, divider up, no way for the world to intrude.

The limo pulls onto the street.

He strokes my cheek, staring into my eyes. "You're nervous."

"Yes."

"I'm not fucking you in here."

His tone is dead serious. I stifle a laugh but it doesn't work. There's something about Nick. He's sweet in such a Nick kind of way.

"Is that right?" I ask.

"You're still going to come." He slides his coat off his shoulders and drags his hand down my neck. "But it's going to be more challenging than I'd hoped." He pulls my seat belt over my chest and clicks it into place.

I stare back at him. "Can't be more than fifteen minutes until we're at your apartment."

"That's ten more than I need."

The confidence in his voice sends a pang to my core. I'm five percent less nervous to be in the backseat of a car. That's still nervous enough to need a distraction.

He cinches his lap belt and turns to me. "Take off your top."

It is difficult to pull my t-shirt over my head without undoing the seat belt, but I manage.

His gaze goes to my chest. His eyes go wide. "I always forget how beautiful you are."

"Me or my boobs?"

"Both." He leans closer, dragging his fingertips down my chest until he's cupping my breasts. "You like it when I play with them."

"No shit, Sherlock."

"You really want to use your mouth to be a smart-ass?" He rubs my nipple over the lace bra.

A groan escapes my lips. "If that's how you're going to respond, yes."

"I'd spank you if it were physically possible. But that's not much of a punishment, is it?"

"Please."

Nick brings his mouth to my neck. He bites me hard. I groan loudly. It's such a release to be able to groan after stifling myself in his office.

"You drive me mad, Lizzy." He scrapes his teeth against my skin. "The way you react to me—" He pinches my nipple over the lingerie. "It's the sexiest thing I've ever seen."

The intensity of the friction sends heat through my body. It collects between my legs.

He rubs harder. Until I'm moaning.

His lips hover over my ear. "That's better." He sucks on my earlobe as he rubs me harder and harder.

He drags his hand down my stomach then plays with the waistband of my jeans. He undoes the button like he's working at quarter speed. I pant, buzzing with desire.

I lift my hips to help him pull my jeans to my knees. Then I'm back in the seat, my legs spread as wide as the jeans allow. I turn to Nick, but his hand goes to my shoulder. He pushes me back in place.

I can work with that.

He brings his lips to mine, kissing me hard. His tongue slides into my mouth. His fingertips slide up my thigh. They drag over me, pressing the fabric against my skin.

I groan into his mouth, digging my hands into the leather seats.

He rubs me over the lingerie. It's smoother and rougher at once. I relax into his touch, soaking in the pleasure building between my legs.

Nick breaks the kiss to bring his lips to my neck. He bites me as he slips his hand under my panties. His fingers skim my clit. It's enough to make me gasp.

He bites me harder.

Something clicks into place. He wants me to scream. Maybe it was killing him too, muffling himself in the office.

When he rubs me, I groan. His touch gets harder. Then it's perfect.

"Nick." I push the word out, arching my back to rub my body against his.

He brings his lips to my ear. "Louder."

He drags his fingers over me with slow circles. They get

smaller and faster, until he's rubbing the spot that needs him the most.

"Nick," I groan as loudly as I can.

He sinks his teeth into my earlobe. The pain sends a buzz through my body. Everything in me is turned on, keyed up, ready to unravel.

I lose track of everything except his lips and hands. He's undoing me in some way I don't understand, but none of that matters.

This moment, right now, is the only thing that matters.

"Nick," I groan as an orgasm rises up inside me. The pressure inside me gets tighter and tighter. Then it's so tight I can't take it anymore.

"Nick." I scream his name again and again.

He bites my neck. That burst of pain sends me over the edge. One last squeeze and I unravel. Pleasure spills through me as I come. It's so intense I forget to breathe.

He drags his hand up my torso, stopping to tease my nipples. His eyes meet mine, an intense look on his face.

He presses his lips to mine and kisses me like we'll never get to kiss again.

———

THIS ELEVATOR IS THE SLOWEST ELEVATOR IN THE history of machinery.

Nick's hand is pressed firmly into my lower back. His body is inches from mine. But we're still in this elevator when we should be tangled up in his bed.

Finally, we get to the penthouse. Nick looks to me, his expression smug and patient at once.

"In a rush?" he asks.

I glare at him.

He smiles. It lights up his face. "We should have lunch. You must be hungry."

"After." I step into the apartment and hang my purse and coat on the rack.

"After what?"

I stare into Nick's eyes, copying his confident posture and tone. "After you fuck me."

His expression shifts. In control. "Go to my room, strip naked, and sit on the bed."

"But—"

"Now. I'll be there in three minutes. If you're wearing anything, I'm not fucking you."

The sternness in his voice sends a rush of pleasure through me. It's like he needs this, like he can't bear anything but me following his commands.

I go straight to the bedroom and close the door behind me. There must be two and a half minutes left. It should be plenty of time to undress. It's harder with all the anticipation coursing through me.

I pull off my shirt, kick off my shoes. It's messy. Too bad.

Then it's socks. And my jeans. The bra and panties. I plant on the bed, my hands in my lap like I'm waiting for my teacher to arrive. It's not the sexiest position.

I want to be ready for him, on display for him, something to drive him as crazy as he drives me.

I lie back on the bed, my hands on my thighs, my eyelids pressed together. My fingers slide up my thighs, my body already craving a release. But I know my hands won't be good enough. The only thing that can possibly satisfy me is Nick.

A moment later, the door opens. I keep my eyes closed but I can hear his footsteps. His sigh of pleasure.

"You want to touch yourself, baby?" he asks.

The term of endearment is new. It does something to me. Makes me feel safe and on edge at once.

"Yes," I breathe. "But I want you more."

"Hands over your head."

I do as I'm told.

Nick sets something on the bedside table. A drink from the sound of it. He sits next to me and restrains my wrists. I blink open my eyes to look at him.

There's desire in his eyes. It only makes me want him more.

He's holding a blindfold. He pulls it over my eyes and around the back of my head. Everything goes dark. I can still hear him. Still feel the warmth from his body.

There's the sound of ice clinking in a glass. The weight on the bed shifts as Nick sits next to me. The soft fabric of his t-shirt presses against my skin.

Something hits the space between my breasts. Something cold and wet.

His hand moves closer and something cold and slick makes contact with my skin.

An ice cube.

It's freezing.

A shiver runs through me. I arch my back, squeezing my toes to contain it.

Nick drags the ice down my stomach. Slowly, it melts, leaving a trail of cool water on my skin.

He reaches for something—another ice cube, from his glass. This time, he starts at my lips. There's the faint taste of whiskey and the overwhelming sensation of cold.

He drags the ice down my neck and to my breasts. It's an inch from my nipple.

I pant, uncertain if I can take it but determined to try. It gets closer. Closer.

He pulls away, towards my other breast. Again, he slides the ice closer and closer.

There.

The ice makes contact with my nipple.

"Fuck," I groan. It's like jumping into the ocean two months too early.

The shock fades to a dull ache. The pain commands me. I have to feel it. I have to surrender to it.

Nick draws circles over me with the ice. I pant and shake. It hurts enough to make me scream.

Fuck it. I do scream.

"Nick. I..."

"You want me to stop, say the word." He takes the almost all the way melted ice and presses it between my lips. "Do you want me to stop, baby?"

I swallow the ice cube. "No."

"You want more?"

"Yes."

His movements get aggressive. He starts at my lip and drags the ice down my neck and collarbones. Straight to my nipple. He presses hard. He presses soft.

I grit my teeth to push through, but it's not working. It hurts too much.

"Yellow," I breathe.

He pulls the ice cube away for a moment then it's back on my stomach.

I relax, settling into his movements as the cold slides over my body.

He leans closer, bringing the full weight of his body onto mine.

His lips connect with mine. They're cold, but the heat of mine warms them. I open my mouth to make way for his tongue and he passes the ice cube from his mouth to mine.

I pass it back.

When there's nothing left but us, Nick pulls away. He takes another ice cube and trails it down my neck, around my chest, closer and closer. It brushes against my nipples for a moment then it's gone.

His lips close over my nipple, warming the coldness. He does it again. Cold then warm then cold again. The back and forth ramps up the tension building inside me. I lose track of everything except the feeling in my body.

I press my wrists against the restraints, arching my body to press it against his. Nick moves lower. Down my stomach. Below my belly button.

No teasing, he presses his mouth against my clit. There's a dull sense of coldness. Like jumping into the freezing ocean, only way more intense. I part my legs to give him room. He sucks on my outer lips. It's a dizzying mix of chill and heat.

Then it's warm. No more ice. Only Nick.

He licks me up and down with soft, slow strokes. Patient. Like he has all the time in the world. His hands go to my thighs. He pries them apart, presses my knees against the bed and holds them there.

I can't move. I'm at his mercy. I groan as pleasure pools between my legs.

Any lingering cold fades away. I'm warm. I'm scorching.

He sucks on my clit until I'm groaning his name.

I arch my back. My hips shift an inch.

His nails sink into the delicate flesh of my thigh. He sucks harder. Faster.

It sends me straight to the edge. I tumble into free fall, pleasure spilling through my body as I come. I scream. I shake. I release everything.

Nick kisses his way back to my mouth. He straddles

me, his thighs outside my hips, his cock straining against me. Only his jeans are in the way.

I rock my hips but he's too heavy. I can't even grind against him.

I can't see him undress, but I hear his clothes coming off. The soft thud of his shirt hitting the ground. The unzipping of his jeans. The elastic tug of his boxers.

I spread my knees as wide as they'll go. No more waiting. I need to feel him inside me.

He reaches for my wrists and undoes the bindings. I reach for him immediately.

My fingers skim his skin. There's muscle then the jut of bone. His hips.

With my other hand, I reach for the blindfold. "Can I?"

He reaches down and undoes my blindfold.

My eyes go straight to his erection. I gawk. I'm pretty sure I'm drooling.

"Come here." He lies on his back and reaches for my hands.

Oh hell yes. I crawl next to Nick. He's practically offering himself to me. I'm not about to miss this opportunity.

He arranges me, so my hands are at his hips, my knees are outside his. He doesn't use words. He brings his hands to the back of my head and guides me into place.

I wrap my lips around him, taking him as deep as I can. With my hands flat in front of me, I only have so much leverage. I let him guide me.

He tastes good.

He groans. His face fills with pleasure. I'm greedy to get him off, but he's in control.

His grip tightens in my hair. "On your back."

I do as I'm told.

Nick shifts off the bed. He finds the wedge he

used the first time we were here. He sets it up with the tall side facing me then presses me onto it, stomach first.

I'm lying at a reverse incline, my head on the bed, my ass lifted enough that I'm on display to him.

His tip strains against me. He teases again and again. It sends a shudder down my spine.

Again.

Until I'm panting.

Until I'm screaming.

And.

"Please," I groan.

His hands go to my hips. They sink into my skin as he enters me.

I sigh with relief.

I can't do anything but feel Nick. I surrender to it, groaning as he thrusts into me. His movements start patient and get faster, harder, deeper.

It's intense, but it doesn't hurt. It only feels good.

An orgasm rises up inside me. This one is fast. It's almost there. I do nothing to extend it. Instead, I groan into it, squeezing him as tightly as I can, screaming his name as loudly as I can.

It only takes a few moments for me to unravel. My legs threaten to go slack. I won't allow myself to melt until I feel his release. I focus on the sounds of our bodies coming together, of sighs and groans escaping his lips. I focus on the feeling of him inside me, of his fingers digging into my skin.

All of it builds to a crescendo. Then he's there, going harder and faster, groaning and clawing at my hips as he comes.

When he's finished, Nick untangles our bodies. He pulls me into his lap and runs his hands through my hair.

A wave of affection rises up in my stomach. But I can't say it yet. It's too scary, too final.

Soon.

I'll say it soon.

———

I SPEND THE WEEKEND WITH NICK. HE SHOWS ME HIS favorite police procedural. I teach him a dozen yoga poses. His balance is good, but he needs to work on his flexibility. I'm sure I can find a way to help him stretch.

He cooks. I make coffee. We have sex half a dozen times. By Sunday night, I'm so sore it's hard to move. I go home so I'll get enough rest to survive Monday.

It's amazing, the two of us together, like a normal couple. Like this could be our life.

My long ignored phone beeps a dozen new alerts. Mostly irrelevant emails, but there's a missed call and a text message from a number I don't recognize. It starts with an address, then—

*Meet me Friday at 10 PM. I have an offer for you. One that can leave Nick with his company intact. It's your choice. If you do what I want, I won't sell.*

*If you mention this to Nick, I'll sell immediately.*

*- Shepard Marlowe*

A chill sinks all the way to my bones. Breathing is difficult. Impossible even.

This is either an olive branch or a hand grenade.

I don't know much about Shepard, besides what Nick has told me. He held his ground against Nick. Yeah, he had Nick's guilt on his side, but that takes considerable strength. Especially for a younger brother.

He's the kind of guy who gets what he wants, whatever it takes.

I should delete this message. Nick cares about me. Meeting with Shepard behind his back could ruin things, convince him I'm not worth trusting.

But the sale is weighing on him. If I can help him...

I can't turn down the opportunity.

I save the address and clear my schedule for Friday night.

I have to help Nick save his company, whatever it takes. Even if it means trusting the enemy.

Even if it means I might lose Nick forever.

# Chapter Twenty-Seven

Monday morning, my Google Alert greets me with a news article that the sale is imminent. *Odyssey Executives Finalizing Details on Sale of Virtual Assistant—Is This the Next Step in AI?*

The article goes on to speculate about the possibilities of the Haley project. There's a quote from an executive at OmniTech that implies they're only buying the company to get their hands on the intellectual property.

Which means Nick will lose the project that means everything to him.

My yoga routine does nothing to clear my head. Neither does my warm shower. I brace myself for the worst on my way to work, but it's more painful than I imagined.

From a glance, everything is the same. Nick is standing at his desk, handsome and imposing in his sleek black suit. There are two cups of coffee, two sesame bagels.

His eyes are on the computer but he's not here. He's off somewhere else, stuck in his head.

"Good morning." There's no enthusiasm in his voice.

"Good morning." I focus all my attention on fixing my coffee.

But he's no more here when we get to work. I try not to let it bother me.

The two hours go slowly. When we're done, Nick nods a curt goodbye.

I have to do something to bring him back.

I stare into his eyes. "I was so sore this morning I could barely make it through my yoga."

Nothing. Not even a hint of a smile.

I keep going. "Did you—"

"Not now, Lizzy. I'm not in the mood."

"Okay. Maybe we can talk later. That theater that did *The Matrix* is doing the second one, *The Matrix Reloaded*, on Wednesday. We could go."

"I'll be busy all week."

"Oh. We could always watch the DVD at your place."

His eyes meet mine. It's like he's staring through me.

Then his eyes go back to his computer. "We'll talk later."

"Yeah, sure."

———

IT'S HARD TO CONCENTRATE. ALL MORNING, I KEEP ONE eye on Nick's office. I need some sign he's okay.

I leave for lunch. My spicy Chinese food is excellent comfort but it does nothing to clear my head.

I take a long walk. It's a nice day. Blue sky. Crisp spring air.

But it feels ugly. The whole world is ugly when Nick is upset.

The elevator is slow. At least I'm riding alone. I check my hair and makeup in the reflective walls. All good.

Finally, the doors ding open. I head straight for my desk, but something stops me.

Nick is at David's workstation, an angry look plastered on his face. "If you don't want to work, you shouldn't be here."

"But, sir—"

"I don't pay you to gossip. Any of you. I don't care what Gizmodo says about the sale. Until it's final, you're an Odyssey employee. Get back to work or hand in your resignation."

"Of course, Mr. Marlowe."

Nick turns to Gabriel. "You too."

Jasmine practically jumps out of her desk. "Mr. Marlowe! I need to speak with you."

He glares at her. "Not now."

"Yes, now."

He ignores Jasmine to stare down the programming team. "This goes for everyone here. If you don't want to work, I expect your resignation by the end of the day, and I expect your desk cleared by tomorrow morning."

He storms past Jasmine. Past me.

Our eyes connect. He looks away like he's embarrassed by his outburst. Then he disappears into his office.

The door slams shut.

The room drops to a hush. Nick is a force of nature, but it's not enough to scare me off.

I move towards his desk.

Jasmine grabs my wrist and pulls me aside. "Miss Wilder, that's not a good idea."

"Do you have a better one?"

"Nick is resilient. He'll be okay."

"'Okay' is relative."

Jasmine leans in to whisper. "You know what it's like with family, the smallest things become so big. When it's already something big... He needs space."

"You loved Shepard, right?"

"Of course, but—"

"Would you have left him alone like this?"

"Nick isn't Shepard. You need to let him calm down."

"No, I need to help him calm down."

"Oh." She nods like she's giving me her blessing. "Be careful. He'll blow a gasket if people start gossiping about you two, and nothing will talk him down." She looks me in the eyes. "This will get out at some point. Tech is still a sexist industry. People will be impressed by Nick's conquest. They'll call you a slut."

"I don't care. I can't let him sit there in pain all by himself." I turn, march to Nick's office, and knock on the door.

"It's Lizzy." I don't wait for a response. I turn the knob. Thankfully, it's not locked.

Nick rises from his seat on the couch. "Go back to work, Miss Wilder."

I press the door closed and turn the lock. "No."

He stares me down.

It's difficult to do anything but melt. Somehow, I hold strong. "You're upset. I want you to feel better."

"Go back to your desk."

This isn't working. I need to get more aggressive. I reach around my back, unzip my dress, and push it off my shoulders.

It falls to my feet.

Nick's eyes go wide. I'm not wearing particularly sexy lingerie today, but he stares at me like I'm in some fantastically expensive silk and lace bra and panty set.

He wants me. It's written all over his face.

But he doesn't move.

I go to unhook my bra. He grabs my arms and pulls them over my head.

"Stop it." He squeezes my wrists. "It's not the time."

"You're hurting. You can use me to feel better."

"I'm not doing that again."

"Why? I liked it. A lot. We'll both feel better." And he'll be here, mine, even if only for fifteen minutes.

"I'm not abusing our relationship like that."

"It's not abuse. I want you to do it." I stare into his eyes. "Please. I want to make you feel better. It makes me feel good."

He releases my arms. "Put your dress back on."

His look is serious. He's not going to budge, and with his history, I know better than to push him.

I slide back into my dress. "This sale is killing you."

He says nothing.

"What if I could help?"

"No."

"Hypothetically."

"The only thing keeping me sane is knowing you're okay." He shakes his head. "Promise you won't get involved."

I bite my lip. "I need you, and you're slipping away."

His eyes go to the window. "Promise."

"Tell me how to get you back and I'll promise."

"Lizzy, no." He raises his voice. "I won't forgive myself if anything happens to you. Promise."

He's practically screaming. I'm sure someone heard.

I stare into those deep brown eyes. All I see is pain. "I have to help."

"You want to help?"

"Yes."

"Then go home."

"What?"

"Go home and don't come back in for the rest of the week. Take a break. Take your sister to a spa. Take a flight to Paris. I'll pay. I don't want you to see me like this."

"But this is what people who care about each other do. They see each other when they're hurting, help each other when they're hurting."

His eyes cloud with frustration. "Do you trust me?"

"Yes."

"Then trust that I need you to leave. I need to know you're okay somewhere else." He reaches for my hand and runs his fingertips over my palm.

The simple touch sends warmth through my body. I move closer. Wrap my arms around his waist.

He brings his fingers to my chin, tilting me so we're eye to eye. "I'll take you out Saturday night. Until then, be somewhere else. Anywhere as long as you're enjoying yourself." He brushes his thumb against my lower lip. "I'll have a credit card sent to your apartment."

"I can't take your money."

"Then don't. But I want you to have the card."

There's so much need in his eyes. I nod.

He leans down to kiss me. He's here. I can feel all of his attention, all of his affection. I melt into his arms.

I need him like this.

I need him more than I realized.

He pulls back and returns to his desk. Already, he's slipping away. Warmth flees my body. I'm cold. Empty.

It's like my insides are torn out.

I want to honor his wishes. I really do.

But I can't watch Nick slip away without acting.

# Chapter Twenty-Eight

Between midterms and the last bits of wedding planning, Kat has no time for a spa day much less a spa week. I'm not feeling very international. I ignore Nick's credit card and use some of the cash I made in the poker tournament to take the train to D.C.

The difference in climate means the cherry blossoms bloom a little earlier here. Most are still white but a few stray trees are a beautiful shade of pink.

I've never been one for history or civics. Touring monuments and museums makes little impression. I take the train home on Friday morning and spend the day watching my favorite sci-fi films.

Nick's impulse was right. It's much harder to survive this in my apartment with my thoughts surrounding me.

I call Sarah.

"Hey, sweet thang," she answers.

"Can we go out tonight?"

"I'm off in two hours. We'll eat, we'll dance, we'll find a nice guy to get your mind off things."

"No guy."

"Things serious with the hot boss?"

"You could say that."

"You little slut! Why didn't you tell me?"

"Maybe I didn't want to get called a slut."

"It's a compliment. You want me to act like Kat." She adopts a prim and proper voice. "Oh my goodness, Elizabeth, you need to be careful. Are you using contraceptives? Are you sure this man is really marriage material?"

"Don't make fun of Kat. She's sweet. And she gets laid more than you do."

"Does not."

"You should see her with Blake. He worships the ground she walks on. And he looks at her like he's thinking about throwing her on the bed and planting his face between her legs." I go to my closet and try to pick out my cutest dress. "You know what, this line of conversation is disgusting. I'm totally done."

"You're not going to abandon me for an engagement, are you?"

"Never." I pick a purple mini-dress and find gray tights to compliment it. "Meet you at Pixie Dust?"

"See you then."

The phone clicks off.

I check the saved text message just to make sure it's still there.

Tonight, 10 PM. The restaurant is a good ways from any club Sarah frequents. I'll have to leave by nine if I want to take the subway. Nine-thirty if I'm willing to take a cab.

I play with my phone, contemplating the merits of calling Shepard and demanding an explanation now. Of calling Nick and begging him to share his feelings with me. The former is too aggressive, the latter too desperate.

He wants me to stay out of this.

But I can't.

———

DINNER IS PIZZA ON THE WAY TO THE CLUB—A LOUD, throbbing dive where the bouncers don't check ID.

I down a double-shot rum and diet and follow Sarah onto the dance floor. There's no mood lighting here. It's dark and dim and sweaty.

For half an hour, I dance with her. We've done this a million times and we fall into a seamless rhythm. It's easy and fun, but it attracts the attention of too many guys. One pair moves in to dance with us.

Sarah looks at me as if to ask if it's okay. I nod *yeah*. It can't be that bad. And it's dancing. Nothing in my relationship with Nick precludes dancing with a stranger.

The guy slides his hands around my waist. They drift to my lower back. I grab them and put them back in place.

The song passes, my hips swaying a foot away from his. He pouts over the distance, but his hands stay put.

The next song is faster. The guy isn't so bad really. Decent height, nice button-up shirt and designer jeans, pretty blue eyes and messy blond hair. Not my type, but anyone can see he's attractive.

My body is magnetically repulsed. I don't want anyone touching me besides Nick ever again.

Fuck it. I nod a goodbye and break to the bar. After two more rum and diets, my head is fuzzy and the room is spinning.

Sarah plops on the seat next to me. "Babe, what's wrong? Talk to me."

I scan the room. We're not in the nicest club in the world, but I should be having fun. Most nights, I'd kill to dance with my friend with no trouble from the bouncers.

I look cute. I have a drink. My back feels fine.

But I'm still heavy all over. I'm still cold all over. It still feels like my insides are ripped out, like nothing will ever be okay.

I close my eyes, willing myself to shake it off.

All I see is Nick. The frustration in his eyes. The slumping of his shoulders. Even over the music, I hear his voice in my head. It's angry. Hurt. Defeated.

I can help him.

How can I do anything besides help him?

"Lizzy!" Sarah hits me in a half-playful, half-*wake the fuck up* gesture. "You okay? Did you leave your drink unattended?"

"No. It's nothing like that."

"Don't tell me you're thinking about the hot boss."

I nod.

"But the blond was panty-melting."

"You know it's possible to feel something for a man besides desire to fuck."

"Possible, but not for you." She looks me in the eyes. "Right?"

God, the room is spinning. I kick back the last sip of my drink. It's not enough. I plop an ice cube in my mouth and suck hard.

Sarah snaps her fingers. "Answer me or I'm assessing you too drunk to stay out."

"I'm thinking." I'm dizzy, but I know it's not from the drinks.

"Oh fuck." She covers her mouth. "You're in love with him, aren't you?"

A dive bar after three drinks is not the most romantic place for a conversation like this.

I've been avoiding the question, even in my head.

I know the answer.

I love Nick.

I'm madly in love with him.

So madly in love with him I can't bear to see him hurting.

I nod a yes. "I am."

"Fuck. Love sucks. It makes you its bitch."

That sounds right.

"Lizzy."

My eyes go to the clock. It's a little after nine. There's still time to get to the hotel.

"Lizzy!!!"

"What?"

"Do you love this guy, like crazy, can't breathe in love with him?"

"I have to go."

"No fucking way, girlie. You're drunk and miserable. You're not leaving my sight."

"What if I swear to go straight home?"

Sarah cocks an eyebrow. "I won't believe you."

I go for another ice cube. Sarah takes my drink away.

She leans in close. "Love can be nice... if he's worth all the pain. Can you see yourself with him for a long time?"

My heartbeat picks up. Yes. I see us in that gorgeous apartment of his in ten years, rings around our fingers. The rest of it is fuzzy. I've never thought about my future beyond a career, but I know I want Nick in it.

I want him happy.

I push off my seat, tugging at my purse to find my phone. "I have to call him. I have to ask him something."

Sarah's expression gets serious. "If you're not back in five minutes, I'm calling the cops."

"Okay." I march to the back door, to the alley reserved for smokers.

Outside, there are two people humping against the

wall. I turn my back to them so as not to ruin their desperate fun.

My hands are shaky, more from the drinks than from my racing nerves. I dial Nick and hold the phone to my ear.

Five rings and I get voicemail.

I call again. Voicemail.

Okay. Third time's a charm.

Ring. Ring. Ring—

"Lizzy, what's wrong?" His voice is equal parts concerned and tired.

"I have to ask you something."

"Are you drunk?"

"Yes, but that's not important." I dig my fingers into the back of the phone. "You told me once... about your company. That if you lost it, it would be like losing a limb. Do you still feel like that?"

"Where are you? I'll pick you up."

"Just answer the question. Yes or no. You've been miserable all week. You're like a different person. You're not here."

"Yes." He pauses. "Baby, tell me where you are. I'll come get you."

The softness is his voice is almost impossible to resist. "No. I'm with my friend. I'll be fine."

But he won't. Not if he loses the company. I take a deep breath, looking around the alley in an attempt to sober up. I can make out the tile walls of the building opposite me. The sighs of the couple next to me. They are not at all bothered by my presence.

I exhale into the receiver. "Nick, do you trust me?"

"Lizzy..."

"Do you?"

"Of course."

"That's all I need to know. I'll see you soon." I hang up the phone before he can object.

I look up directions to the hotel. The subway is a mess. There's no time. I have to take a cab.

Fuck.

I hightail it to the street and throw my arm into the air. How the hell do people hail these things?

Somehow, a cab stops in front of me. I take a deep breath as I slide inside.

The cabbie takes the address and the car pulls onto the street.

I close my eyes. I can do this. For Nick, I can do this.

Once I'm calm enough to breath evenly, I send a text to Sarah.

*Lizzy: Sorry, but I have to take care of something. Take the blond and his friend home. I bet they'll be into a threesome. I promise I'll call if I need you.*

*Sarah: I'm going to rat on you to your big sister.*

*Lizzy: No, you're not.*

*Sarah: Fuck you. I might. Call me when you get home.*

*Lizzy: Use a condom.*

## Chapter Twenty-Nine

My cell buzzes frantically the entire ride to the restaurant.

Pressing "ignore" and counting the seconds until the next call is enough to keep my attention off the possibility of a crash.

When the cab arrives, I pay and turn off my phone.

At ten on a Friday night, the restaurant is crowded. New Yorkers love eating late.

Still, I spot Shepard in a booth in the back of the room. His bright blue tie draws my attention to his eyes. He looks so much like Nick.

He's just as handsome, just as strong and in control.

It's not smart being here drunk, but it's better than leaving Nick to disappear into his pain.

I walk through the restaurant. Shepard rises and shakes my hand.

"Thanks for coming. Do you prefer Miss Wilder or Lizzy?" He motions for me to sit.

I do. "Lizzy."

"Can I get you a drink or something to eat?"

"No thank you. I'm not in the mood."

Shepard slides back into his seat. He's nursing a soda in a large glass. No alcohol, most likely. He must hate it that Nick forced him into rehab. More that it worked.

There's no malice in his expression. No sign he's after hurting Nick. No clue as to what he's after, actually.

"I'm not sure why you want to meet with me." I cross my legs. "What could I possibly have to do with you selling Nick's company?"

"It's our company. We grew it together." Shepard shifts like he's fighting a frown. "You must care about him to meet me here."

"Yes."

"Do you love him?"

My cheeks flush. It's like it's national Ask Lizzy if She's in Love Day.

I look back to Shepard. "Yes, I do."

He frowns with sympathy. "This isn't personal. I'm not trying to hurt you."

I don't like the sound of that.

"I'd like you to break up with Nick."

My stomach twists. "Are you trying to hurt him?"

"That isn't my priority."

"Is it about money?"

He stares back at me, totally unreadable. "If there's something you want more than me backing off the sale— money, another job, information you can use for leverage—"

"No. I want you to back off the sale. Nick is miserable over this. I..." I don't want to share my feelings with someone who is so blasé with other people's, but I can't have everything on my chest. "I can't lose him to this."

"Then leave him."

I can't lose him like that either. My body goes cold. "At least tell me what you get out of me leaving Nick."

"Look at it this way. If he loves you, he'll fight to get you back. You'll make up and be happy."

"And you'll get...?"

"What I want."

"Which is?"

His expression hardens. "Jasmine."

"How will this get you Jasmine?"

"I need to know if he loves her. If she loves him."

"She loves you. She practically told him that."

"Words are cheap. I need to see what she does. What he does. Letting her leave was the worst mistake of my life. I'll do whatever it takes to win her back, no matter what you or anyone else suggests." He stares back at me. "I hope that Nick really does love you. That he fights for you and you end up happy together."

"Because it will be easier for you to get what you want?"

"Yes. And because he's my brother. I do care about his happiness."

"But not as much as you care about her?"

He doesn't blink. "I care about her more than I care about anything."

"I believe him when he tells me he never touched Jasmine. And he doesn't look at her like he's ever wanted her."

Shepard's expression fills with frustration. "I'm sure you're a lovely person, but we're not friends. This is a business arrangement."

"Fine." It's not like I want someone like Shepard as a friend. "What are the terms?"

"Break up with Nick. You have until the end of the weekend. If you do, I'll step off the sale on Monday."

"What if he fights me?"

"Fight back."

"What about him fighting for me?"

"Make him work for it. Give it two weeks. If he's still fighting, do what you want. I'll call off the sale as soon as I get word it's over."

I bite my lip.

It makes sense... in a twisted kind of way.

He wants to know if Jasmine loves Nick. If she'll run to him as soon as he's available. Or if he'll seek comfort in her.

But what if he's right?

What if Nick wants to fuck his way out of his pain with the closest available woman?

He might not forgive me for this.

He might not fight.

I might not get him back.

"How do I know I can trust you?" I ask.

"You don't have another option."

He's right. I'm stuck. And I'm a pawn. It's awful.

"If I don't hear from you by start of the day on Monday, I'll assume you decided not to do it, and I'll sell."

"Doesn't the money you could make mean something to you?" I ask.

"You have my number." He slides out of his seat and offers his hand to shake. "It's your decision."

I shake his hand with a weak grip.

The world goes cold as I watch him leave. It's my decision. Either I leave Nick, or he loses his company. And I lose him.

It takes ten minutes for me to regain my breath. I can't stomach another cab ride.

I take the subway to Kat and Blake's place.

When the doorman assures me that they aren't home, and thus aren't fucking on the couch, I let myself in.

Sure enough, the penthouse is empty. That beautiful blue New York light streams through the windows.

Even that is ugly.

I'm numb all over. My thoughts are in messy squiggles, so far from the straight lines I need to figure out what to do.

A hot bath does nothing to wake my senses. I wipe off my makeup and climb into the empty spare room.

There are pajamas somewhere, but I can't bother. I pull the blanket over my head and press my eyelids together.

There's no way out.

No matter what I do, I lose Nick.

## Chapter Thirty

It's too bright in here. It should be illegal for fluorescent lights to be so bright.

My head is pounding. From the hangover or the misery, I'm not sure. No matter what I do, I lose Nick.

It hurts to think. Hell, it hurts to breathe.

There's a knock on the bedroom door. It's followed by a soft voice.

"Hey, Lizzy. You up?" Kat asks.

"I am now." I throw the comforter over my head, inspecting my cocktail dress.

There's no time to change or make up a believable cover story.

Kat enters the room with a glass of water. She sits on the bed and hands me the drink. "Want to tell me what's going on?"

"I went out with Sarah and felt like coming here."

She opens her palm to reveal two ibuprofen. "Want to try again?"

"I wanted to see you, but you were out."

Despite the doubt in her expression, she hands over the

pills. I swallow them and down all the water. The pounding in my head lessens by three percent. It's enough to motivate me to find my glasses and drag my heels to the kitchen.

According to the microwave, it's almost noon.

Kat pours and fixes two mugs of coffee. "You have ten messages from Nick. Does that have anything to do with your appearance here?"

"My phone was off last night."

She pushes my drink across the counter. "Sue me. I was worried. I've been caught up with wedding stuff and we haven't talked much."

"Two weeks from tomorrow."

She nods. "Not going to distract me." She sips her drink. "What happened?"

The squiggly thoughts in my brain straighten out. It's bright. I have coffee. I can think clearly, even with the pounding in my head.

There's really no decision here.

Nick loves the company more than anything. More than he'll ever love me.

I stare at my coffee. It's dark and deep, like Nick's eyes.

There's a pang in my chest. This is going to hurt so fucking bad, but it's the only thing that makes sense.

I look back to Kat. "I have to break up with Nick."

"Why?"

I struggle to find an explanation that won't give anything away. "He's in love with his job."

"So?"

"So? Didn't you break up with Blake because he was in love with his job, and he didn't love you or something like that?"

"Technically." She points to her engagement ring. "But I did give him another chance."

"He got lucky. You're forgiving."

"What about your internship?"

"I'll find another one."

"You're only halfway through the semester. What about school?"

"I don't know." I press my fingers into my mug. "Maybe... I wasn't learning anything. Maybe school isn't right for me."

"Elizabeth Marie Wilder! You are not dropping out of college because a guy broke your heart."

"It's not because of a guy. It's because the classes are worthless. I'm better off getting a junior programmer job somewhere. I'll learn more."

"I don't believe you."

I stare into my coffee, willing some kind of contentment to form in my expression. It's all true. I was thinking about skipping college for an internship before I got that scholarship to Stanford.

"Blake's gotten better about work. Maybe Nick can—"

I stare her down. "Why do you care anyway?"

"You were happy last time you talked about him. I want you to be happy."

I study her expression. There's something she's not telling me. I'm sure of it.

"Is that all?" I ask.

"He sounded so worried about you, Lizzy. Like he really loves you."

"When did he sound worried?"

She blushes, embarrassed. "I might have listened to his voicemails."

"Snooping brat."

"I'll make you pancakes."

"Won't Blake freak about the mess?"

"Let him." She slides into the seat next to me and looks

me over like she's inspecting a torn painting. "There's more going on. You can tell me."

"It's the only decision that makes sense." I play with the bottom of my cocktail dress.

"Feelings aren't logical."

"No, but decisions should be."

"Lizzy—"

"I've made up my mind. Now make me pancakes if you want me to forgive you for invading my privacy."

She frowns but gathers a bowl and flour.

I give Kat a few minutes to get started, but she has no idea what she's doing.

I take over the process, measuring, stirring, and flipping until my entire world is pancakes.

I'm almost finished when the intercom buzzes.

Kat excuses herself to answer. "Yes."

The doorman speaks. "Katrina, there's a Mr. Marlowe here to see Miss Elizabeth Wilder about a personal matter."

I can't breathe.

Not now. Not here. Not yet.

She turns to me. "Do you want me to let him in?"

I turn off the stove and take a deep breath to collect my senses. There's no way to stop this. Maybe it's better to get it over with, so it's not hanging over my head all day.

I nod. "Yes."

"Are you sure?"

"Positive."

Worry flashes over her face, but she turns back to the intercom. "Let him up. But give us two minutes first."

"Of course, Ms. Wilder."

She unlocks the door and makes her way to the kitchen. Her eyes bore into me, examining me the way she examines something she's going to draw.

"You know, if you do love him, you might be able to work this out. Whatever it is," she says.

"I made my decision."

"You look like you're going to cry."

"I have to do this!" I bite my tongue. I can't get upset. That will bring questions, from Nick or from Kat or both. I have to convince them that I'm okay with this.

My stomach twists. It must be the hangover. I tear a pancake in half and stuff it into my mouth. It's perfect. Fluffy and slightly sweet with a warm burst of blueberries.

"Do you want me to go?" she asks.

"You can stay on the couch."

There's a knock on the door. My chest tightens. The room goes cold. I'm not sure I can do this.

Kat answers the door with a polite handshake hello. Nick is ragged. He's still handsome and well-dressed— jeans and a sweater today—but his eyes are tired and he's at least two days without a shave.

He'll be happy soon.

He'll have the company back, and he'll forget about me, and he'll be happy.

That's what I want.

A tear forms in my eye. I wipe it away. I'm not crying. Not yet.

He comes closer, until there are only three feet between us. "Lizzy, what happened?"

"Nothing. I went out dancing with Sarah. I guess I was a little drunk. Just one of those drunk phone calls."

His brow furrows. His eyes fill with doubt. He's not buying this story.

I step back. "It's good you're here though. I have to talk to you about something."

He moves closer. Until he's six inches away. His finger-tips slide over the side of my cheek. My body fills with warmth. God, he feels good. I fight my desire to wrap my arms around him. That will only make this harder.

"You've been crying." His voice is soft.

"It's just a hangover."

"You're a terrible liar." He wipes a tear from my eye. "Tell me what's wrong, baby. We can fix it together."

I shake my head.

"We can."

"No, we can't."

"Lizzy—"

I step back, breaking from his touch. At once, I'm cold. My back tenses. My stomach churns.

"Did you come here because you thought I'd come looking for you at your apartment?"

"Did you?"

"Yes." He stares into my eyes. "What happened?"

"I realized something."

Dread spreads over his face.

I want so badly to wipe it away. I want to run my hands through his hair, to wrap my body around his, to soothe him today, and tomorrow, and every day, forever.

But this is the way I can make him happy.

The only way.

I stare back at Nick. "I think we should. No, there's no think, no should." I gather every ounce of strength in my body. "I'm breaking up with you."

Kat jumps towards the bedroom. "I'll give you guys a minute. Sorry." She slams the door shut on her way out of the room.

Nick moves closer. His hands go to my lower back and he pulls my body into his. "Tell me you don't feel something right now." He leans down and presses his lips against mine.

God, how I feel something. I feel everything.

I step back. "I care about you, Nick. That isn't the problem."

"Then what is?"

"Your life is full. You have your company. That's your priority. That's what makes you happy. There's no room for anyone or anything else. And I have a lot on my plate too. Figuring out what I'm doing with school. This relationship was never going to work. It's better if we end it now."

His eyes fill with sadness. "You don't believe that."

"Yes, I do." I try to convince myself. I make my voice as loud and confident as possible. "You'll be happier when you can focus on your work."

"And what about your internship?"

"If it's still there after this sale stuff settles down... I'll ask another one of the programmers to teach me."

"None of them know AI like I do."

"I know." I bite my tongue so I can focus on how much that hurts instead of how much my heart hurts. "I'll find another internship."

His eyes go to the floor. "Is there any way I can change your mind?"

I rack my brain for something, some bone I can throw him so that he can fix this.

Nothing comes.

"You have your priorities," I say. "I have mine."

He steps back. "I respect your decision." His eyes meet mine. He opens his mouth like he's going to speak, but he says nothing.

"I'll walk you out." I press my hands to my sides so I won't be tempted to touch him.

Nick waits until we're at the elevator to speak. He turns to me, his eyes wide with something I don't recognize.

His voice is soft. "This could be forever."

The elevator doors slide open. He steps inside, his eyes on the floor.

"But if this is what you want—" his eyes bore into mine "—I do trust you."

The doors slide shut.

Nick is gone.

I make it all the way to the spare room before I curl into a ball and cry.

# Chapter Thirty-One

Kat brings me coffee and breakfast. "Do you want to talk?"

I shake my head and stuff my face with pancakes.

She sits with me until I finish my brunch, then she takes the plates and makes herself scarce.

I lie in bed with my laptop, watching the first season of *Battlestar Galactica* in an attempt to think about anything besides Nick. My eyes are tired. I drift in and out of sleep. It's not even a little bit restful.

Mid-afternoon, an email grabs my attention. From Phoenix Marlowe, to the entire Odyssey team. We're off Monday and Tuesday. The sale is still in the air. He'll have final word first thing Wednesday.

That's two days to breathe before I have to see Nick.

Maybe it's enough.

A little after seven, Kat drags me to the living room for dinner. It's something she made herself—pasta with meat sauce and a giant bowl of green salad.

I sit at the table with her and Blake, stabbing my food with my fork and not at all paying attention to the conversation.

When we're finished, I clear the plates and wash the dishes. The scalding water barely makes an impression. I know it's hot, but I'm too numb to feel it.

Kat settles in front of the TV with her sketchbook, half watching a teen soap, half drawing. She pats the spot next to her. I look to Blake for some sign I'm encroaching on his turf.

He slides out of his seat. "I'm going to put in a few hours of work." He goes to the couch to plant a kiss on Kat's lips. "There's a lot to do before the wedding."

She beams. "I love you."

"I love you too."

It's sweet enough to make me sick. I raid the fridge for something to counter the bile rising in my throat. Coffee ice cream. Perfect.

"You want dessert?" I ask no one in particular.

"Sure." Kat kisses Blake again. "None for Blake. He can't get his desk dirty."

He smiles that devious *this is really about sex* smile. It's been over a year since they met, and they still look at each other like they can't wait to tear each other's clothes off.

It's sweet.

But gross too. I don't need details on my sister's sex life.

I focus on scooping ice cream. Once Kat and Blake are finished with their long goodnight, I make my way to the couch and hand my sister her mug.

The dessert is cold and creamy, but it has no taste. Nothing about it makes me feel good.

Kat sets her half-eaten treat on the coffee table and slides her arm around my shoulder. "You're growing up. You don't tell me everything anymore."

"I haven't told you everything for a long time."

"Still." She glances at the screen. "I'm getting married. You'll go back to Stanford. We'll have our own lives."

"I want to stay in New York."

"You can stay here. Or at the Brooklyn place. The sublet goes through June." She slides back into the couch. "Lizzy, I want to sell the Brooklyn apartment. Unless you want to live there."

"What? It's where we grew up. Everything last year—"

She turns to face me. "Half that money is yours. That's more than enough for college anywhere you want."

"But—"

"I don't care how much you fight me. I'm not going to let you take on the whole world alone. You're my best friend. You'll always be my best friend. I'd rather have you in New York, and I'm not afraid of using any tool in my arsenal to keep you here."

"Including that one—" I nod to Blake's home office.

She nods. Her expression gets serious. "If you want to talk about Nick, I'm here. I'll skip school, and we can go shopping. My treat. I need to pick up some honeymoon stuff."

"Do I have to talk about Nick?"

"You don't have to do anything. But I'm here. I'm always here." She throws her arms around me in a tight hug. "I've never seen you this miserable. Not since the accident."

"Yeah."

"I'm worried."

"You're always worried."

She grabs her ice cream and settles back into the couch. "I'm trying to respect your boundaries, you know."

I nod.

"You might feel better if you talk about it."

"I might."

I focus my attention on my ice cream. When I'm done,

I drag the spoon around the porcelain cup, drawing circles in the melted dessert.

Maybe I'll feel better if I talk about it.

Like it's not impossible.

At the next commercial break, I take a deep breath. "I just want him to be happy."

Kat nods, attentive and sweet as always. I start talking and I don't stop until I've got nothing left to say.

———

MONDAY, KAT SKIPS HER AFTERNOON CLASSES. WE TAKE the subway to Midtown and dig through a dozen boutiques and department stores in search of the perfect beach clothes.

Kat makes a point of asking my advice on every single article of clothing. The second my mind drifts back to Nick, she's there with a question about a style of bikini or the best pattern to match with white shorts or some inquiry that I can explain in great detail.

After three hours of shopping, I'm exhausted. I leave her to try on a dozen bikinis to find some caffeine. I pass the lingerie section on my way to the coffee shop.

The colorful lace catches my eye.

My head flashes with all sorts of mental images that were totally delicious two weeks ago. Right now, the thought of Nick with his pupils dilated and his lips parted only makes me feel heavy.

It hurts. It hurts a lot. But this is the only way I can help him. This is what will make him happy.

I can't bring myself to order a hot drink. I'm too cold to bear any threat of melting. I dump simple syrup into a cold-brewed iced coffee and plant in the tiny wooden chair to drink it.

Eventually, Kat finds me. She's holding half a dozen shopping bags. She drops them in a mess on the floor to slide into the seat next to mine.

"You want to talk?" she asks.

I shake my head.

Her eyes go to the clock on the wall. "I have a meeting for a group project. You okay to leave?"

"You can go straight there. I'll take your stuff home."

"You sure?"

I nod.

She squeezes me in an incredibly tight hug. I scoop up her bags and follow her to the subway. I plant in a seat on the 6 train. She leaves at Times Square to transfer.

The tiles whiz by. The people who enter and exit the train whiz by. Somehow, I get off the train at the right stop. It's cold today. The sun sinks into the horizon with a streak of red, like it's bleeding and broken and about to disappear.

Once I'm in the penthouse, I drop the bags by the front door and I bury myself in my room.

There's a breaking news story about Odyssey on my Google Alert. The headline tells me all I need to know.

*CFO Shepard Marlowe Decides Not to Sell Odyssey and Controversial Virtual Assistant Project. Claims Company is Worth Five Times the OmniTech Offer.*

Nick's company is safe. I should feel better. Freer. Calmer. Something.

But I still feel heavy. I still feel so heavy I can barely breathe.

## Chapter Thirty-Two

I'm halfway through season two of *Battlestar Galactica* when a knock breaks my concentration. It's too early to be Kat. But what the hell could Blake want with me?

I yell in the direction of the door. "Kat isn't here."

"I know."

The door opens. Blake is standing there in his expensive black suit, his expression fire and steel.

"I want to talk to you. There's Thai food on the table." He moves to the living room like he's sure I'll follow.

I curse my hunger and my undying love of spicy shrimp dishes.

There's even a can of diet soda.

Fine. That earns my future brother-in-law exactly twenty minutes of my attention.

I fix my plate with a giant scoop of brown rice and another of green curry. It smells good and, right now, I'll take any hint of good I can get.

"I heard about Odyssey." He pours himself a glass of whiskey on the rocks. "Is that good news?"

I nod.

"Lizzy, I'm not going to waste your time." He settles into a seat at the table. His voice is even, like he's talking about the weather. "I transferred two hundred thousand dollars into your checking account."

"You what?"

He holds his expression. "With you and Kat owning the Brooklyn apartment, you no longer qualify for need-based scholarships. I did that. You're a smart young woman and you deserve options. I'm giving yours back."

"Get the 'I told you so' over with."

"You followed your heart. I can't fault you for that."

"Ugh. You sound like Kat."

Blake smiles. His expression is light, like he's so happy he could die. On him that's a slight crinkling of the eyes and a slight upward curve of the lips. But it's happy. There's no mistaking that.

"She already offered to sell the place in Brooklyn." I look Blake in the eyes. "Do you think she really wants that?"

"She's always wants the best for you."

"Yeah. She always wants the best for everyone else." I play with my fork. "Do you have any idea how lucky you are to have her?"

"Luckiest guy in the world."

"At least you realize that." I take a bite. Red peppers, green peas, and the rich taste of coconut. It's good. Really good.

Blake pulls something from his laptop bag and slides it across the table to me. "You got into NYU, Hunter College, Rutgers, and a dozen other schools within two hours of the city."

"Funny, 'cause I don't remember applying to any of them." I throw him a death stare. "What did you do?"

"I copied your Columbia essay and input your information. It only took an hour." He makes eye contact. "NYU is thirty minutes on the subway, and Hunter is less than twenty blocks away. You can stay here if you'd like."

"You'll be newlyweds."

"There's space."

"You'd really want me in your fancy apartment, cock-blocking you twenty-four/seven?"

He smiles. "You won't manage to cock-block me. I'll soundproof our bedroom."

"Please stop."

"It's official in two weeks, but as far as I'm concerned, you're already family. You're always welcome."

Some of the coldness melts away. I'm family now. It feels real. Hell, it's the first time I've ever seen Blake as more than that guy who makes Kat happy.

He's really going to be my family.

Maybe... maybe I don't have to do all of this alone. Maybe it's okay to accept someone's help.

I take a long sip of my soda to cool my scorching taste buds. My attention goes back to Blake. He's unflappably calm, but he's also sincere.

For the first time, I understand what Kat sees in him.

He's sweet.

We finish dinner in silence. After, I take my *Battlestar Galactica* marathon to the TV in the living room.

Blake joins me until Kat gets home. Then they go to their room, probably so he can prove just how little I am able to cock-block him.

———

THERE'S NO ONE AT ODYSSEY WHEN I ARRIVE Wednesday morning. Of course there's not. It's eight, and start time is nine.

There's a light at the end of the hall. Nick's office.

I take a deep breath, gathering my courage, but I'm not ready to face him. I wait at the coffee shop across the street. One vanilla latte, and I'm a little more awake.

It's only eight forty-five. I order a second drink so I won't be tempted to text him and confess everything.

I don't know much about Shepard, but I'm positive he won't give me any wiggle room with this arrangement. That means I need to keep Nick at a distance for two weeks.

And that's if he wants anything to do with me.

My drink is good. Warm, sweet, robust. I savor it as much as I can. The caffeine has me on edge. I take a long walk around the financial district. It only helps makes me extra late to work.

It's ten-thirty when I step into the elevator.

Oh well. It's not like attention is on me.

I go straight to my desk, but it's already impossible to concentrate.

There's coffee and a bagel on my desk. Next to it are two packets of half and half and two of brown sugar. Exactly how I fix it every morning.

The last thing I need is more coffee. I drink it anyway. At least needing to pee every thirty minutes gives me something to do. There's plenty of work. I'm in the middle of a project and I have another week or two before I need guidance from a senior programmer.

I get sucked into coding until I hear his voice. It's loud, booming.

Angry.

"Was I unclear last week?" Nick stares down David. "Don't come to me or to Ms. Lee with questions about gossip."

"Mr. Marlowe, I'm only asking about official word from the company."

Once again, Jasmine rushes into the fray. "Nick, maybe we should set a meeting for this afternoon. People have questions."

"Yes, I have a lot of questions as well." He stares at her like he's asking for an explanation.

"I didn't have anything to do with this," she says.

Poor David blinks with confusion. The guy has no clue what is going on.

He returns to his desk and whispers something to another programmer. Nick watches them with a glare. He and Jasmine whisper something.

Then he looks straight at me. It's obvious I'm watching. Everyone in the office is watching.

But he says nothing. Heads back to his office and slams the door so hard the wall shakes.

He has his company.

He shouldn't be angry.

Maybe he needs time for it to sink in.

That must be it.

———

HABITS ARE HARD TO BREAK. THURSDAY, I ARRIVE AT Odyssey at eight.

Once again, the floor is empty except for the light in Nick's office. The door is open a sliver. I'm here. He's here. Let's get this over with.

With a deep breath, I knock on his door.

"Is that you?" He asks. The soft tone of his voice makes it clear that he means me.

"Yeah. Can I come in?"

"Of course."

I push the door open and step inside the office. Nerves flutter in my stomach. I swallow hard to shove them down.

His eyes aren't quite as tired. His posture isn't quite as slumped. He's not ecstatic, but then who is at 8 AM?

Nick points to a cup of coffee on his desk. There's a bag next to it. A bagel.

"In case you skipped breakfast." His voice is flat, impossible to read.

"Nick, I—"

"You'll be working with David starting today."

"You yelled at him yesterday."

"I shouldn't have lost my temper like that. It was out of line." He taps his fingers against the desk. His expression stays irritated. "He's in charge of voice recognition. Not the most interesting work but useful to know. He can't come in early or stay late. You'll have a stable nine to five schedule."

I nod.

"He's a good programmer. You'll learn a lot."

"Sure." I grab the coffee and the bagel and take a step backwards. So I won't be tempted to touch him. "Thanks for the breakfast."

He nods. "I'll miss our mornings together."

"Me too." I bite my tongue. The pain calls my attention. No touching Nick. No telling him I care about him. Nothing that will make this more difficult than it has to be. "I'm really glad you didn't have to sell. I know how much this company means to you."

His eyes turn to the floor. Regret flares in his expression. "Thank you."

Every ounce of me wants to run into his arms. I turn and rush back to my desk. I can't give in to that temptation. Nick is already doing better. By the end of the week, he'll be back to his old, ruthless self.

He'll be happy.
I can't ruin that.

———

DAVID IS A GOOD PROGRAMMER, BUT HE'S NEW TO BEING a mentor. He's patient with my endless questions. I'm patient with his slow responses. He unloads a lot of grunt work on me. At least it's a distraction.

Friday morning, I make a point of doing an extra-long yoga session so there's no way I'll get to the office before nine.

Sure enough, there's coffee and breakfast on my desk. I try to resist Nick's offering. I try not to wonder what it means. I fail on both accounts.

I take lunch at my desk. I drink half a dozen cans of diet. I work until I'm too tired to think, then I work some more. It's dark when I finally break. After seven.

The office is empty, but I don't care. I'm still thinking. That means I need to work more. I take a break to use the bathroom and get a snack.

When I return to the main room, all the lights are off. Even the one in Nick's office.

Huh? I didn't see him leave. Hell, he never leaves this early. I try to forget about it on the way back to my desk.

But he's there, leaning over the computer, tapping something into the keyboard.

I move next to him, but there's no way I can get into my chair. Not with him in that position. He'll be leaning over me, his hands on my shoulders, his breath on my neck.

The thought is enough to light a fire in my body. All that coldness melts away.

I want him.

I want him enough to scream.

I sink my teeth into my apple, chewing as loudly and unattractively as possible.

Nick points to a line of code. "You missed a semicolon."

"Is that it?"

He nods. He shifts so he's standing and we're face to face. His eyes scan by body, half desire, half concern.

I gnaw at my apple until it's a tiny core then I wrap it in a napkin and drop it on my desk.

"How's working with David?" His voice is even.

"He's not as good as you, but I'm learning."

A minute passes. Two even.

There are so many things I want to say to Nick and all of them are impossible.

His eyes bore into me. "Why is it you look even more miserable than I feel?"

I press my hands into my sides. "That's in your head. I'm fine."

Concern spreads over his expression. "You're a terrible liar."

I swallow hard. "You seem happier. You're in control again—"

"If I was in control, I'd have you."

My legs threaten to give out. I press my hand against my desk for much needed support. "You have Odyssey and Haley. You must be glad Shepard backed off."

He stares at me. "Do you want to tell me what you had to do with that?"

"Nothing. His greed got the best of him."

"Lizzy, please don't lie. It infuriates me."

"I'm sorry, Mr. Marlowe, but I'm afraid that's all I can say. It was the best decision for everyone—"

"Don't do that—"

"Do what?"

"Pretend like you never mattered to me." He shakes his head. "What did you do, baby? What did you do to make this happen?"

"Don't call me baby. We broke up." And it makes it impossible to keep up my poker face.

I bite my lip, praying he'll buy that I'm okay. That he'll walk back to his office and bury himself in the work he loves more than anything.

No such luck. He stands firm, his posture strong, his expression demanding.

*Order me to tell the truth. Order me onto my knees. I don't fucking care, just make me feel something else.*

I stare at the lines of code. Anything to keep from verbalizing my thoughts.

"What would you like?" he asks.

"What are you talking about?"

"Sweetheart? Sweetie? Darling? Honey? Sweet pea? Just Lizzy?"

"It's Ms. Wilder." I play with the pocket flap of my blazer. Stupid fucking thing is fake. "Isn't that what we do in this office? Everyone is on a last-name basis."

"Yes."

"And aren't you all about the rules and keeping your personal life and professional life separate?"

"Did you fuck him?"

"How could you ask that?" I turn to Nick. There's no malice in his expression. Just hurt. "I would never do that to you. I—" I bite my lip until the pain is too much to take. "Never."

He moves closer. Until he's six inches away. "I still trust you, Lizzy, but you shouldn't have done this. Whatever it was."

I can't move. I want to be near him more than I've ever

wanted anything. "You have your company. That's what matters to you."

"You're what matters to me."

I shake my head.

Nick leans closer. Until he's two inches away. His hands go to my hips. One moves to my lower back. The other moves to the back of my head.

He undoes my bun so my hair spills over my shoulders.

His hands feel good. I press my eyes closed, unable to do anything but soak in the sensation.

He digs his hand into my hair. "You're still reacting to me." He drags his hand down my neck until I groan. "You want this."

I look up into his eyes. It takes my breath away. "You're hot. I can't help it."

"I'm going to kiss you." He brings his hand to the back of my head and uses it to pull me closer. "You remember how to say no to me?"

"I remember." But I can't do it. No way in hell.

My eyes flutter closed as Nick leans closer. The connection of our lips sends a spark through every inch of my body.

For the first time all week, I'm awake and alive. I want something I can have. In theory.

I part my lips to make way for his tongue. I slide my hands around his waist and hold on tightly. Nick, Nick, Nick. It's my world. It's everything.

The kiss breaks. He stares into my eyes, his expression equal parts desperation and desire.

He slides my blazer off my shoulders. It falls behind me on the floor.

I press my body against his. "This doesn't mean anything. It's break up sex."

He pulls my zipper all the way down my back. "It means something."

"But not that we're together. We're not. It's just tonight. It's just because we're both miserable."

"You're miserable?"

"Don't pretend like you can't tell."

He drags his fingertips up my back. "Why are you running away from what you want?"

I hold Nick's gaze. "You have your priories. I have mine."

"What are they, baby?"

God, I like the way that sounds. I swallow hard. "Stop that."

"Priorities can change."

"Call me when they do." I step back. "Until then, I'm not discussing it."

Nick moves closer. He pulls my dress off one shoulder then the other. His eyes go to my chest as he pushes my dress to my waist. "I want you to feel better."

"Then fuck me."

"Do I need to get a condom?"

He might as well ask "have you fucked someone else?" I'm tempted to slap him. Is that really what he thinks of me?

I hold strong. This is the Nick I know. The one who only takes necessary risks.

He's already back to his normal self.

This was the right decision. No matter how much it hurts me.

I reach around my back to unhook my bra. "No."

He nods. His expression changes. Stern. "Strip. I want you naked in front of me."

That's the Nick I know.

I slide my bra off my shoulders and toss it aside. I push

my dress to my knees. It's impossible to take off my tights and boots in a graceful manner, but I get my groove back as I slide my underwear off my hips. It falls to my feet.

I kick all the clothes away.

Nick scans my body the way he did that night in San Francisco, like he's taking a mental picture, like he believes this is the last time.

Tension threatens to consume my back. The moment Nick presses his palm into my skin, my muscles relax.

Fucking body. Why can't the thing respect my wishes? Instead, it's on fire. It wants him and nothing else will do.

Nick brings his hands to my chest. He cups my breasts with a gentle touch. His eyes go to mine as he plays with my nipples. It starts soft. Then it's harder. Faster. Rougher.

Pleasure builds between my legs. I fight my desire to close my eyes. I want to see the look on his face. The mix of control and ecstasy in his expression.

I groan, pressing my knees together. He's fucking good at this.

I forget about tomorrow. I forget about next week. I forget about everything but his moment.

It means something.

It means everything.

He toys with my nipples until I'm panting. One hand goes to my chin, tilting my head so we make eye contact.

"What do you want?" he asks.

"Right now?"

"Period. What do you want, Lizzy, more than anything?"

# Chapter Thirty-Three

I turn away, pressing my eyelids together.

How am I supposed to answer that?

He rubs me until I can't bear the silence anymore. I groan. I arch my body into his.

"Right now—" I look back at Nick. "Right now, I want you. I want your hands on me. Your mouth. I want you inside of me until I'm coming so hard I can't stand it."

"Is that all you want from me?"

I want everything from you, Nick. *I love you.* "I don't want to talk. I want you to fuck me."

His hand slides down my stomach and below my belly button. Almost.

Then he's touching me properly. His fingertips skim my clit. He presses his palm against me.

He groans. "Jesus, Lizzy. The way you respond to me." He teases my sex. "You really want this to be the last time?"

"Ask that again, and I'm leaving."

I lean into his touch. I press my eyelids together so the rest of the world disappears.

All I feel is Nick's hands on my body. Fuck the rest of it. I'm going to enjoy this if it kills me.

He slides one finger inside me. Then two. I cry out. My hands go to his suit jacket. That same expensive wool.

I tug at his tie to undo the knot. My hands go to the buttons on his oxford shirt. I undo two before he grabs my wrists and brings them to my sides.

Nick shoves everything off my desk. He pushes the monitor aside, so there's nothing in the way

His arm slides under my ass. He lifts me and places me on the desk.

I spread my legs to make room for him. He slings his hands under my knees, bringing my body onto his. I'm naked on this desk, and he's fully dressed in front of me, and I fucking like it.

He kisses his way down my neck and chest, stopping at my breasts to suck on my nipples. It's intense. His mouth is soft but the pressure is hard.

When he bites me, I groan.

He bites harder.

I can't feel anything but him. The burst of pain. The pulse of pleasure.

I dig my hands into his hair as he tortures me with his mouth. When I'm certain I can't take it anymore, I press my hands against his head to tell him to go lower.

His lips press against my stomach. My belly button.

The inside of my thigh.

He drops to his knees. His hands close around my thighs. He drags me forward, pulls my legs apart. I'm splayed for him, on display for him.

My breath hitches. My pulse races. The closer his mouth gets to my sex, the more unbearable the anticipation. I'm on fire. I'm going to ignite.

I plant my hands behind me to stay in place. He nips at my inner thigh with desperate, hungry motions.

"Nick," I groan. I arch my back, shifting my body just a little closer to his mouth.

He's almost there. He catches the delicate skin of my inner thigh between his teeth. Pain bursts through me. My sex clenches. I need him. God, how I need him.

Then his mouth is on me. My arms go slack as his tongue slides over my clit. I collapse on the desk with a thud. It does nothing to slow him. He slides one hand under my ass and uses it to bring me closer. The other hooks my knees around his shoulders, one at a time.

I press my thighs against his ears as he licks me. He's damn good at this. In moments, my body is pulsing with bliss. The knot inside me pulls so tight it hurts. I squeeze him harder.

"Nick," I breathe.

He sucks on my clit. It's intense enough to take my breath away. I grab onto the edges of the desk, something to convince me I've got my balance.

He's soft and warm, and he's working magic. The next lick pulls that knot so tight I can't take it. The tension unravels, my sex pulsing with pleasure as I come.

I squeeze my thighs around his head. Whatever it takes to hold him against me.

He licks me again. Again. It's too much, but I can't bear to tell him to stop.

I squeeze the table. Not enough. I scream.

He's still licking me. I reach for Nick until I find his hair and I tug hard. He moans against my skin.

Another orgasm builds inside me. I press my heel into his back. I tug at his hair.

And I scream. I scream his name as I come. It's intense. It hurts. But it hurts so fucking good.

Pleasure spills through my body. Such a wonderful high when I've been so fucking low.

He's the best comfort in the world. So much better than ice cream or movie marathons. So much better than anything.

Nick pulls back. He rises to his feet and presses his crotch against mine. I shift so I can feel the hardness in his slacks. I need that too. I need to make him feel as good as I do.

He tortures me, undoing his shirt as slowly as humanly possible. I wait on my back, my tongue sliding over my lips, my sex throbbing.

Finally, he slides his shirt off his shoulders. I reach up to touch him but he shoves my arms back onto the desk. I squeeze the edge as he does away with his slacks and boxers.

There's no patience left in his movements. He grabs my legs and presses them to his chest, so my ankles are at his ears. His hands go to my hips, and he pulls our bodies together.

His cock strains against me.

There.

I sigh as he enters me. The look on his face is exactly what I feel. Like the world finally makes sense.

He stares into my eyes, daring me to shy away from the intimacy.

I don't. I stare back. It hurts all the way to my bones, but I stare back.

I need to be his, even for a moment, even if I'll be more miserable when it's over.

He drags his hands up my thighs, over my knees, all the way to my calves.

I'm powerless to do anything but feel him thrusting into

me. It's the only thing I want. I hold his gaze. He digs his nails into my calves. He sighs. He groans.

He fucks me.

I can't keep my eyes open any longer. I press them together, moaning and groaning and screaming in equal measure. The only comprehensible sound is "Nick."

This could be the last time we're here.

The last time he's mine.

I soak in the ecstasy of our bodies joining until it's too much to take. This orgasm is hard and fast. Sensation over-whelms me as I come but I don't dare say "yellow." Not until I feel his release.

Nick's nails get sharper. His groans get louder. I open my eyes to watch his bliss. It's the best sight in the world. The way his lips part. The way his shoulders shake. The way his eyelids press together.

One more thrust and he's there, pulsing inside me.

"Lizzy." He groans as he fills me.

Our bodies slow. Our eyes connect. That look is enough to undo me but I manage to stay silent.

He shifts, breaking out touch. I get back into my clothes. He gets back into his.

He leans down and presses his lips to mine.

His kiss is still the best feeling in the whole fucking world.

Even if it is the last one.

———

BETWEEN POURING MYSELF INTO MY LATEST AI PROJECT and helping Kat put the finishing touches on her wedding planning, the weekend passes quickly. I barely think about Nick and how horrifically awkward things will be on Monday morning.

*Hey, how was your weekend? How much of it did you spend thinking about fucking me on my desk? How much do you want to do it again?*

The subway ride is a lesson in managing anxiety. But Nick isn't at Odyssey when I arrive. He's not there at lunch. He's not there for my afternoon coffee. He's not there when I leave.

Tuesday is the same. No Nick.

Wednesday, no Nick.

Thursday, no Nick.

I relax. Without him around, I'm able to focus completely on my programming. I'm not a master, but I'm competent and I'm learning a lot. This is a good internship. I'm lucky to have it.

Friday, Nick sends a company-wide memo.

*From: Phoenix Marlowe*

*There is a mandatory meeting at 4 PM today for an important announcement about the Odyssey team. We'll have coffee and pastries.*

He wastes no words, as usual.

There's no time to analyze it. My phone buzzes with a new text.

*Nick: Be in my office in five minutes. I need to speak with you.*

Sure enough, three minutes later, Nick steps out of the elevator. He's back to his normal self. His posture is strong and confident. His eyes are bright, full of life. He's the guy who can take on the world.

He's happy.

I smooth my dress and check my hair. Here goes nothing.

I walk to Nick's office.

The door is open. Still, I knock.

"Come in." His voice is all business.

I step inside. It's as bright and clean as it always is. Nick is standing at his desk, all his attention on me.

"Please close the door." He steps out from behind his desk.

I do. "I'm not going to lock it."

"Of course." His eyes find mine. "I trust you to keep a secret." He steps closer until we're two feet apart. "I'm leaving Odyssey."

What? There's no way I heard that right. There's no way Nick is leaving the company. It means everything to him. I pinch myself to make sure I'm awake.

I am.

"I've found a new CEO to replace me. And a new lead programmer to run the Haley project."

No. This doesn't make any sense.

This isn't the Nick I know.

"Lizzy, are you all right?" His voice is soft.

"But you... you can't leave your company. It's everything to you."

"I thought about what you said." His eyes burn with intensity. "This company has been a weight around my neck. I don't want to put work ahead of everything. I don't want those priorities."

I stare at him like he's speaking a foreign language.

"I sold my third of the company to an investor I trust. I expect Shepard will back off, but there's no guarantee of that."

"When are you leaving?"

"Today is my last day." His expression softens. "I spoke to your adviser at Stanford. With all the hours of overtime you've worked, we agreed that you'll get full credit as long as you stay through the end of the month."

"Thank you."

"You're welcome to stay as a paid intern through August. The salary won't be a fortune, but it will be enough to keep you in New York." He moves back to his desk and fishes through one of the drawers. He clears his throat. His voice returns to an even, all-business tone. "The apartment is yours through June. If you stay with Odyssey, you can rent it at a discount starting July first."

I nod.

He pulls something from his drawer. An envelope.

His eyes focus on mine. This look isn't business. It's personal.

He hands me the envelope. "The tickets are transferable if you'd rather take someone else."

I open the envelope. There are two plane tickets to the Virgin Islands and a reservation for a hotel suite in my name.

One ticket is made out to Phoenix Marlowe, the other to Elizabeth Wilder.

I try to find the meaning in Nick's eyes. I can't. "What is this supposed to be?"

"A second chance."

The room is spinning. This is too much, too fast. I take a step back, squeezing my fingers around the plane tickets. Slick paper. They're here. They're real.

His fingertips brush my cheek. "You would be my priority, Lizzy. My first priority."

The words rise up in my throat. *I love you. Do you love me?*

I swallow them down. I'm not ready for that.

The silence hurts. The words claw at my throat, desperate to escape.

A knock on the door calls my attention. I sigh, pushing the sentiment back to the bottom of my stomach.

"Mr. Marlowe. There's more paperwork for you to sign." Jasmine clears her throat. "I'm going to come in."

"Of course." Sadness flares in Nick's eyes. He shakes it off. "Enjoy your sister's wedding. I'm sure it will be beautiful."

"Thank you."

I stare back at him, willing my thoughts to go from messy squiggles to straight lines. There's so much I want to say to Nick, but the words stay trapped in my throat.

I go back to my desk so I won't implode.

## Chapter Thirty-Four

Screw the mandatory meeting. I leave early. The apartment is mine for another three months but it doesn't feel like home anymore.

I find a suitcase in the corner and start packing a bag for the weekend. The wedding is Sunday afternoon, and I won't have a moment of breathing room until it's over. It's good being busy. Better seeing Kat so happy.

My bridesmaid dress is in her closet. I find my shoes and my purse and toss them into a pile on my bed. I need something for the bachelorette party. A black cocktail dress and matching heels should do the trick. I need something to sleep in. Something for our spa day.

And something to wear under my clothes. I dread opening that particular drawer. There's no resisting the flood of memories as I paw through the lingerie Nick bought me.

*You would be my priority, Lizzy. My first priority.*

The memory of his voice nearly undoes me. But he didn't say he loved me.

He's good at getting what he wants. If he really loved me, he would have said it.

I find something practical and zip my suitcase.

It's still early. Kat must be home. Her last midterm was Wednesday, and she's technically on spring break. Lucky her, the school's schedule lined up perfectly with her ideal wedding date.

It's possible that she and Blake are currently having crazy sex in the living room. I can't bring myself to potentially cramp their style.

I find a paper notebook and a pen on my desk. I have a maid of honor speech to write and no time to waste.

For two hours, I stare at the neat lined paper. For two hours, nothing comes. I'm so happy for my sister, for this wedding, for everything it means, but I can't manage to string my thoughts together.

———

SATURDAY IS DEVOTED TO THE FINISHING TOUCHES OF beauty. We spend hours at a spa—on Blake's dime, of course.

It's too awkward to be relaxing, but I do my best to keep Kat's attention on anything but the wedding.

With every passing hour, her nerves shoot into overdrive. She is a thorn in the side of every masseuse and esthetician.

She's always worn her heart on her sleeve, but this is a whole new level of emotional honesty.

We finish with just enough time to get to the rehearsal dinner. All those nerves fade away the moment we arrive. Well, the moment her eyes lock with Blake's. They're both so happy. It's plain as day. Our parents were like that, all gooey in love, ecstatic just for the chance to be together.

A warmth spreads through me. The lingering hurt over Nick fades away, and I'm confident it will stay away for the next twenty-four hours.

They're so in love they radiate positive energy. It's infectious enough that the food tastes better, the air smells sweeter.

Dinner is small. It's me, Kat, Blake, and Blake's sister Fiona. She was a certified super-bitch when we met, but she's come around. We're actually friendly. And she seems to like Kat. A lot.

She's happier without her ex-husband around.

She's even dating... as far as I can tell. She doesn't exactly hang out to chitchat.

She and I take turns embarrassing our respective siblings. There are no speeches, no toasts, just the awe of seeing two people so totally perfect for each other.

It's overwhelming. I back off after Fiona picks up the tab—technically, she is the groom's family—to give them space.

It's a private moment, Kat and Blake staring into each other's eyes, whispering softly. I force myself to look away, but my gaze keeps going back to them. It's still such a wonderful sight—my sister so happy. I never thought she'd have that again.

I never thought either one of us would do anything but struggle.

I stare at my phone to keep myself occupied. There are a few confirmation emails about the bachelorette party.

And there's a text message from Nick.

*Nick: Are you giving a speech tomorrow?*

Not exactly a declaration of love, but it is sweet.

I reply.

*Lizzy: A big one. Haven't started yet.*

*Nick: You have sixteen hours.*

*Lizzy: Give or take. Luckily, I'm terrible with words.*

*Nick: You have enough charm to make up for it.*

*Lizzy: Are you trying to make me blush?*

*Nick: No. I don't want to distract you, but I'd regret not wishing you good luck.*

*Lizzy: Thanks.*

*Nick: I'm sure that whatever you write will be beautiful.*

———

WE MEET HER FRIENDS, PLUS SARAH, AT AN ALL-MALE strip club at nine o'clock. Kat and her friends take the front entrance. Sarah leads me around back, to the stage entrance. I don't bother wondering how she knows her way around this place. It's Sarah. It has to be sex.

The place is surprisingly clean. The furniture is red velvet, the walls are mirrors, and the black stage is lined with little yellow lights.

Our table is plenty big for the six of us. Kat has three friends from school with her. They all seem nice.

A waiter clad in only a bowtie and a pair of black-and-white briefs stops at our table. He kneels in front of Kat like he's about to propose.

"Are you the bride to be?" He smiles.

She blushes. "Oh my God, Lizzy. Remind me to kill you after the honeymoon." She turns to the buff man, her expression polite but not at all interested. "I am."

"This is for you." He pulls a "Bride" sash from a hook on the wall and drapes it over her shoulders. "And what are you drinking on your last night of freedom?"

"Gin and tonic."

He nods to note her order then goes around the group. Each of us gets a flirty smile and a word of encouragement.

The man is good at his job. He's cute—green eyes, brown hair, huge muscles—but my body is entirely apathetic to his hand on my wrist.

When our drinks arrive, Sarah busts out her offering to the festivities—penis-shaped straws. Kat turns as red as a tomato but makes no objections.

"Why do you think all this bachelorette shit is cock-shaped?" Sarah pulls a massive penis-shaped lollipop from her purse and hands it to Kat.

"Thanks." Kat passes it to one of her friends. "I have plenty."

"It's to remind you that you're stuck with one dick for the rest of your life." Kat's redheaded friend giggles.

"Do you worry about it, Kat? Only one guy for your whole life. Won't that get boring?" Kat's black-haired friend asks.

"Nope." Kat downs her gin and tonic in one long sip. "He's perfect."

"Him or his—" Her black-haired friend waves the penis lollipop.

"The whole package." She laughs. "Oh, fuck. I didn't mean it like that."

The lights dim. A smoke machine kicks on, filling the room with haze. Music starts.

And then there are four men on stage in Western jeans and cowboy hats, grinding and thrusting to the beat. Kat covers her face with her hands, barely peeking.

"I can't believe you talked me into this," she says.

"You love it." I knock back my rum and diet.

She giggles. Her hands stay over her eyes.

The show is more cheeky than it is sexy. The men do a coordinated routine then strip to their underwear. They strike a pose as the music ends. A moment later, they're back on stage with a new routine, stripping off a new set of clothes.

Our waiter is incredibly attentive. I make an effort to pace myself, and I'm still three drinks deep by the time the dancers break. I excuse myself to the bathroom to pee and check my phone for texts from Nick. There's nothing, of course. He was clear enough.

*You could be a priority. My first priority.*

I stare at my phone, my thumbs hovering over the keyboard. I can't say this in a text. And I can't say it right now.

On my way back to the table, I run right into my sister. She slides her arm around me, smiling wide and slurring her words.

"Lizzy. You're such a hard-ass sometimes, but you don't fool me for a second. Not even one second." She wavers. "You are being so fucking stupid right now."

"How many drinks have you had?"

"Too many." She looks me in the eyes. "You're not fooling me for shit. I know you're in love with Nick."

"Do you?"

"That's right. And I know... I know that you still believe there's a chance."

"You've veered into drunk, sweetie."

She shrugs.

I check the time. A little after ten. The hair and makeup person will be in the apartment in twelve hours.

In theory, it's plenty of time. But I'm not risking it with Kat this tipsy.

"Okay. Time to go home. You want to say 'bye to your friends?" I ask.

"No. I want to talk to you."

"Let me pay, darling."

I drag Kat back to the table and settle the check. It

takes a while to get through the goodbyes. Everyone wants to hug the bride to be. We're not safely in a cab until nearly eleven.

"You're really stubborn. You know that?" she asks.

"You're really drunk." I give our address to the cabbie and turn my attention back to Kat. "You nervous?"

"Really nervous." She plays with her seat belt. "It's crazy how much everything costs, how big a deal it is for this thirty-minute ceremony. And then you're married and that's so real."

"Blake loves you a lot."

She smiles. "It's really nice, you know, when you find that person."

I nod.

"And if you do... you have to hold on and never let go. Okay, Lizzy?"

"But you left him. Last year, you left him. You loved him, but you left him."

She looks out the windows as we breeze through Times Square. Her eyes are wide. Her face is filled with wonder.

She's not drunk. She's just Kat.

"I couldn't be with him unless he loved me back," she says.

I nod. "What if he'd said no?"

"It would have hurt, but it felt good to say those words. I had to do it. No matter what happened after."

I settle into my seat, watching the city whiz by.

The drive passes quickly. In minutes, we're at the penthouse apartment. I pay the cabbie and help Kat to the curb.

It doesn't occur to me until we're in the penthouse elevator. I was in a car without batting an eyelash. It didn't worry me at all.

Some of it must be my focus on the wedding. But the rest I owe to Nick.

In the apartment, I force Kat to drink half a gallon of water, eat a snack, wash off her makeup, brush her teeth, and get promptly to bed.

The living room is mine. I pull out the empty notebook and I channel all the feelings whirring around inside me.

And I write until my hand goes numb.

## Chapter Thirty-Five

I zip Kat's dress and take one last look around the apartment. We have everything. It's go time.

Downstairs, the limo is waiting. Flutters are building in my stomach. My sister is getting married. I'm walking her down the aisle. I'm standing with her at the altar. I'm giving the speech.

It's a big fucking deal.

Her dress doesn't have a train. A good thing, because it's raining.

It's April. Of course it's raining.

I close my eyes and listen to the drops pound against the aluminum roof.

"You okay?" she asks.

"Yep. You?"

She nods. "I feel like I'm going to throw up."

"Glad you skipped lunch?"

"Very glad."

"You look beautiful. Really beautiful." I fight my desire to cry. Plenty of time for that later.

Instead, I check my purse for my speech and my extra

copy of Kat's vows. I'm under strict orders not to read them, so I zip my purse, toss it on the bench seat, and rest my head on Kat's shoulder.

She plays with her engagement ring.

"You should put that on your right hand," I say. "Don't want to upstage the wedding ring."

She switches the rock to her right ring finger. Her eyes stay on the sparkly gem. "Is this really happening?"

"It is."

"Are you sure I'm not dreaming?"

I smile. "Positive."

"I'm really young to get married. Mom and Dad would be freaking if they were here."

"They were like twenty-three. Barely a year older than you are now."

"Yeah."

"You love him, right?"

"Like I love breathing."

"I've never seen two happier people." I squeeze her. "Do you really doubt your decision, even for a minute?"

"No." She takes a deep breath, her expression softening. She looks down at her dress. "It feels like I'm dreaming."

I pinch the back of her neck.

She yelps.

"You're not dreaming."

"You're a brat."

"Love you too."

The car stops for a solid three minutes. That was fast. I collect my purse, smooth my dress. This is happening and I'm ready.

The limo door opens. There's a smiling woman in a black pantsuit, holding a pink and white bouquet with a big pink bow.

She's one of the wedding planners. She introduces herself as Shelby Something—I'm too nervous to catch the last name—and hands us each a bottle of water.

I chug half of mine, but my throat still feels dry. There's no way I'm calming my nerves today. Might as well enjoy the ride.

Shelby presses her earpiece to her head and speaks into the receiver. "Okay. Get everyone seated." She offers Kat her hand. "We're ready for you."

Kat look at me as if to ask "is this really happening?" I nod.

She takes Shelby's hand and steps onto the curb. The rain is still pounding, but it doesn't seem to bother either of them. Shelby hands Kat the bouquet and helps me out of the limo.

"You're walking your sister down the aisle?" she asks.

I nod.

"How sweet." She leads us through the back entrance then points to the ceremony site, about five hundred feet away. There's a pink tarp tied to the blooming cherry blossom trees. The few dozen guests are seated in plastic folding chairs. Half of them are holding pink umbrellas.

"You'll get a little wet," Shelby says. "But we have a portable wooden walkway on the grass. Your dresses are safe."

We move closer, until we're about two hundred feet away.

There's a small guesthouse shielding us from view. We come to the corner. The next step is onto that walkway. Then it's one long path down the aisle.

Kat holds the bouquet to her chest.

I sling my arm with hers. "You got this?"

She nods.

It's pouring too hard for me to hear anything.

Shelby taps us on the shoulder, and then it's our turn.

Kat is really getting married.

I squeeze her as we make our way down the slippery wooden path. The world becomes a blur.

The cool colors of the rain. The soft pink of the petals blowing in the wind. And Kat standing across from Blake, both of them so happy they could die.

I'm too nervous to hear a word the officiant says, but I can feel all the love between my sister and the man who is about to become her husband. The way they stare at each other, with so much honesty, so much vulnerability.

When they read their vows, I start bawling. I don't even try to blame the rain. I used to think this kind of thing was cheesy bullshit, but it's so sweet, so beautiful.

He slides the ring onto her finger. "I do."

And then it's her turn, and her smile is so wide I almost worry her cheeks are going to break off.

She slides the ring onto his finger. "I do."

And then they're kissing. It's like a fairytale. I can see the magic swirling around them. I can see that everything in the world is exactly where it needs to be.

It's a tender moment, one that would usually be theirs alone.

But they're sharing it with the world.

That's love. You share it with the world.

A tear rolls down my cheek. I do nothing to stem it. My sister is married, and she's happy, and no matter what happens—

She's gonna be okay.

———

THE NEXT TEN MINUTES ARE A BLUR. I POSE FOR A FEW

dozen pictures, then wait as the photographer focuses solely on the bride and groom.

For a few minutes, I watch Kat and Blake pose. They both look so happy, so natural, so free.

Maybe she's right, and I have to tell Nick how I feel, no matter the results. It's possible he'll hate me for interfering with Shepard. It's possible I'm about to lose any chance we have at any kind of relationship—

But it's a risk I'm willing to take.

I step under the now empty altar and look up at the transparent pink tarp. The rain is down to a drizzle. It makes tiny drops on the tarp, that same pitter-patter, only softer.

I pull my phone from my purse and call Nick.

*Ring. Ring. Ring.*

Voicemail.

"Hey Nick. It's Lizzy. I'm at the wedding. It was beautiful. Reception starts in forty-five minutes, but that's not why I'm calling. It's because I have something to say."

I take a deep breath, willing my thoughts to straighten.

They do.

"I talked to Shepard. He made me a deal, to leave your company alone if I ended our relationship. I thought it would make you happy. It did. But it made me miserable. Nick... I don't want to say this over the phone. I'll come over after the reception. I have to see you. Please, even if you hate me for getting involved." I dig my hand into my phone. "Let me know where you'll be tonight. The reception ends around seven. I can get anywhere in the city by seven-thirty."

I end the call and hug the phone to my chest. My heart is racing. My breath is totally uneven.

Whatever happens, I have to tell him today.

## Chapter Thirty-Six

The reception is in a solarium. There's hardwood floor beneath us and a beautiful curved glass ceiling above us. The dance floor is surrounded by tables with soft white cloths.

The cake is sitting against the wall, right in the center. It's white and pink, and it's decorated with cherry blossom petals.

It's so Kat. The ceremony, the reception, the dress—all of it is perfect.

The sound system reverberates as the DJ steps up to the mic. "Now arriving, Mr. and Mrs. Sterling."

Blake and Kat step through the doors. They go straight to the dance floor. They dance to Etta James's rendition of "At Last." It's seamless and sweet. The whole time, they're staring into each other's eyes like they're lost in a different world.

When the song ends, they mouth "I love you" and take their seats.

The DJ speaks. "The salad course will arrive in ten

minutes. But first, some words from the best woman and the maid of honor."

A coordinator brings a mic to Fiona. I find my speech in my purse and read over it. I'm so focused I don't hear a single word she says. I don't even look up until I hear clapping and cheering.

She passes the mic to me.

Here goes nothing.

I stand up and look over the reception. "I'm sure you've heard this story, but I was in an accident four years ago. It killed our parents. Almost killed me. Doctors told me I'd never walk again." I dig my fingers into the mic. "It gets better, I promise."

The tension in the room eases into a laugh. "Kat was only eighteen, but she was there every day when I woke up, and when I fell asleep. She took me to every physical therapy session and every doctor's appointment. For a long time, I was sure that no one would ever take care of us but each other. I was protective of her too. When she met Blake, I didn't want her to have anything to do with him."

Everyone laughs.

"I never thought I'd be okay with anyone else taking care of my sister, but when I see her and Blake together, I know I can pass the torch. He appreciates everything that matters about her. The way she sees all the magic and beauty in the world. The way she loves with her whole heart. I've never seen two people more perfect for each other. A year ago, I didn't believe that kind of happiness was possible." I look over to them. They're smiling. Blushing even.

"You guys made me believe in love. You made me believe enough that I fell in love. That wasn't possible last year. And that's worth more than all of Blake's money. Which is a lot." I swallow hard. Almost done. "I'm so happy for you both. It couldn't happen to two better people."

People are laughing. Kat is crying. Blake wipes a tear from her eye and presses his lips against hers.

It's too hard to breathe in here. I lock eyes with Kat then motion to the door. I mouth, "I'm going to get some air."

She nods okay and mouths, "I love you."

Everyone is looking at the food. It's my only chance for a break. I go straight to the main entrance and slip outside.

The air is still cold and damp, still drizzling. I wipe my glasses on my dress but it doesn't help.

"Here."

Huh? That's Nick's voice.

I look up. That's him. That's Nick.

He takes my glasses, wipes them dry on his shirt, and slides them back on my face. His touch is gentle, affectionate.

"Your speech was beautiful," he says.

"You heard that all the way over here?"

He nods. "I didn't want to interrupt." He runs his fingertips over my cheek. "Did you mean the part about falling in love?"

My cheeks flush. "It would be wrong to lie in my maid of honor speech." I lean into his touch. "I'm sorry about everything with Shepard. I should have respected your wishes."

"You were trying to protect me. I would have done the same thing."

"I thought it would make you happy."

"I thought so too." He slides his hand around my neck. "I was a wreck over losing the company, but that was nothing compared to losing you. I haven't slept. I can't eat. I can barely think."

I stare into his eyes. They're honest. They're earnest.

"I didn't know what you'd done, why you'd left, but I knew you were right. Odyssey was my first priority. It made me happy once, giving everything to the company. But not anymore."

I'm warm everywhere. I squeeze Nick's hand. I suck in a shallow breath.

"I want to be a better man, a man who deserves you. I want to put you first, Lizzy, before everything."

"Before work?"

"Before breathing." He drags his fingers to the back of my head, tilting me so we're eye to eye. "You're everything to me."

I melt into his touch.

"I'd give up anything before I'd give up on you."

"You make me want to be better, too."

"I know, baby." He digs his fingers into my hair. "I want to be with you. All yours. And you're all mine. Is that okay?"

I nod.

He leans closer. "Elizabeth Wilder, I love you. I love you in a way I've never loved anyone."

"I love you too."

He presses his lips to mine. All the cold melts away as I kiss him back. Nick is mine. And I'm his.

Whatever happens, we belong together.

When the kiss breaks, we go back to the reception and we dance the night away.

## Epilogue

---

My knuckles are white as I pull the car into the narrow parking space. I practiced this a hundred times with Nick.

Foot on the brake, hand on the center console, I put the car in park and turn off the ignition.

Done.

The DMV employee checks boxes on her clipboard. She looks to me with a smile. "You passed, Miss Wilder."

Holy shit. I passed. According to the state of New York, I'm a licensed driver.

"Thank you." I shake her hand and get out of the car.

There's Nick, standing on the curb of the Brooklyn DMV.

The rain has his dark hair sticking to his forehead. Otherwise, he's no worse for wear. He looks impeccable in his black trench and jeans.

Better out of them, of course.

I throw my arms around him. "I passed."

"I'm so proud of you, baby." He squeezes me tightly and presses his lips to mine. "I knew you would."

"I don't know how you talked me into getting a license. I go to school eighty blocks from our apartment." I decided to go to Hunter College. It's not the best school in New York, but it's a state school, which means it's in my price range. Between the money I saved working at Odyssey, and me and Kat selling the Brooklyn apartment, I have enough to put myself through grad school.

He's running another start-up. He's passionate about the project, but he still turns it off when he gets home. He still gives me his weekends.

And he's even speaking to his brother again.

I'm not sure exactly where they are. But they're friendly.

As far as I can tell, Shepard is still trying to win Jasmine back.

I haven't decided if I'm rooting for or against him.

"Because you knew how we'd celebrate." He slides his hands to my lower back and plays with the bottom of my t-shirt.

It's cold today, but even with my coat in the car, I feel damn warm.

"Miss Wilder." The DMV employee calls for me.

"Coming," I yell back.

Nick winks. "Not yet."

My cheeks flush. It's difficult to focus on paperwork. The fifteen minutes feel like hours. When we're done with the DMV, I hand Nick the keys to the car but he won't take them.

"Your turn to drive." He motions to the driver's seat.

The rain is pounding, but I can manage. I slide into the car, buckle up, turn the ignition. Nick is next to me the entire ride. He holds my hand when it's not glued to the steering wheel.

It's early afternoon. There aren't many cars on the road. Driving is still far from my favorite activity, but there are moments—like when Nick squeezes my hand—when I like it.

We park in his garage. Our garage. He asked me to move in last July. It's perfect. I have my own office for schoolwork, a gorgeous room in shades of purple and silver.

But I'm not ready to get back to the apartment yet. Not when the sun is shining through the clouds, and the trees in Battery Park are blooming.

I lead Nick across the street. It's pouring rain. My canvas sneakers are not at all helpful in staying dry, but I don't care.

The cherry blossoms are clouds of pink. The whole park is lined with them. It's just like last year, at Kat's wedding. Just as perfect.

There's a great view from Nick's apartment, our apartment, but it's nothing compared to being here. It's like the world is flourishing in front of us.

The sun casts a glow over the park. Over Nick. He looks like an angel, backlit and surrounded by soft pink cherry blossom petals.

He is an angel. He saved me from losing touch with the world.

I reach up to my tiptoes so I can whisper in his ear. "I love you."

"I love you too." He slides his arm around me and holds me close.

We stay like that until we're soaked to the bone.

He brings his mouth to my ear. "How about we get you out of those wet clothes?"

"Only if you go first."

He takes my hand and leads me back to the apartment building.

Glass walls be damned, the second the elevator doors slide shut, I undo the buttons on Nick's coat and slide it off his shoulders.

He grabs my hips and presses me against the wall. My coat is too slick for me to stay in place. I slide down. Right back into his arms.

A laugh escapes my lips.

"I warned you about the wet clothes." He does away with my coat.

"My turn."

I pull his t-shirt over his head and press my hands against his broad chest. His eyes are wide with desire. No hesitation. No fear.

He's mine.

And I'm his.

And nothing else matters.

I go slow as I unbutton his jeans and slip my hand inside. He's already hard.

He groans into my ear. For a second, I think he'll tell me to stop, that he can only handle me touching him if he's one hundred percent in control.

But he doesn't.

He groans my name.

The elevator dings. Finally. I kick our coats into the penthouse and step inside. He follows right behind me.

I shove his jeans to his knees then rub him over his boxers. He wraps his arms around my waist. Then they're at my ass, pulling our bodies together.

He looks into my eyes. "You want me in control today?"

I nod. "As long as I get to touch you."

Nick must be impatient. He grabs my hips, presses me

346

against the wall, and kisses me like the ship is going down. I kiss him back, my hands digging through his hair, my body melting into his.

He talks in between kisses. "Take off your top."

I fling it over my head. It lands on the floor with a thud.

"I like you soaking wet."

My cheeks flush. "Me too."

His hands go to my zipper. My jeans are soaked through. They don't want to budge. Nick has to drop to his knees to get them to my ankles.

He drags his hands up my hips, grabs my panties, and pulls them to my ankles. "Step out of your pants."

I do.

"Spread your legs wider."

I do.

Starting at the inside of my knee, Nick trails kisses up my thigh. Until his lips are on me, working their magic.

I dig my hands into his shoulders. His skin feels so good against my fingers. Somehow, it makes the motions of his tongue feel even better.

Pleasure fills my body as he licks me. Almost. Almost.

"Nick," I groan.

There. An orgasm spills through me. I scream his name again and again as I come.

He doesn't waste any time. He rises to his feet and kicks off his boxers.

"Come here, baby." He takes my hand and wraps it around his cock.

Hell yes. I stroke him until his eyes flutter closed and a groan escapes his lips.

His hands go to my hips. "I need to be inside you, now."

He places my hands on his shoulders and pins me to the wall.

I stare back at him, into those deep brown eyes of his.

The world is where it needs to be.

He stares back as he enters me. There's no doubting what's passing between us. We have the words, and we have our bodies. Two different ways to say I love you.

I hook my arms around his neck and hold on tight. He kisses me hard and deep as he drives into me. I kiss him back, lost in pleasure, lost in him.

My world is a dizzying mixture of color and light. The most wonderful shade of purple. I'm not intellectual. Only physical. Only emotional. All I feel is his body. His breath, his hands, his fingers, his cock, his teeth.

His love.

The way he shakes when he's about to come.

I'm almost there. I arch my hips to press my clit against his pubic bone, so I can come with him.

An orgasm rises up inside me.

His eyes go wide. His teeth sink into my neck. His shoulders shake.

I can't fight it anymore. I come, my sex pulsing around him. He's there seconds later, filling me as he rakes his nails across my skin.

———

We take a long shower. Nick makes excellent use of the detachable showerhead. When we're done, I've come so many times that I can't stand.

He carries me to the bed. I expect him to toss me pajamas, but he brings me a dress. That gorgeous purple dress I wore during our poker night.

"This is a bit much for lying around the house," I tease.

"It's our anniversary."

"Our what?"

"A year ago, today, I told you I loved you."

He's right. A year ago was Kat's wedding, the day he told me he loved me, the day the world starting looking beautiful again.

She and Blake left for a trip to Japan last week. The exact date must have slipped my mind.

I sit up. "You're cheesy."

"I don't care. You're the best thing that ever happened to me. I'd celebrate you every day if I could."

"What about selling three start-ups for what—ten billion dollars?"

"Better." He sits next to me.

Naked.

He's naked.

Somehow, I keep my eyes glued to his.

He presses his lips to my forehead. "You're better than ten billion dollars."

"Twenty billion?"

He nods.

"A hundred billion?"

He shrugs, teasing. "Don't get greedy." He sits up and puts on his boxers. "We have a dinner reservation."

"To celebrate our anniversary?"

"Yes. Get dressed. I don't want to be late."

His cheeks turn red. Nick is nervous? Nick is never nervous.

Suddenly, I'm motivated. My legs are jelly, but they cooperate enough to get into my dress and my shoes. I don't bother with underwear.

After ten minutes with my blow-dryer and makeup brushes, I'm ready. Nick is waiting for me in the living room. He's as handsome as ever in his sleek black suit, his tie the same amethyst shade as my dress.

"Are we walking or driving?" I ask.

"Up to you. I reserved a limo."

I look out the window. It's raining. That puts a cramp on walking. "The limo."

He leads me to the elevator, then the lobby, then the curb, where a shiny black limo is waiting for us.

I'm not quite relaxed enough about driving to spend the ride doing anything fun. We're in our seat belts, our hands intertwined, my head on his shoulder.

It's only ten minutes to our destination. The building looks familiar, but I don't place it until we're on the top floor, in the middle of the hallway.

It's the restaurant where we had our first official date.

Nick presses his hand into my lower back as he leads me inside.

My eyes go wide. The furniture is arranged so there's only one table in the center of the restaurant. It's just us. All ours.

He pulls my chair out for me. It's tilted slightly, so it's facing the windows more than it's facing the table.

I take my seat, my eyes fixed on his.

But he doesn't sit.

He squeezes my hand, drops to one knee, and pulls a purple ring box from his pocket.

Oh, my God.

Nick smiles wide. "I meant what I said earlier. You are the best thing that ever happened to me. I'd be a fool not to make things official."

He pops open the purple box. The ring is beautiful. A princess cut solitaire. It's beautiful, modern, and feminine at once.

He stares into my eyes. "Lizzy Wilder, will you marry me?"

My body fills with warmth. "Yes. Of course."

He slides the ring onto my finger. It's gorgeous, but it's not as gorgeous as the joy in his expression.

I lean down to press my lips to his. "I love you."

"I love you too."

I kiss him until my lips are numb.

## Want More?

Thank you so much for picking up *Dirty Boss*. I hope you love Lizzy and Nick's story as much as I do.

If you enjoyed the story, please help other readers find it by leaving an honest review on Amazon or Goodreads.

Want to talk books? Awesome! You can find me at CrystalKaswell.com

## Acknowledgements

My first thanks must always go to my husband, who not only tolerates but loves all my weird quirks (even my rants about grammar). Kevin, I couldn't do it without you. And the second goes to my father for always encouraging me to follow my dreams and especially for taking me to the book store when I was supposed to me grounded.

To my editor, Dee, thank you so much for the quick turn around with this manuscript. It looks amazing. My beta readers—there are too many to name--thank you for helping me make this book the best book it could be.

And a special thanks to Hang Le for the gorgeous covers.

And my biggest thanks goes to all the readers for taking a chance on a new book.

Printed in Great Britain
by Amazon